9-90

M000203783

MURDER IN A GOOD CAUSE

By the Same Author

MURDER IN FOCUS
MURDER ON THE RUN

MURDER
IN A GOOD
CAUSE

MEDORA SALE

Charles Scribner's Sons • *New York*

Maxwell Macmillan International
New York   Oxford   Singapore   Sydney

Charles Scribner's Sons
Macmillan Publishing Company
866 Third Avenue
New York, NY 10022

Collier Macmillan Canada, Inc.
1200 Eglinton Avenue East, Suite 200
Don Mills, Ontario M3C 3N1

This is a work of fiction. Names, characters, places, and incidents either are the product of the author's imagination or are used fictitiously. Any resemblance to actual events or persons, living or dead, is entirely coincidental.

Library of Congress Cataloging-in-Publication Data
Sale, Medora.
    Murder in a good cause / Medora Sale.
        p.   cm.
    ISBN 0-684-19216-0
    I. Title.
PR9199.3.S165M85   1990
813'.54—dc20   90-31107   CIP

10   9   8   7   6   5   4   3   2   1

Printed in the United States of America

to Anne,
filiae meae dilectissimae

MURDER IN A GOOD CAUSE

CHAPTER 1

When Mrs. Martha Wilkinson awoke suddenly in the night, groggy with codeine and sleeping pills, she heard voices whispering above the hum of the air conditioner in a language she could not place. There is nothing odd about that. Toronto is—at least in some senses of the word—a cosmopolitan city. Italian is everyday, Chinese ordinary, Greek more common than French. And although Mrs. Wilkinson might have recognized French or even guessed at Portuguese or Italian (her housekeeper was Portuguese), the language was none of these.

But the question should never have arisen. Martha Wilkinson shouldn't have been there at all, listening to any conversation. She ought to have been sleeping peacefully in an airy summer house on an island in Georgian Bay, except that a stabbing pain in her jaw had forced her to drive back to Toronto to see her dentist. In a day or two she would return to Georgian Bay. Of course, the speakers of the strange language shouldn't have been there, either. They were under the impression the house was empty.

Terror cleared the drug-induced fog from Mrs. Wilkinson's mind, but with the return of rational thought, terror disappeared again. Whoever was in the house felt quite at home. What had sounded at first like whispers were voices in another room speaking at normal volume. And the footsteps on the hall floor were neither furtive nor hesitant. The wild pounding of her heart settled. Christopher. He had come back unexpectedly with some of his friends from McGill.

Foreign boys. Dear, soft-hearted Christopher. He had always collected waifs and strays for her to look after. It used to be puppies and kittens; now it was lonely young men from overseas, feeling lost at university. She smiled and climbed out of bed, wincing a little at the pain in her jaw when her feet hit the floor; she put on the light and struggled into her dressing gown. "Christopher, darling, is that you?" she called as she opened the door. The three men who were systematically going through the contents of her husband's study froze, and then moved gingerly out of the room they were in. One of them picked up a small wrought-iron statue from the desk—a triumphant Viking warrior with a crested helmet—and raised it above his head. They met halfway down the corridor. The crested helmet caught Mrs. Wilkinson on the temple, and she fell to the floor. She lay still for a moment; then, lifting her head an inch or two from the floor, she tried to drag herself back to the safety of her bedroom. The second man took two steps nearer to her, pulled a pistol from his jacket, and fired. The one who had hit her leaned over her solicitously, picked up her hand and felt for a pulse, and then shrugged his shoulders. He dropped the hand carelessly back again and returned to the study. The third man remained where he had been, standing inside the study with a box in his hands and watching with grave eyes.

Twenty-five minutes later, a dark-colored van pulled out of the driveway of the house and drove sedately away in the darkness.

"The pattern is exactly the same as the others, eh, Tom?" said Sergeant Adam Volchek of the Break and Enter squad.

Sergeant Tom Gardiner nodded morosely. "Pretty much," he said, glancing from the body lying on the strip of Persian rug over to the inspector from Homicide.

"People off at the cottage." Volchek counted off the items. "They go through the security system like a knife through butter; clean entry, no mess; and only the most expensive, negotiable things gone—silver, jewelry, paintings, cash. Most of the houses had safes, neatly opened. They do their homework, go in and get what they want, and they're out again with a minimum of damage. They have access to a pretty high class fencing operation, too," he added.

"I wouldn't have thought they'd attack someone like that," said Gardiner. He sounded disappointed in them, as though they had failed to live up to the high standards expected of them. "I mean, that's downright stupid. But I guess this'd be the first time they've hit a house that wasn't empty." He looked down at the body on the floor. "I wonder if they knew she was here?"

Inspector John Sanders from Homicide looked down as well. "Who knows?" he said. "Have you spoken to the neighbors? Got anything from the family yet? Any idea who this fence would be?" And the usual routine quietly replaced the futility of speculation.

That evening, a dark brown van backed up to a building in a completely different section of the city. The driver—a tall man with longish dark hair and a matching dark mustache—jumped silently out and eased his door shut, then walked back to the entrance and knocked softly. The door opened instantly, and the tall man disappeared inside.

In two or three minutes the driver emerged again, followed by a young man whose boyish good looks were clouded by the frowning concentration of his expression. They both stopped in the doorway and stared gloomily at the van. The young man ran his hand indecisively through his curly brown hair, and then, with a sudden, angry movement, stepped over to the back of the van and wrenched open the door. The driver, one beautiful dark eye twitching nervously, moved a few feet away and leaned against a tree. The young man looked inside the van for several long seconds. "Are you guys crazy? What went wrong last night? And what in hell are you doing here?" he said finally.

The two men sitting inside the back of the van looked up.

The one closest to the back door grinned. "Hey, *Buru* . . . No sweat. Last night was great. We brought the new stuff. It's good. Even Carlos says so. And a pile of cash. Safe wasn't worth a pinch of shit." He was a thin, wiry man somewhere in his twenties, neat, small and clean-cut.

"It is not important—not at all—how good it is, Don. Not anymore. Can you not understand that? You're in every paper in the city." The buru paused and looked thoughtfully at the two men inside the van.

"You gonna just stand there and gawk at us all night?" said Don defensively. "Or do we bring the shit in?"

"We are alone here tonight. There is no one around. It does not matter how long we stand here. I want to know what happened," he repeated, his voice quiet, controlled.

"I dunno," Don said impatiently. "We were pretty sure the place was empty, and so Manu came in to help carry things." The tall, dark-eyed man leaning on the tree looked up sardonically at the sound of his name. "And this lady came out of nowhere. . . . I dunno what happened. I just gave her a little whack with this statue thing I was carrying, kind of to get her out of the way, and Carlos— Well, you know what Carlos is like." Don shrugged. The fourth man, who was lounging, relaxed, on an air mattress at the other end of the van, looked up and smiled. "He shot her. But no one heard. The goddamn place is air-conditioned; no windows open or nothing like that. No one saw us. There's nothing to worry about."

The man they called Buru replied with a flood of obscene invective both in English and his native language. Don stayed passively where he was, crouched on the floor of the van, waiting. "You cannot leave that stuff here," the buru said at last, his voice calmer. "The whole operation will be ruined if it is found here." Then he shone a powerful flashlight beam into the interior. His quick eye caught the signature on one of the paintings stacked against the wall. He jumped in and picked up a Georgian silver teapot, hefted it, and shone his light on it. "Okay," he said reluctantly. "I will take it, but you have made it much more difficult to move any of this now. It was a very stupid thing to do. It will be impossible to meet for a while, as well. And certainly not here. We will meet at Carlos's place, if necessary. Okay?"

The man lounging toward the front of the van, a dark-haired man with lazy eyes, looked up again, acknowledging his name, yawned, and nodded. "Whatever you say, Buru," he drawled. In his mouth the epithet was an insult.

The buru's reply was curt. "Move it quickly," he said, and stepped back. They nodded. Manu strode rapidly to the door, Don jumped to the ground behind the van, and even Carlos moved lightly to his feet, crouching under the van's too-low ceiling. They began transferring last night's haul smoothly and quietly into the building.

On the night of August the fifteenth, a choking pall of damp, hot, and dirty air lay heavily over the city, shortening tempers, shortening breath, and making sleep impossible for all but the efficiently air-conditioned. The dispatcher on duty at the Thirty-third Division stared heavily into the distance. There was a lull, as though the whole area had grown too hot even for thieves and muggers. He yawned and looked over at the constable writing up a report on the other side of the room. "Maybe it's going to be a quiet—" he started, and was interrupted by the telephone. As he wrote, a look of exasperation passed over his face. "Christ! That's the third time since I got on nights that goddamn alarm has gone!" he said to the voice of Mid-City Security Systems on the other end. "Either you guys get that system back in adjustment, or we stop responding." He cut the connection and turned back to the constable. "Shit. The bleeding poodle has tripped over the burglar alarm at 47 Rosefall Road again. I wish these people would figure out how their systems worked."

"Maybe the lady of the house gets lonely," said the constable with a mildly lecherous grin. "And gives it a kick every once in a while."

"I should leave those bastards at Mid-City to do their own investigating," the dispatcher muttered, shaking his head. "Next time . . ." And with a sigh he began to relay the message out to the nearest patrol car.

When Constable Jim Underhill got the call to proceed to 47 Rosefall Road, he was parked only a block away. "Shit," he muttered; luck had sent him there only three nights before, and he had not enjoyed dealing with the irritable and defensive owner of the premises that time. He started up the car, glumly wheeling it around and turning down the street. Rosefall Road was a celebration of excessive wealth: six vast houses squatting in privacy on million-dollar lots. At its dead end, the world plunged off into a ravine. Tonight the area was dark and very still. The street lighting had become strangled in the lush growth of summer, and the road was deserted. All the residents appeared to be off at summer cottages, abandoning their city properties to the raccoons and the house breakers.

As he pulled his cruiser smoothly up to the turning circle at the end, he could hear the muted buzzing of the alarm. The house looked dark and empty. He wondered what had set the alarm off this time; three nights ago it had been a teenaged daughter forgetting about the existence of the new system and casually opening a door. The time before that it had been the humidity. It would be something just as stupid tonight, he thought philosophically. He got out, flashlight in hand, and started up the front walk. As he reached the halfway point, Mid-City Security Systems finally deactivated the alarm from their end. He paused uneasily. The silence, as menacing and oppressive as the heat, was suddenly broken by a low thumping sound. His uneasiness vanished; now every sense was agonizingly alert. He stepped onto the lawn in the shadow of a large shrub and listened. Another muted thump. He slipped around the corner of the house, very quietly. There was a window wide open. Inside he caught the suggestion of a fluttering movement. Jesus! he thought, his heart pumping with mounting excitement. I've caught those bastards right in the act, hands in the goddamn cookie jar. They're getting sloppy, he reflected happily. This time they hadn't even worried about the alarm. He reached down to unfasten the flap on his holster, keeping his eyes fixed on the almost-silent figure edging over the sill. The man behind him—the one he hadn't seen in the darkness— didn't give Underhill a half second to respond before the bullets crashed through his spine.

Inspector John Sanders stood in the cemetery, stiff and uncomfortable. By some malignant trick of fate, if he raised his eyes from the ground, they would fall directly on the smooth dark hair and bowed and trembling shoulders of Jim Underhill's young widow. Then his guilt—for as he saw it, he was responsible for her widowhood—compounded itself with his private misery. Heather Underhill's dark hair and slender body reminded him painfully of Harriet; the sight of her inevitably summoned Harriet up from the deep recess in his brain where he had hidden her all summer. Harriet, who had so mysteriously and maddeningly made herself unavailable. Every time he telephoned, no matter what the hour, her answering machine repeated the same monotonous message. No human being could be out that much, he had concluded, and tormented himself with visions of her wandering restlessly about in her apartment, listening to her phone ring and not answering it—to avoid him. And every time, he obstinately refused to confide his loneliness and heartbreak to a piece of magnetic tape.

Five minutes of this and he eased himself out of the crowd, trying to placate his conscience by getting a good look at each one of the people he edged by. Not that it was necessary. There wasn't a face that hadn't been videotaped at least once since the funeral began and wouldn't be studied, analyzed, and if possible, identified. But the murderer of Jim Underhill had better things to do than titillate himself with morbid thrills by attending the funerals of his victims, Sanders suspected. The only faces here that had been at

Mrs. Wilkinson's funeral would be his, and Dubinsky's, and the other members of the team from Homicide. He backed farther away until he was out of the crowd, away from the reproach of those thin shoulders in black. If he had tracked down the men who had put a bullet in Mrs. Wilkinson's back, they couldn't have just as casually murdered Heather Underhill's husband. "Dammit! What do they think I am? A goddamn magician?" he muttered. He turned and walked quickly away.

He paused at the sound of longer strides behind him and waited for his partner to catch up. "It's no use, John," said Dubinsky. "We're not going to get anything solid until they start fencing the stuff. Then we'll get them. Come on. Let's have some lunch."

Twenty minutes later, Sanders was looking at his pastrami sandwich as if he were contemplating arresting it for an offense against decency. He tried the dill pickle, put it down again, and shoved his plate away. "For chrissake, Ed, where in hell are they getting rid of the stuff? Nothing has turned up. They're not selling it back to the insurance companies. And there can't be a fence in town who'd touch any of it."

"They're not hungry," said Dubinsky philosophically. "Whoever they are, they can afford to wait. Besides, the stuff'll all be in the States by now. If it was sitting anywhere in Toronto, Volchek would know. He knows everybody and what they're up to." By now he had finished his corned beef and was casually helping himself to Sanders's french fries. "Anyway, these guys are amateurs."

"Amateurs?"

"Sure. You know. Pros always expect to be caught at some point. They keep their asses covered. I mean, look at them. They go into that house on Rosefall. They know it's alarmed and pay no attention. They plant someone outside to dispose of that poor bugger Underhill when he turns up, and then they stroll off with $350,000 worth of paintings and stamps. That wasn't a panic killing; they plucked him off like a crow on a fence." He helped himself to another french fry. "Bastards."

"What if Underhill hadn't turned up by himself? What if two cars had responded?"

"They wouldn't have, though, would they? You saw the report. That alarm system had gone off three, four times in the ten days before the robbery. Owner kept forgetting it was on, it malfunctioned in the heat, whatever. The dispatcher knew no one had broken in, didn't he? Minimal response guaranteed."

"And how do these guys know that?" said Sanders. Only it wasn't a question. "If they aren't working for the security company. And they can't be. Volchek's been over there a hundred times. He's shaken every employee they've got until his teeth dropped out."

"Yeah," said his partner. Doubt oozed out of the syllable as he pronounced it. "And speaking of Volchek, a call came in just before I left. Wilkinson wants to know when he can have his wife's ring back."

"What ring?"

Dubinsky pulled his notebook out of his pocket. "One woman's ring, gold, set with a large emerald flanked by two diamonds inside a knotlike design, valued at approximately eight thousand dollars." He closed his book again. "He said he could get a more precise description from the jeweler who designed it. He had it made for his wife as a birthday present, and he would like it back so he can give it to his daughter."

"I didn't see anything about a ring. Did you?"

Dubinsky shook his head. "I called Volchek, who knew nothing, and I called the morgue. The guys at the morgue swear there was no ring on either hand except for a narrow gold wedding band and that they can vouch for the honesty of everyone who works there. They're paranoid sons of bitches, those guys at the morgue. The detailed autopsy report indicates some damage to the knuckle—the ring might have been forced off her hand during the robbery. Anyway,

I called Wilkinson back and asked him how come he waited so long to mention a missing eight-thousand-dollar piece of jewelry, and he said that when he'd asked the undertaker about it before she was buried, the bastard had said that we'd kept it as evidence. So I called the goddamn undertaker, and he said that he didn't *know* that, he just thought it was the sort of thing we'd be likely to do."

"Wonderful. Add it to the list of stolen property," said Sanders. "The more the merrier."

"I did already," said Dubinsky. "Here, have something to eat before we go over to Mid-City." He pushed Sanders's lunch back in front of him.

CHAPTER 2

Harriet Jeffries stiffened uncomfortably as Irene's strong fingers massaged her scalp. The whole process of having her hair "done" seemed entirely too self-indulgent, almost decadent. Even if it was straggly and long and hung in her eyes every time she tried to work. Self-indulgent and time-consuming. She began to count up the projects she had to get finished before the end of September and chewed nervously on her lower lip as the list mounted. In her business, either you worked yourself to death, or you starved. Everyone wanted you, or no one did. And as her professional life flourished, her love life went to hell. She had spent an exuberant night with John after she had returned to Toronto in June, a magic night that swept away past doubts and hinted at a glorious future. Then a promise of a phone call and John Sanders had disappeared. As if he had never been. He hadn't called—not even an insincere "Sorry, I'm too busy" call—and he had been impossible to reach through his department. She burned with embarrassment at the memory of the snickering voice that had answered his telephone and of her cowardly refusal to leave a message. A jet of hot water on her head deflected her momentarily from her gloomy reflections.

Once she had been parked in the main part of the salon to wait for Rudi, she closed her eyes and tried not to think about the amount of time she was going to be spending in the darkroom this afternoon and tonight. One of her most important clients expected a hundred black-and-white prints by nine tomorrow morning; she had been up until one last night finishing the last phase of the shooting, and now the film was processed and dry, ready for printing. Of course, it was pure luck that they hadn't wanted the prints this morning. Except that she would have stayed up all night and been finished by now instead of putting off the agony until this afternoon. Why in hell hadn't she canceled the appointment and started printing right away? "Because you're a lazy, decadent sybarite, that's why," she muttered to herself.

The mutter produced the receptionist, with an air of polished distress. "Terribly sorry, Miss Jeffries," she murmured. "I think he's almost ready for you."

"Don't worry about it," said Harriet. After all, she thought sleepily, if you have zero hours to spare, then what difference does it make how you slice them up? As she puzzled over the mathematics of this, she was distracted by the sound of a throaty laugh followed by a flood of German. Harriet couldn't catch the words, but she recognized the voice and the impenetrable dialect. The speaker occupied a chair halfway down the row, and from it she dominated the entire room. She was an erect and handsome woman, lost somewhere in the indefinable recesses of middle age, with dark, clearly delineated features and a great deal of thick black hair slightly tinged with gray. Her name was Clara von Hohenkammer, and she was the current owner of a magnificently renovated house that Harriet had lovingly captured in both color and black and white, a project so successful that it had prompted her to consider putting together a book of interesting renovations. Maybe she should call the editor who was working on her current book and— No, Harriet, she said to herself, no more projects, and turned her attention back to the woman. Rudi was presently occupied in piling her hair up in an extravagantly Edwardian hairdo, apparently much to her amusement.

"It's Miss Jeffries," she said, catching sight of Harriet in the mirror. "My dear, how delightful to see you." Her English was fluent and graceful, although too mannered to be native; her accent fluctuated between controlled Ox-bridge and recognizably German. "Is this not the perfect look to go mad and die in?" She gave a little pat to the ring of hair piled on the top of her head. "Tonight I read Lady Macbeth to finish my performance, and I must look the part, although I don't think I will appear in a nightgown." Harriet gave her a blank and baffled stare. "You haven't heard of my great Toronto debut, then?" She shook her head mutely. "Never mind. Since it is almost entirely in German, I believe it was mentioned only in the German press. But I am giving a reading tonight at the Goethe Institute, and you, my dear, must come. Your German is certainly good enough, but even if it weren't, that wouldn't matter. The important thing is that I am giving an impromptu party afterwards. Rudi is com-ing, isn't he?" She cast an upward glance into the mirror.

The hairdresser nodded as he rearranged the last few drooping curls at her hairline.

"That's very kind of you, Frau von Hohenkammer," said Harriet, moving automatically into refusal mode. "Unfortu-nately, I'm in the middle of a very time-consuming project—"

"Nonsense! Of course you must come. You can't work all the time. Your buildings will wait; they are not going any-where." There was a tinge of contempt in her tone. Harriet and Clara had already had a small and stubborn confronta-tion on the subject of architectural photography and Harriet's refusal to do portrait work. "The reading is at eight o'clock. There will be a brief reception after and then a not-so-brief affair at the house. You haven't had a chance to see what it looks like now that it's been lived in a little. I've left the Mondrian where you so cleverly put it, by the way." She turned again to Rudi. "That house is marvelous. A wonder-ful bargain, and it's already increased greatly in value, you know. And it is such a"—she flipped hastily through her English vocabulary for the right word— "well, sympathetic house to live in. I don't know how else to put it."

Harriet choked slightly at the thought that a house that cost $650,000 four and half years ago, when prices were much lower, could be considered a bargain. But she had enjoyed photographing Frau von Hohenkammer's art, and she was curious to see it all again. "Thank you very much," she said at last, trying to look enthusiastic. "I would love to come. I didn't even know that you were back in town."

"I came down early. I suddenly realized I had many things to do before the reading. Like coming here." She frowned as she craned for a sideways glance at her hair. "And calling you. My nephew will be in town. . . . He, too, is a photographer. I need to talk to you about him a little." She glanced sideways at Harriet and dropped her voice slightly. "So you understand, it is important that you come this evening. I shall stay until the season starts again in Munich," she added loudly. "To see my grandchildren, you know. You will have to look at pictures of them when you come tonight. Even if you won't take pictures of people, you can't object to looking at them, can you?" She smiled and turned away in a definitive gesture of dismissal. She and Rudi retreated cozily into the dialect of the tiny corner of Bavaria they both came from.

Inspector John Sanders lifted a pile of reports and dropped them on the floor beside him. He sorted through the rest of the material still in front of him and took out four sheets of paper; these he placed carefully in a file folder under his right elbow. With his left arm, he pushed aside everything else on his desk until it piled itself up against the heating unit on the wall. With great deliberation, he moved the file folder from under his elbow over to the center of the desk. "This is it," he said. "Unless you have more. The rest is worthless crap."

Dubinsky gave him a martyred look from the safety of his own desk but remained silent.

"I told you. We've been through those sons of bitches at Mid-City until we knew everybody's grandmother's maiden name," said Sergeant Volchek resentfully. "And what she ate for breakfast. But if you bastards think you can find your way around better than we can, be our guest."

"Sorry," said Sanders wearily. "Of course you know what you're doing. But for chrissake, we can't just shrug our shoulders and say okay, you look after it. Not when it's an officer shot on duty. You know that. And it has to be connected with Mid-City. . . ." He shook his head. "Come on." His voice quivered with impatience. "All but two of the big money break-ins since May were into houses that had just bought or updated their security systems from Mid-City. And except for the house on Rosefall Road, they were all entered at some weak point in their system. If you want me to believe that's a coincidence—"

"That house didn't have any weak points," said Volchek. His voice was getting more sour. "Except that the system was too good. Mid-City's deluxe model. Too goddamn sensitive to function."

"Anyway, what in hell are we supposed to think?"

"Believe it or not," said Volchek, "we figured that out. We were the ones who fed you that information, remember?" He pulled his chair closer to Sanders's desk and hunched forward. "Only three guys had access to all those installations, and they all have alibis for most of the robberies. What in hell do you want us to do? Harrison has gone in undercover," he added. "If there's anything sour in that company, he'll find out."

"Well, maybe someone at Mid-City has just been setting them up," said Sanders, "and—"

"Come on. If someone at Mid-City is just selling plans and stuff like that, it could be any one of the people who work there," said Volchek. "And Harrison will get him. I mean alibis don't come into it, then, do they? Besides, that would mean the person involved at Mid-City didn't kill Underhill or Wilkinson."

"Of course not." Sanders ran both hands through his hair and then began to massage his scalp. "I can't think anymore."

"Have you checked out the people who quit recently?" said Dubinsky.

Volchek gave him a look of infinite long suffering. "Yes.

Back to April third. After that week, two systems were installed into houses that have been broken into."

"No one quit?"

"Just one. And he's left the country," said Volchek. "But if we're not worrying about alibis," he added, "then my money is on him." One large hand hit the list sitting in front of Sanders, its index finger stabbing the name "Don Walker."

"Who's he?" said Sanders, startled.

Volchek smiled. "A lousy little punk who was in and out of juvenile court until he was eighteen. No record, because he hasn't been caught once since. He sure learned a helluva lot in those detention homes. I damn near died laughing when I saw that Mid-City had hired him."

Dubinsky and Sanders leaned over the file, staring down at it. "You think he's the organizer, then?" asked Dubinsky.

Volchek shook his head slowly. "I don't know. It doesn't figure, though. Don was never a great brain. A greedy little bugger, all right, but not the guy I'd pick to be running an operation like this one. I mean, where would he find the kind of fences you'd need to get rid of all this art and shit like that? We've been keeping an eye on him, but he couldn't have been doing anything but peddling information to someone else about how the Mid-City systems work. He had alibis for three of the robberies." Volchek pulled out his notebook and extracted a folded piece of paper from it. "Okay. Forget the one on Post Road the twenty-fourth of May weekend. It wasn't the same crew; they took a lot of audio equipment and stuff like that. For the big one in Rosedale on the first of July weekend, no alibi. There was a second one that weekend up in Aurora that they probably did as well. But the second in our jurisdiction was the Wilkinson house, at the end of July, and for that one he was playing poker with four other guys. We interviewed two of them *and* the landlady, and it all checks out. And then for the one on the Scarborough Bluffs and that massive haul over by the Kingsway on the Civic Holiday weekend, August fourth or fifth, Walker was away for the long weekend at his sister's cottage and right under her nose all the time. Or so she says. And a couple of other people up there saw him around. So they say. No alibi for the eleventh. But the night Underhill was killed he was working. He had taken over for a friend whose wife was having a baby. On the phones, even though he was actually an installer."

"And he worked on all the houses?" said Dubinsky. Volchek nodded. Dubinsky looked down at his own notes again. "I wonder what they were doing," he said, "between July fourth and July twenty-fourth?"

Volchek shrugged. "Who knows? Taking a holiday. Now what happens?"

"We're taking four days off," said Sanders. "That's what happens. For the last month we've been working eighteen-, twenty-hour days."

"Lucky bastards," said Volchek. "Give my love to your girlfriends." Volchek stood up, stuffed his sheets of paper back into his pocket, and walked out the door.

Sanders gave his retreating back a vicious look. "Arrogant son of a bitch," he muttered. The word *girlfriend* had scratched open an uncomfortable wound on his soul. "He can go to hell."

An hour later, Clara von Hohenkammer's voice filled the sunny conservatory in her elegant house on the ravine, but someone who had heard her talking to Rudi might never have recognized it. The flow was just as overwhelmingly fluent, but the vowels and consonants were now precise and educated, the vocabulary extensive, and the tone very irritated. "Now let me see if I understand what you are trying to tell me, Theresa." Clara stared unblinking for a few moments across the room at the tall, vaguely pretty woman who squirmed in the chair opposite her. "You are trying to tell me that Milan, that brilliant designer, that wonderful engineer, who is so clever with money—I am only trying to remember exactly the way you used to describe him to Papa—has managed to sink all his money, and all the money he could borrow, and the money your father left you, in a scheme so bad that he has lost it? All of it? And you want me to supply you with even more money so he can have a chance to lose all that, as well? And just why do you suppose I should do that, Theresa? If I might ask." Her voice rose to second-balcony level, then sank again in pure scorn as her peroration came to an end.

Theresa's cheeks flamed in splotches of angry color. "You don't need to be so unpleasant about it, Mamma," she said, sulking. "It could happen to anyone. You just don't know what interest rates were like here when we started the company. Or what's been happening to the Canadian dollar. And when the market went down, well, that wasn't Milan's fault. He couldn't foresee that. We should have made millions on this already, and we will, if we can keep the project going. But if he doesn't get some money quickly, he'll lose everything. We'll even lose the house. And the banks just won't listen to him right now. And Mamma, it would only be for a short while. He'd pay you back. He's got options on all the land for a major development—well, almost all the land—and once he gets started, he won't have any trouble getting investors. And the economic climate is improving here. He is sure that he can attract investors from the U.S." She leaned forward in her chair, her voice throbbing with sincerity.

"If he is so sure that the economy is improving, then why doesn't he wait a little while before going ahead? That sounds like the sensible way to do things."

"Mamma, you don't understand. He can't wait. These people are just not willing to give him any time to find refinancing. We'll be ruined." At this, her voice rose in a small shriek, and then she subsided into tears.

Her mother continued to look at her in a detached and interested sort of way. "You'll have to excuse me if I don't find that very comforting, Theresa. I have great confidence in bankers' instincts, even when I don't necessarily admire their intellect. It seems to me that if they thought that their money was safe with your husband, he wouldn't be in this situation. And you two seem to expect that I will be stupider than the banks and will throw my money down the drain with yours." She turned her head impatiently away from her sobbing daughter. "Will you stop that noise! I will consider the whole thing. Tell your husband I will make an appointment for him to discuss the matter with Frank and the accountant, who will no doubt want to look at his books. If there seems to be a reasonable chance of the business being salvaged, I might do something about it, but this would be the last time—the very last time—that you could possibly count on me to rescue you. I have to think of Nikki, you know, and Friedl and Klaus, as well. You cannot expect to get everything for yourself, especially after your father treated you so generously."

A look of sullen mutiny settled grimly on Theresa's pretty face. "Thank you, Mamma" choked itself out from between her tight lips. "We'll see you tonight."

"Certainly, my dear. I would appreciate it if you could keep Milan from discussing this tonight. I will have other things on my mind. Give the children a kiss from Grandmamma and tell them I will see them tomorrow." She made a slight gesture of dismissal, as though to an annoying housemaid, and opened the drawer of the small desk in front of her.

A black Porsche was drawn up in the broad half circle of gravel in front of the house. It lay open to the September sun and breezes, which played on the short dark hair (thinning at the crown) of the man waiting in the driver's seat. But the sun, the birds, the breezes, the spreading trees didn't seem to be bringing him much joy and comfort. His handsome, gently Slavic face was screwed into an expression somewhere between cold rage and furious impatience. Theresa came hurtling out of the house, saw the unpleasant set of his shoulders, stopped, and sauntered over to the car. The slight scuffle of her feet on the gravel cut through his obviously unpleasant reverie, and he turned and snapped a terse "Well?" at her.

She shrugged her shoulders. "I don't know. You know what Mamma's like. Hard as nails when it comes to cash. She said a few nasty things about throwing money away and then that she might consider the idea, but she wants Frank to look at the books with the accountant—her accountant."

He reached over and flung open the door for her. "Shit! That's all we need." He nibbled at a fingernail for a second before starting the car. "How good is the accountant?"

Theresa shrugged again. "I don't know. I can't remember who he is. But you won't get much past Frank. He's as suspicious as hell, and he's even tighter than Mamma with her money."

"Screw Frank," said Milan Milanovich. "He's a half-assed, stupid bastard. It's the accountant we have to worry about."

"Maybe. But Frank Whitelaw still figures that he's going to marry Mamma, you know. Then all her money will be his one day, he thinks. So every minute that a penny of hers is invested in the company they'll both be breathing down your neck to see what you're doing with it. But I can't help that. I've done all I can."

"Did you happen to point out to her," he said in a low voice, slowly and emphatically, "that when the whole god-damned thing starts coming apart, I could end up in jail?" He eased the car into gear and started down the driveway.

"Good God, no!" said Theresa. "If she heard that, we'd never get a cent out of her. Mamma may look all broad-minded and cosmopolitan to you, but she's just a school-teacher's daughter who never did anything illegal in her life. That's why Nikki's always in so much trouble with her. But, you know," she said, shifting to another train of thought, "today she was talking about being fair to Nikki . . . and to Klaus. Klaus! He's just a lousy nephew. And to Aunt Friedl. I wonder what's happened." Her look of vague sulkiness disappeared in frowning worry. "Damn. I should have spent the summer at the cottage with her; we made a bad mistake there." She ducked instinctively as the Porsche leaped out onto St. Clair Avenue in dangerous proximity to a moving van and a fast-traveling motorcycle and then went back to what was troubling her. "Six months ago she was talking about disinheriting Nikki, you know. And she had no use for Klaus at all. In fact, I was sure we could count on Nikki's share. Dammit!"

"Is Nikki still up at the cottage?"

"She's coming down tonight for the stupid reading." She paused while Milan negotiated a turn that involved ducking around, then cutting off, a cab and a stretch limousine in order to get into the newer, quietly expensive area where their splashy house was located. "I'll take the kids over tomorrow. She'll have recovered by then, and she'll be more in the mood. She's in a foul temper today. It was stupid of me to try, I guess."

"Well, we can't wait forever for her to be in a generous mood. I have to have something positive to say to Grantly and to the bank by Monday, and this is Thursday."

"Okay," she said irritably. "Don't push me. Look what happened today because you got impatient. I'll get around her one way or another in time for that meeting." She reached for the door before the car came to a halt. "And tonight, not a word about business or money. Just keep telling her how wonderful she was and keep your temper."

"Christ, how stupid do you think I am?" His wife raised one contemptuous eyebrow in his direction and strode briskly along the path that bisected the perfect lawn and led into the neat and perfect house.

Clara von Hohenkammer set the phone down in its cradle and made a minute note in her desk diary. Then she pulled a flimsy airmail envelope from the narrow top drawer, took a sheet of paper from it, and read it slowly, smoothing the paper several times as she read. She folded it again and slipped it into the center of a novel lying by her elbow. For a moment, she sat staring at the blank surface in front of her before passing her hand over her brow in a gesture of exhaustion or despair. A young man walked briskly into her line of sight, heading purposefully southwest, across the back lawn, in the direction of a large coach house in the back of the garden. Clara got up and walked over to an open window. "Paul," she called peremptorily. "I would like to see you."

He looked up in surprise and changed his course for the main house. "Yes, ma'am?" There wasn't much of the faithful servitor in his bored gaze. "You wanted to speak to me?"

"Yes," she said irritably. "I was kept awake for hours last night by some sort of party. The noise came from the coach house, and your lights were on. I will not tolerate rowdiness on the premises, whether you think I am going to be here or not."

"In the coach house?" he said, opening his dark blue eyes wide with surprise. "Oh, no, Doña Clara. Certainly not." His soft voice throbbed with sincerity. "There was noise last night, yes. Around midnight." He nodded emphatically. "I went out to look, and I left my lights on while I did my round. But it was a party in the ravine. Kids, probably," he added, pointing to the fence perched just above the ravine that formed the southern border to her property. "They go there with cases of beer, and sometimes they are very loud, especially on warm nights. It is very noisy in Toronto on warm nights." He said this almost reproachfully.

"This was not in the ravine," said Clara firmly. "I heard car engines and doors slamming. It was up here."

"That could have been the people next door. Was your air conditioner on?" he asked casually.

"No. I had my windows open, and you would think that they were in the room with me. It was not next door. Where were the dogs?"

"They were locked up, ma'am," he said.

"What's the point of that if there are people prowling around outside? And why weren't the police called to get rid of whoever it was? Do you realize how many houses have been broken into this summer? And how many valuable paintings stolen? You have little enough to do around here for the enormous salary you get paid. I should at least be able to sleep peacefully at night."

"Yes, ma'am," he said with a nod of his head. "But if you kept your air conditioner on, you wouldn't notice these little noises."

"Little noises!" she snorted. "I have no intention of using an air conditioner in weather like this. From now on do what you are paid for." With that she turned from the window and pressed the bell on the underside of her pretty, white-painted desk. The gardener, uncowed, stared at her erect back with expressionless eyes before resuming his interrupted walk.

After a long pause, during which Clara von Hohenkammer stood impatiently staring at the plants and hanging pots that filled the room, a short, very blond woman waddled into the room. Her face was round and pale and choked with pinkish powder; floating in the center of it were a pair of round pale blue eyes. Her hair lay in neat waves grimly secured in place by a hair net. Her round and powerful arms were bursting out of a white uniform. She stared in the direction of her employer, her lips quivering with annoyance at being dragged from her kitchen.

Frau von Hohenkammer scarcely glanced in her direction. "Bettl, there will probably be five for an early dinner tonight. Mr. Whitelaw, my daughter and her husband, Fräulein Nikki and my nephew, if he drives her down from Muskoka. I will take some soup in my room at five-thirty. That is all." She waved a hand dismissively.

The formidable Bettl did not dismiss that easily. "I am," she said, "to prepare dinner for five extra people and get ready for a party tonight? I cannot do it." She turned to go. "They can eat in a restaurant."

Her employer whipped around and looked at her steadily. "Bettl," she said in a poisonously calm voice, "I would ask you to remember that I pay you very well and that you have little to do, looking after me and the occasional guest. You can be replaced very easily, and I shall not hesitate to do so, I assure you. You know perfectly well that most of the food for the party is being done by the caterers. I shall expect soup in my room at five-thirty and dinner—a decent dinner, not some warmed-over goulash—for my guests at six-thirty. Fruit will suffice for dessert, since there will be cakes and pastries later at the party. Do you understand that? Because if you do not understand, then my guests can indeed go to a restaurant, and you can pack your bags and go back to Pfaffenhofen on the next plane."

Bettl's wide expanse of throat and neck turned scarlet as she backed wordlessly out of the room.

Clara lowered herself slowly into her chair behind the pretty desk; the muscles in her cheeks sagged minutely, and a twitching flutter started in her lower right eyelid. In spite of her careful makeup, her face looked slack and gray with fatigue. Once again she rubbed her hand absentmindedly over her forehead, then picked up a folder sitting in the corner and flipped it open. Never taking her eyes off the page, she slowly rose again, moved over to a small couch by the glassed-in south wall, and arranged herself comfortably, with her feet propped up on cushions. Her lips moved soundlessly as she studied the pages in front of her, oblivious to the sound of a car tearing up the gravel drive. She started slightly when the door to the conservatory was flung open by an out-of-breath, smaller and younger version of herself.

"That's where you're hiding yourself, Mamma. Well, we're here, both of us, starving and dying of thirst, but we never stopped a second on the way down. How are you bearing up?" She leaned over, gave her mother a kiss, and stepped back to observe her critically. "You look very white. Are you ill?"

"I'm fine, Nikki, dear. Just suffering from lack of sleep. There seemed to have been rowdy hoodlums partying in our garden last night, and I lay awake until the noise quieted down. I warn you that I am in something of a temper as a result. . . . I almost fired Paul, and then Bettl, one right after the other." She laughed. "It will do them good."

Nikki dropped into a white wicker armchair. "Are you sure there isn't something else wrong?" she asked, bending forward and looking more closely at her mother.

"Certainly," said Clara firmly. "I have things on my mind, but nothing is *wrong*. There are matters to be worked out, that is all. At times, life becomes rather, well, complicated and one needs a certain amount of strength and ingenuity to manage it."

"Whatever are you talking about, Mamma?" An expression of blended amusement and alarm spread over the girl's face. "Strength and ingenuity? What has happened?"

"Nothing." Clara suddenly looked deathly tired. "It is always difficult to judge," she said, allowing hesitation to creep into her voice, "how one should behave in a foreign country. One never knows exactly how seriously certain things are viewed by the authorities. It was foolish of me not to hire a local manager. One forgets that the British are foreigners here, too, even if they do speak the language. That's what sentimentality gets you. And another lawyer. I need someone like Peter Lohr over here."

"Lawyer? Mamma, what's going on?"

Clara glanced at the puzzled, worried face of her younger daughter and shook her head cheerfully. "Nothing at all. I was considering purely theoretical problems. How was the drive? And did you say 'we'? Klaus has come with you?"

"I wouldn't miss this for the world," said the slightly rumpled young man who had just wandered into the room. "What is country scenery compared to civilization and culture? Besides, it is cold at night up there now, and too chilly to swim." He embraced his aunt and then sat down. "And I have decided it is time to seize life by the horns."

"That sounds impressive," said Clara. "But perhaps you should have some lunch first."

"Good idea. I'll just duck into the kitchen and see if Bettl can throw together some sandwiches for us, right, Nikki? Do you want something to drink?"

"Bring me a beer. I'm dying of heat and thirst."

"Your servant, gracious lady," he said, withdrawing with an extravagant bow and click of the heels.

"Klaus looks much happier these days, don't you think, Nikki?" said her mother, firmly heading off a reversion to their earlier topic.

"Definitely," she said with a quick glance at the door. "He's actually been talking about settling down. He asked me if I thought Toronto might be a good place to live in. I wonder if he met a girl while he was wandering around the city in July and August." She yawned and stretched her legs out in front of her. "I think he wants to talk to you about it." She was talking in a soft voice, and rapidly, with one eye on the door in case he returned.

Klaus walked in carefully balancing two bottles of Kronenbourg and two tall glasses on a tray. Eventually he was followed by Bettl, who stalked in, slammed down a plate thinly covered with sandwiches, and wordlessly stalked out again. "This isn't much," said Nikki as she scooped what she considered to be her fair share from the plate. "Bettl must figure we're all going to eat too much tonight."

"She didn't look very happy when I asked for that," said Klaus. "I guess we can't complain about what we got."

"That's because Mamma almost sacked her today," said Nikki, and settled down to her modest lunch.

Nikki finished the last drop of beer in her glass, put it down, and stretched extravagantly. "Now I am off to take a bath and generally get myself looking more civilized. Mamma, you should take a nap and stop even looking at that stuff. You could read it with both eyes shut if you had to, couldn't you?"

Her mother waved good-bye to her. "I'm going to do that in just a minute. As soon as Frank comes." Clara watched her out of the room before turning to her nephew.

"When is he coming?" asked Klaus, glancing at his watch.

"Not for twenty minutes," she replied. "Did you want to see me?"

"You're sure you're not too tired? We could easily talk tomorrow, when you aren't getting ready for a performance." He fidgeted uneasily in his chair.

"Not at all," she said. "I have nothing to do until seven but dress and get worried." She shrugged her shoulders irritably. "I detest these small performances when you're only a few feet from the audience. Now, Nikki tells me you have an idea, she thinks. What is it?"

"It's hard to know where to start, really," he said, leaning forward, looking anxiously at his aunt. "But ever since I came here I've been thinking seriously about getting myself established."

"Doing what?" she asked in a carefully neutral voice.

"Oh, photography, of course. I've had several pictures published here and there, and I've made some money doing portraits—little girls with their dogs and so on. I'm pretty good . . . they thought I was very good at the institute, even though I hated it by the end of the course. But I did finish. I am capable of finishing something that I start." He gave her a self-conscious smile and sat back in his chair.

"I thought you were considering something like this. And it would be expensive to set yourself up as a photographer, is that what you're saying?" She laid the book in her hand down on the floor and looked steadily at him.

"Well, not exactly. I'm not asking for money, Aunt Clara."

"That's strange. Everyone else is," she said with a touch of bitterness. "But what was it you wanted if not the other half of my fortune?"

"Actually, there are two things. Remember I asked you if I could store things in a room in the basement?" She looked up sharply, studied his face for a moment, and then nodded. "Well, while I was here in the summer, I took one of the empty rooms and turned it into a darkroom, using the bathroom next to it for washing film and prints. It's on the other side of the basement from your storage room. I wouldn't get in your way. I put in some secondhand equipment and used one of the cupboards for chemicals and things like that. And there's a whole lot of color film in the freezer, too, all packaged and labeled. If Bettl hasn't tried to cook it, thinking it was lamp chops." His aunt smiled. "I should have told you sooner, but I intended to clear it all out before you came down again."

"My dear, don't look so worried. I don't care how much film is in the freezer, and I don't suppose I should ever need that room in the basement. I hate rooms in basements. It's not one that Bettl uses to do the wash in, is it?"

"No, Aunt Clara, she does the wash upstairs, behind the kitchen."

"Then go ahead and use it," said Clara impatiently. "But is that your great plan? Really, Klaus, it wasn't worth all this buildup."

"No. I want Nikki, too. She could work as an assistant for me—or as an apprentice. She has a very good eye, you know, and she's quick and clever. It would keep her out of trouble," he added.

"In what way?" At the mention of her daughter, her face and body stiffened, her voice deepened.

"I don't think she should go back to Munich," he said cautiously, keeping a wary eye on his aunt's responses. "I think she could get herself in real trouble this time if she does."

"What do you mean by real trouble?" Clara's voice was glacial.

"Look, I know these people she's mixed up with. She's half in love with Christian, and he's crazy about your money and planning to blow up the world in the name of peace and justice when he can afford to buy enough explosives. I never said anything when she was just flirting with radical ideas and going off to meetings or rallies or whatever and feeling very righteous. I mean, she got a big charge out of it, and I think she was lonely and unhappy there for a while." He looked nervously at his aunt, expecting a truly grand explosion, but she merely nodded.

"She took her father's death very hard. And she hasn't quite forgiven me for being out of the city when it happened." Her tone was still mild and reasonable.

"Well, Christian's after her to move in with him, more or less permanently, and to help finance the movement. I think that's why she suddenly decided she wanted to spend all summer looking at rocks and pine trees. Well, I thought if I could talk her into staying here and helping me—not with money but really working at something, establishing a business—she might forget him. He could very well land her in jail."

"How much would all this cost?" she asked briskly.

"Well, to buy first-class equipment and rent space enough to do commercial photography—large product and specialty work—would cost twenty to thirty thousand dollars, but I am planning on getting started with much less. Especially if I can use your space here as a darkroom and if Nikki would accept a share in profits instead of a salary. Which would mean that she'd need an allowance so she could eat. But I was thinking of getting a bank loan, if you would consider backing it for me." He leaned forward in his eagerness, letting his light brown hair fall into his large brown eyes, so that he looked like an overanxious sheepdog.

"I'll think about it." Her tone was lively and amiable now. "It sounds as if it might be a good idea. We'll talk about it tomorrow, shall we? Be prepared to come up with some figures, and if it seems possible, we can go to the bank in the afternoon." There was a thoughtful smile on her face as she waved him out of the room.

She settled herself comfortably in the chaise longue and once more picked up the text she had been studying. When she heard the doorbell and familiar footsteps in the hall, she let it drop on the floor with a sigh and called, "Come in, come in," almost before the discreet knock sounded on the conservatory door. "Hello, Frank, darling. I do wish you would stop creeping about that way. It's very unnerving."

Frank Whitelaw smiled and bent over to kiss her on the shoulder. "I was afraid you might have dozed off and didn't want to wake you. How are you, my dear? You look absolutely ravishing." He stepped back critically a pace. "Although you do appear a trifle tired. Shouldn't you be resting this afternoon? You don't want to look like that this evening, do you?"

"What do you mean, 'look like that'? Really, Frank, you are a most tactless person. Besides, I won't look 'like that,' as you so gracefully put it, this evening. I shall look stunning as always. How do you like what Rudi has done to my hair?"

"Not a trifle too *belle époque*? I should have thought something simpler might appeal more to the natives. It is, nonetheless, charming." He bent down to pick up the folder. "But you really should be in bed, not going over your texts," he repeated in reproachful tones. "You'll only get stale."

Clara regarded him without emotion. "I was merely passing the time waiting for you, Frank. Sit down, please. Over here so I don't have to peer sideways at you. I have business we must discuss." As he opened his mouth to object, she raised her hand in a silencing gesture. "Next week I must reevaluate my financial position. Both the girls seem to be at crisis points in their lives, and before I tell them what I am prepared to do, or not to do, I must know where I stand." Her manager nodded briefly. He did not care for his employer when she was in one of these competent moods. He preferred the fiction that she was an emotional, fragile artist, not to be tormented by sordid details about money and contracts. "I don't like what is happening to Theresa and Milan at all," Clara continued. "He has gone through a great deal of money and will probably go through even more if he can get his hands on it. I am tempted to let him fail and suffer the consequences, but I must think about my grandchildren, who should not be paupers because their father is a fool, or perhaps a thief. Did you find out anything significant?"

Frank Whitelaw shook his head. "Not very much. But the rumor is that the project, and Milan, are in deep trouble."

"Just what does that mean?"

"Fraud. He could end up in jail."

"I see. Well, I have no desire to be there while you and the accountant are going over the company position with Milan, but this is what I want you to keep in mind: If the project can be rescued without bankrupting me, I might do it, but I want effective control. He must be removed. The company could go into Theresa's name, but I would insist on fifty-one percent in the restructured organization. Otherwise, we will have to see what can be done for Theresa. I have no intention of giving her a substantial amount of money; she is too silly. I have considered setting up a trust fund which would go eventually to the children." Frank Whitelaw had taken a small notebook from his pocket and was rapidly jotting down the points as she made them. "The other thing is setting Klaus up in business. It might be a good thing, but I want to consider the state of my finances before I make a commitment. Now I think I will go to bed. I am terribly tired."

"Would you like me to massage your shoulders?" he murmured, leaning closer to her as he tucked his notebook away. "You seem tense."

"Thank you, Frank, but I doubt if that would help. Perhaps instead you could check my exact position in the European and North American markets and we'll go on from there tomorrow." She slid gracefully to her feet, moved over to her desk, picked up the novel she had been reading, and quickly left the room. Frank Whitelaw sat where he was for a long time, his eyes fixed on the point at which he had last seen her.

CHAPTER 3

Klaus stood in front of the bedroom door, bouncing back and forth indecisively on his toes; finally, he tapped lightly. Putting his mouth close to the edge of the door, he whispered, "Nikki, are you in there?"

There was a soft scuffle on the other side, and the door eased open. She dragged him in, holding up one hand for silence, and shut it again. "For God's sake," she said, "don't wake up Mamma. You know what she's like before a performance." She padded back to the rumpled side of the big double bed, settled herself comfortably up against the pillows, and picked up a nail file from the table. "And to what," she said, concentrating on her fingernails, "do I owe the honor of this visit?" She patted the other side of the bed. "You might as well sit down, too."

He kicked off his running shoes and sat cross-legged at the foot of the bed. "Do I have to have a reason to come and talk to you?"

She glanced up for a moment. "Of course not. But you're obviously up to something, and you must have been down there spilling it all to Mamma. Do I get to find out what's going on, too?" Then she jabbed the file at him for emphasis. "And if you're thinking of marrying some girl you met over here, I claim the right to inspect her first. You have no taste or judgment in these matters at all."

"Marrying someone?" He straightened up in surprise. "Good God, no!" Then he laughed. "In fact, you were the only woman we were discussing."

She looked up sharply and went back to her nails. "And just what were you discussing about me, may I ask?" she said in the direction of a now perfectly formed little fingernail.

"I shouldn't have put it that way," he said hastily. "We weren't actually discussing you." He was treading on dangerous ground. "I was really just talking about settling down here and establishing myself as a photographer. I've found a place where I can rent studio space on a share basis cheap, and Aunt Clara said I could have that corner of the basement as a darkroom." He ran his hands nervously through his hair. Veronika's attention never strayed from her nails. "All I need, then," he said almost casually, "is a small apartment and an assistant. The trouble is, I can't afford to pay a real salary for a little while. So I need someone whose family would continue to support her until the profits started rolling in." He stopped, unsure of the reaction he was getting.

"I see," she said. "So you and Mamma cooked up this scheme to give little Nikki useful employment in nice safe Canada instead of letting her go back to nasty Munich. She bankrolls you as long as you look after me. Very clever. But suppose little Nikki doesn't want to be your assistant?"

"Come on, Veronika, you know that's not what I meant. Aunt Clara is not bankrolling me. I need an assistant, you know your way around a lab, and you're careful. Besides, you have a good eye. And I would rather work with someone I know and can trust." She continued to bend over her nails. "Listen, sweetheart, if you don't want to do it, just tell me. There are plenty of people I can hire part-time. The city's full of art students who can use the money, and you can go to hell. I don't need you or the rest of the goddamn family." He leaned back on the footboard and glared at her.

"Are you seriously trying to convince me that this isn't a scheme designed to keep me away from Munich? Because if you are, I just don't believe you." She put down the nail file and looked steadily at him.

"No, I won't say that." He ran his hands through his hair

again. "Of course I was thinking of that. But it was a side issue. I thought that since I was going to stay here anyway, you might like the chance to get away from everyone. I mean, this is the easy way to do it. But if you want to go back and crawl into bed with that sewer rat and ruin your life, that's all right with me. You never could tell the difference between a bastard after your money and someone who cares what happens to you. Go ahead, trust all your good friends in the movement instead of your family. I'll come and visit you in jail." He glowered and then uncrossed his legs and planted them on the bedroom floor.

"Klaus, you are the filthiest, most narrow-minded, unenlightened—"

"Stop." He held up a hand as he got to his feet. "We'll just leave it at that, shall we? I had an idea; you didn't like it. That's all." His posture was that of a deeply offended man as he stalked toward the door.

Veronika von Hohenkammer sat in the oversized bathtub and stared glumly at her feet. There was nothing in particular wrong with them except that they were, at the moment, conveniently in her line of sight. The bracing and mood-lifting bath compound, essence of mare's milk or Dead Sea salt, or whatever, which she had poured with reckless extravagance into the steaming water, didn't seem to be doing its job. Her mood was foul and plummeting lower. She picked up a pumice stone and began to attack a callus on her foot with the zeal of a preacher attacking unlicensed sex. "Damn it all, anyway," she said, and heaved herself out of the tub, abandoning all those expensive additives. She climbed dripping wet into a terry-cloth robe and headed across her bedroom rug for the door, leaving damp footprints behind her. She tiptoed down the narrow corridor toward the back of the house and knocked very softly on the next door she came to.

"For God's sake," she said, once she was safely in with the door shut, "I don't know why you had to storm off like that. I didn't say I wouldn't do it. Just that I resented people planning my life behind my back." Klaus Leitner was lying on his bed, his hands behind his head, glaring furiously at her. "Anyway, when is all this supposed to start?"

"I see. Now that the poor relation has been made to feel his place, milady is prepared to help him out," said Klaus. He looked grimly and stubbornly outraged. "I told you, no thanks. I can manage on my own."

"Come off it, Klaus. I think I'd rather like to stay and help you become rich and famous—for a little while, at least. And you're right that you need me, but not in the dark-room. You can do that yourself. You need someone around with some business sense, and I'm even better than Mamma at money and things like that. Which is more than anyone can say about you." She sat down at the foot of his bed and looked speculatively at him. "You could live here, you know. It would be cheaper, and Mamma wouldn't mind. In fact, she'd prefer to have someone living in the house. She doesn't entirely trust the crew that look after things. Bettl would be back in Munich with her, so we wouldn't have to put up with her. It sounds like fun. Where is the nearest decent place to ski?"

He shook his head gloomily. "Hours away, I think, and no real mountains." Then his face brightened. "But we could go to Davos at Christmas and spend a few weeks."

"Marvelous. I think I'll call Theresa and tell her the happy news. Won't she be pleased to have her very favorite relative in her hair all winter." Grinning, she reached for the phone and picked it up. "No," she said, putting it down again. "Let's wait and spring it on them at dinner. That should do something for Milan's digestion."

Five people sat around the enormous dining-room table in Clara von Hohenkammer's house. The men were all elegant and correct in black tie; Clara liked that sort of thing, and even Klaus Leitner had exchanged his shorts and running shoes for shirt studs and cummerbund. Theresa Milanovich was looking thin and pale, almost sickly, in a light blue silk that emphasized her fragile prettiness, and Veronika was looking boisterously healthy in red. They were all contemplating a thick and cream-filled, flavorless soup and making desultory tries at conversation. What little speech there had been gave way to uncomfortable silence as Bettl snatched the soup plates away and replaced them with dinner plates. These she covered rapidly with food, then slapped the serving dishes onto the table, clapped a bottle of wine down beside Klaus, and slammed out of the room.

"I don't understand why your mother, with all her money, doesn't get rid of that woman and replace her with someone who can cook and is at least minimally respectful," said Milan, staring uneasily down at the mess of food on his plate. Bettl had interpreted the instructions from her employer on the subject of proper dinners in her own way, and on that warm September evening, after the thick soup, they were each facing fried potatoes, overcooked carrots, and a large slab of braised pork, heavily sauced with cream and paprika.

"She doesn't want to get rid of her," said Theresa. "Look at the way she drags her around with her everywhere she goes. Anyway, who else would she find who was willing to work seven days a week all year?" she added nastily. Theresa had problems with housekeepers.

"Besides, she can cook and be perfectly polite if she wants to," said Klaus, pouring some wine into his glass and casually passing the bottle on around the table. "This is her revenge because she's annoyed at Aunt Clara, and she figures it's perfectly safe because none of us can do anything about it. No doubt Aunt Clara is dining on some light and flawlessly prepared delicacy while we suffer. One of these days, if Bettl gets mad enough at *her*, there'll be a few hundred grams of rat poison in *our* béarnaise. She has a nasty temper, that woman does."

"I wish you wouldn't say things like that at dinner, Klaus," said Theresa, looking down at the gray meat in front of her.

"Now every time I eat here I'll be wondering if the food has been poisoned." She speared a small piece of carrot and regarded it doubtfully.

"That's easy," said Veronika. "I'm sure that rat poison tastes awful. To poison us you'd have to put it into something with flavor. So, you see? You only have to worry if the food is good. This," she said, jabbing her fork into the meat, "has no taste at all. Rat poison would be a distinct improvement."

"Must you, Nikki?" said her sister, looking greenly at her dinner. She put her fork down and pushed her plate away slightly. Her husband leaned over her solicitously, murmuring in her ear, then reached over and refilled her wineglass. She took a hasty gulp and with an effort at friendliness turned back to her younger sister. "Have you decided when you're going back to Munich yet, Nikki? Are you going to wait until Mamma leaves?" She turned to Frank Whitelaw, who was toying with a rubbery triangle of overcooked potato and ignoring the conversation. "Nikki really has become enamored of the New World. She's never been here this long before. Have you, Nikki?"

Veronika von Hohenkammer, with her mother's flawless timing, smiled agreeably and produced her bombshell. "Actually, I'm not going back—not for a couple of years, anyway. Klaus and I are staying here and setting up a family business, aren't we, Klaus? He's going to turn his photography into a paying affair, and I will look after the financial end of things."

There was a profound silence as this sank in. Klaus smirked; Whitelaw gave Veronika a quick, searching glance and went back to his rubbery potato. "Does Mamma know about this?" asked Theresa sharply.

"It was partly her idea," said Veronika maliciously. "She and Klaus came up with this marvelous scheme. We'll be working out of the house so that expenses won't be too high at first." She returned to the attack on her braised pork.

"That sounds like an interesting business," her brother-in-law said casually. "Tell me, does it involve heavy start-up expenses?"

Klaus, to whom this remark was addressed, pushed his plate away and replaced it with his glass. "That depends," he said, "on the scale of your operations and the type of photography. I'm interested in commercial work, and that involves hefty expenses for equipment and studio space. To get completely set up could cost over fifty thousand dollars. Canadian, of course." There was a gasp from across the table. His cousin Theresa was staring at him openmouthed. "But I won't be working on such a scale, and I already have a certain amount of equipment. Anyway, I've spent most of July and part of August making contacts and seeing people. I'm pretty optimistic about our chances. There's a girl at one of the advertising agencies who is impressed with my work."

"I'll bet," muttered Veronika.

"My camera work," he emended with a wink, "and she hires a lot of photographers. That will be a good start."

"I'm ashamed of you, Klaus," said Veronika, "prostituting yourself like that."

"Really, Nikki, I wish you wouldn't talk that way," said her sister automatically, and turned her attention back to Klaus. "What did you mean about working out of the house?" she asked. "Are you going to have models coming and going all the time? I'm sure Mamma won't like that."

"Not at all," he said with a wave of the hand. "That's fashion photography you're thinking of, which is definitely not my thing. Besides, I'll be renting studio space. No, it's just the processing that will be here. In fact, it's here already. I have a pretty complete darkroom down in the basement now."

"What?" said Theresa. Alarm sprang into her face. "Do you mean the basement is full of chemicals? And the children are here all the time, playing? They could blow themselves up. I hope everything is locked up. If Mamma can keep her old junk locked away from the children," she said resentfully, "you at least could keep that sort of thing out of reach."

"I guess I should," he said, looking slightly worried. "I never thought of the kids. I'll get a padlock for the room tomorrow. Not that they could blow themselves up, though. Nothing down there is explosive, even if you mix it all together—I think." He smiled brightly at everyone. "But I wouldn't recommend eating the chemicals. They might disagree with you. Drastically," he added thoughtfully.

"Fascinating though this is," said Veronika, "Mamma will never forgive us if we're late. I suggest we escape before Bettl can serve us any more horrors." There was a sudden scrambling as they all heaved themselves out of their chairs and toward their coats.

Harriet Jeffries pulled the last prints out of the wash water and set them carefully in the print dryer. Yawning, moving like an automaton, she began to clean up her mess, dumping out the large plastic trays, rinsing them, and putting each one on its own section of shelf. Last of all, she covered the enlarger and looked around her. All finished. Time for bed. She left the darkroom, walked through her bedroom, which occupied the other half of the ground floor, and headed up a flight of stairs that divided her living room from her kitchen area. Bed, but first something to eat.

Before turning left into the kitchen, she noticed the polyethylene bag filled with clean clothing tossed over a chair. Her light wool dress. The one she had picked up on her way home from Rudi's because she needed something to wear tonight to Clara von Hohenkammer's party. Damn! She liked Clara—she enjoyed talking to her—but she was too bloody tired to go out tonight. Even if, especially if, Clara wanted to foist some hopeful young amateur photographer on her for help and comfort.

She opened up the refrigerator and extracted a couple of radishes. Munching reflectively, she tried to consider the problem. In one sense, it didn't matter if she offended Clara, who hadn't, after all, been her client. But then, what's the point of offending a nice lady, a rich, nice lady, when you didn't have to? And Clara von Hohenkammer would be offended. She opened the sliding door to her deck and stepped into the warm evening. Suddenly, another factor entered the equation as she leaned over the decorative wooden rail to look down at the garden below. Harriet lived in a structure that had once been the oversized garage to a large house. Some zany or greedy previous owner of the property had built a second floor onto the garage and created instant, rentable living space, adding a second garage onto the structure for good measure. Her car was in the second garage, and its roof had become her deck. The original garage had been turned into her bedroom and darkroom; her kitchen and living room sat on top of it. The resulting creation was odd looking but comfortable. She was rarely aware of her landlords except on those occasions—too frequent occasions—when they had parties. Especially in the summer. And tonight there were unmistakable signs that they were having a party. Her landlord was firing up two barbecues in the back garden. Her landlady was setting bottles onto a table. Might as well try sleeping on a camp bed at the corner of Bloor and Yonge as in her room tonight. Confused guests would be knocking on her door, looking for a washroom. Drunks would be peering in her bedroom window, or worse, crawling through it if she were foolish enough to leave it open. She couldn't bear the prospect of being kept awake, alone with her thoughts, while mirth and jollification were going on all around her. Might as well go to Clara's bloody reading.

The black Porsche pulled up in front of the Goethe Institute and stopped. Milan leaned over and opened the door on his wife's side. She stayed where she was and gave him a worried look. "I wish you'd come in with me. I'm sure it won't put Mamma in a very good frame of mind if you aren't there for the reading."

"How will she know?" he said. "Unless you tell her, of course, which would be very stupid." He put his hands on her shoulders and gave her a light kiss. "I can't stand these things—you know that. If she notices that you're alone, tell her I dropped you off and had to go back and park the car, so I sat by myself at the back." He smiled winningly. "Come on, don't worry. In a way it's true. I do have to go and park the car. Only I think I'll park it at your mother's and get myself a drink. You can come back with Nikki."

Theresa's face distorted with anger. "I don't understand how you can be so stupid," she hissed. "Here's Mamma putting up the money for some sort of business for Nikki and Klaus—it had to be Mamma, because he hasn't got a cent—fifty thousand dollars. Did you hear him say that? Fifty thousand dollars. And that will just be the beginning. And do you know why she's doing it?" She didn't give him a chance to answer. "Because right now she's planning to let us go under." She turned to face him, her hand clutching the door handle. "She worries about money. She's not going to let a whole lot of it go at once. I'll bet she has just so much that she figures she can squander on her children and that's that. She has no intention of being poor in her old age, let me tell you. I know her. If Klaus gets that money, we'll wait until she drops dead before we get a penny. And she's very healthy."

He gave her a little push toward the door. "You worry too much, sweetheart. I'll see you later. Just keep acting as though I'm there and they'll all believe it's true." Silently, she pulled her black silk evening wrap around her and got out of the car. The Porsche roared off, then screeched to a halt at the red light on the corner.

Carlos was sitting on a battered steel-and-plastic kitchen chair in front of a grubby child-sized desk. He held a pen in his hand, poised over a pad of paper. Every once in a while he altered one of the figures in the column on the page and bit his lip as he stared at the result. Beside him, the television flickered gloomily. Its sound was turned off.

The doorbell rang. Carlos stood up, automatically ducking to keep from hitting his head on the low eaves, and crumpled the paper in his hand. He shoved it into his pocket as he walked over to the door.

Don was the first to arrive. "Christ, it's dark in here," he said. "You can't afford light bulbs or something?"

"Go on into the kitchen, then," said Carlos easily. "Help yourself to a beer while I let the others in."

Don shifted his shoulders uneasily and looked up at the taller man, trying to assess what degree of insult, if any, had been intended by those remarks. He hated being towered over, and he hated arrogant sons of bitches like Carlos who always made him feel stupid. The doorbell rang once more, and Carlos ran lightly down the stairs, two at a time.

Manu came up first, stooping to get through the low doorway. The buru walked in right behind, followed by Carlos. A silent procession.

"So where's the fence?" asked Don. He hated silence. "You said you were going to bring him tonight." It was an accusation, and he stared hard at the buru when he made it. "I want to find out from him what the hell is going on. I work on these jobs, I take the risks, and what happens? The stuff gets dumped off with *him*"—he pointed at the buru— "and then fucking well disappears. I want to know where it goes, and I want my share of the money. The real money. Not a few thousand for 'expenses.' I want to talk to the guy who's running things, okay?" He headed into the kitchen, opened the refrigerator, and took out a beer.

"I'm running things," said the buru with a calm voice as he moved into the kitchen after Don. "I ran things at home, and I run them here. Right, Manu?" The tall man nodded. "The fence is just that. A convenience. A necessary and expensive component in this operation. Like Carlos over here. Who doesn't give a shit who he works for but who knows what to take and what to leave behind." Carlos smiled, as if he appreciated being viewed in this light. "And the reason for this meeting is not to reassure you," he said, nodding at Don, "but to deal with potential problems. Sit down." The buru pulled out a chair on the far side of the table, turned it around and sat, leaning his elbows on the back.

Manu sat far back from the table on the other side, one long leg bent and perched on his knee. Don squeezed himself into the end nearest the wall. Carlos pulled several bottles of beer out of the refrigerator, which he set unceremoniously in the center, before taking the opposite end.

"So what's the problem?" asked Don, once again breaking into the silence.

"There are many problems," said the buru. "And the biggest is you. I am canceling the last two strikes. You may not know it, but the police are getting closer and closer. I have had some experience with them—"

"You have!" interrupted Don incredulously. "Listen, you snot-faced brat. I've been dodging the cops since I was twelve, and I know what I'm doing."

The buru paid no attention. "The fence becomes increasingly nervous. He doesn't want to make any more trips for a while, and we cannot afford to pile up too much anymore."

"How do we know that?" asked Don. "Or is this just more of your bullshit?"

"You know because I tell you," said the buru quietly. "He can hold a little more, but otherwise . . ." He took a small calendar out of his pocket and et it down on the table. "One possibility is that we start moving the goods across the border ourselves, although with our accents Manu and I are likely to be searched. Still, if we . . ." He began rapidly sketching out possibilities on the back of the calendar page.

Harriet sat entranced as Clara von Hohenkammer stammered out her tormented vision of the sleepwalking Lady Macbeth. Orders tumbled from her lips in a rising tide of guilt and panic: "Wash your hands, put on your nightgown, look not so pale: I tell you yet again, Banquo's buried; he cannot come out on's grave." She was standing behind a lectern in the pleasantly civilized room under a bright spot, her hair and sweeping black gown elegant and formal, yet, with voice and expression and gesture alone, she evoked the bedroom, the nightgown, the wild disarray of the distraught queen so strongly, that Harriet could feel the dank chill of the cold castle chamber and shivered. It was uncanny. The earlier readings had been a trial. She could certainly follow Clara's beautifully enunciated German, but the texts were too old, too complex and difficult for easy comprehension. This, however—this compelled her, in spite of hunger and exhaustion, to feel the actress's feigned torment. Then Clara came to the last brokenhearted "to bed, to bed, to bed" and a wild surge of applause greeted her. The spell was broken.

She bowed gravely and stepped out of the spotlight, walking without ceremony toward the chairs in which the audience was seated. There was a slight turmoil in the corners as discreet floor lamps were turned on, and the play suddenly turned itself into a well-behaved party. Clara was immediately claimed by officialdom and the representatives of the German and Canadian governments, while Harriet tried to make her discreet way over to the coffee and biscuits.

With a cup of strong coffee and a couple of substantial fruit tarts in her hands, Harriet settled into one of the chairs pushed up against the wall and prepared to observe the crowd. About half of it was drifting toward the exit, doubtless strangers who had not been invited to Clara's "impromptu" party. Harriet finished the pastry on her plate and was considering helping herself to more when suddenly Clara detached herself from the mob surrounding her and began to work her way over toward the exit. A tall woman in a black silk coat clung to her arm with the desperation of a lost child. Suddenly, everyone in the room developed that oh-dear-I-must-be-going look and started searching for coats and gloves scattered around on chairs. Harriet looked at her watch; she was never going to survive another two hours of polite partying.

*   *   *

And now she was standing in the palatial bathroom next to the guest room and surveying herself critically in the mirror. Too thin, too pale and exhausted looking, she decided, and there was not much to be done for any of it until she managed to get some sleep. She ran a finger lightly over the dark smudges under her eyes and tried to decide whether she had developed more lines since the spring. She had certainly lost weight, weight she couldn't afford to lose. This dress had been almost provocative looking when last she wore it; it had made her feel charged with desirability; now it hung on her like a particularly unappealing sugar sack. She ran her hands over her bony hips and wondered if John would object to her scrawniness. Or if she would ever see him again. "Dammit, anyway," she muttered, overwhelmed with tired anger and frustration. She took out a comb and flipped her hair out of her eyes. It made no difference to her appearance, but it gave her the sense that a ritual had been successfully performed; she was prepared to meet the throng downstairs.

It had been more than three years since she had been in that house. A substantial but conventional—in fact, very ordinary—house that had been tiled, plumbed, carpeted, painted, and curtained into a soft, cool fantasy straight out of a design magazine. She had come in to photograph it right after the furniture delivery men, chasing the last workmen out of the place as she went. She had shifted furniture, borrowed plants, rehung the paintings, created a sort of minimalist clutter, and had begun to feel as if the place were hers. Now curiosity enlivened her, and she ran quickly down the stairs in the direction of the living room.

The room was lit with many-branching candelabra that soared over strategically placed tables, and a small fire burned cheerfully in the large fireplace in spite of the warm night. There were probably fifty people there, she reckoned, easily swallowed up in the broad space. Amid them all, a tiny army of unobtrusive women in the severe black cotton and frilly white aprons and caps of a local, expensive catering service wove their way through the mob with trays of food and drink. The bar, she decided, must be located in the dense crowd to her right. She drifted over, secured a Campari and soda and a handful of hors d'oeuvres, and then found herself a large, comfortable-looking chair near the back of the room.

From her vantage point she saw her hairdresser talking to a group of three women—all customers, no doubt. She wondered which of the women in the room was the mother of the famous von Hohenkammer grandchildren. The short, dark-haired girl gesticulating animatedly by the fireplace was clearly a copy of Clara von Hohenkammer, reduced to three-quarter size, but she looked very young to be the mother of two children, the younger of whom must have been more than four; it had been the birth of that child that had impelled the actress to buy a house in the city. She was talking to a taller woman, fairer and somewhat wispy in appearance, who bore a vague resemblance to her. The other daughter. And she, of course, was the black-cloaked creature who had left with Clara. The least interesting member of the family, thought Harriet meanly. Getting bored with long-distance character analysis, she began trying to match everyone up with possible husbands and lovers, but the choice was too great, and the game began to be a chore. What I need now, she thought, is to close my eyes for a few minutes. . . . Suddenly a voice bounced off her eardrums.

"Harriet, my dear, why are you cowering—that is the right word, is it not?—here in the corner?" She opened an eye and saw her hostess looming over her. "You look splendid this evening. I don't know how, with your dark skin, you can wear gray and not look dead or jaundiced." Clara glowed with health and expansive energy.

Harriet rose politely to her feet. "Frau von Hohenkammer, you were magnificent. I cried over your Lady Macbeth. She was so real, so beautiful, that she was almost painful to watch."

This elicited a gratified smile. "You must call me Clara,

you know. And you are quite right. I have always done Shakespeare well, I thought. Such a pity he wasn't German. Or I wasn't English, perhaps." She winked at her. "You mustn't be shocked at my egotism. I can't help it when I have given a good performance and carried everyone along with me. Even just a small audience like this one. I am drunk with success tonight." Then she grasped Harriet by the arm. "Now come and see these pictures; you promised me you would, you know. I have a splendid album of them in the library. Bring your drink." She was propelled at high speed through the door into a small room, softly lit and pleasant looking, just behind the living room. In one corner, at a small round table, there was a pile of old-fashioned photo albums, one of which the actress picked up and spread open. Harriet walked behind the table, pulling a small chair with her, and opened up the next book.

"These are all of you, aren't they?" she said. "May I look at them?"

The actress waved an imperious hand. "Only after you have seen Michael and Mariana; then you may look at them. That's just a collection of old publicity shots. Rather a mess. The children wanted to see them, or so their mother led me to believe." Her sardonic expression made Harriet wonder if her devotion to her family was as blind as she permitted people to assume.

"What is this?" asked Harriet, pointing to a black-and-white of a young and very slender Clara dressed in a black leotard and tights, crouching by a gray plaster rock, staring upward. "It's beautiful. Superb tones."

"The fool," she said, a dreamy look on her face. "*Lear*, you know. I played the fool once, at a drama festival in Chichester, when I was young and thin enough to be taken for a boy. The director wanted a girlish voice with an accent—to make the fool seem more vulnerable, he said. It was a lovely part. That picture was taken by—" Her face softened for a second; then she turned abruptly back to the first album, pushing it in front of Harriet.

"It doesn't matter. But now that I have you to myself," she said, "I—"

There was a knock at the door, and a sour voice murmured, "Frau von Hohenkammer . . ."

Clara frowned. "Anyway, I shall leave you here, because pictures of children are self-explanatory, and the others are not really improved by being discussed. Don't go away. I have questions to ask you about my nephew Klaus."

Harriet was left alone to plough through the two albums. The children's pictures were like children's pictures anywhere and everywhere. She refused categorically and without exception to photograph children herself and found no solace in looking at other people's work. The subjects themselves were neither surprisingly homely nor surpassingly beautiful. Nice children, no doubt, and a credit to their parents, but as photography, basically dull. She made quick work of that one. The other album stopped her completely. There were publicity shots, extravagantly posed and not quite human. Among them was interspersed a wildly varied collection of pieces, some of them done by people whose names made her pause in awe: of Clara working, face twisted with agony, or clowning for the camera or smiling archly. She was clad in everything from elaborate historical costume to the most casual of rehearsal garb. Hers was a face and body that the camera loved. Harriet smiled. What a hell of a manipulator that woman was, leaving all this temptation lying out on the table. And if I ever had any inclination to do some studies of people, she began, looking at a shot of Clara standing in trousers and a sweater, alone on a stage, desolate in the harsh light of the spot, she'd certainly be— But her thought remained unborn.

Outside the room a pair of female voices, spitting angrily at each other in subdued tones, approached the library. At first, all Harriet could hear was meaningless babble, but as they came nearer, the babble formed itself into words—snarled words in rapid and almost incomprehensible German. Curious, she strained to catch the drift, and her ear began to adjust itself to the dialect. One voice, slower and more defined in speech, was easier to understand, and that voice suddenly said, deliberately and clearly, "You two won't succeed in this. I'm going to make sure of it." One pair of footsteps clicked angrily away down the uncarpeted hall; another swept a couple of steps into the room where Harriet still sat in front of the photo albums. It was the dark young woman who was obviously Clara's daughter. Her cheeks were scarlet and her lips tight, but as soon as she saw Harriet, an automatic smile of welcome flashed across her face. "Excuse me," she said. "I didn't realize there was anyone in here. I am Veronika von Hohenkammer," and she approached, hand outstretched, graciousness intact.

"I was just looking at some pictures of your mother and her grandchildren," Harriet said, taking the proffered hand and feeling, irrationally, that she had an obligation to explain why she was hiding around the corner, listening to a quarrel in the hall.

"Aha," Nikki replied brightly, "you have fallen victim to Mamma's pride in her grandchildren. On behalf of the family, I apologize. They are really quite awful kids, you know, spoiled and horrid, but Mamma can see no flaws in them. She'll be devastated if you don't tell her that they are the most beautiful children you ever saw."

"Don't worry," said Harriet, "I will. I'm Harriet Jeffries, by the way. The person responsible for that," she added by way of justifying her presence, pointing to a sixteen-by-twenty black-and-white print of the staircase hanging on the wall.

"Ah," said Veronika. "The photographer. My cousin Klaus is very interested in meeting you. Did you enjoy the reading?" she asked.

"I was overwhelmed by the Shakespeare," she said. "The German passages went by me, I'm afraid. I don't understand the language as well as your mother thinks I do," she added, not quite truthfully. The taut expression on Nikki's face relaxed suddenly, and the social temperature in the room rose by several degrees.

"Yes, Mamma's pretty extraordinary, isn't she?" her daughter remarked as she dropped into a comfortable chair.

"I'm impressed with your English," said Harriet. "I wish my German were half as good."

"Oh, well, Papa insisted that we both go to English schools and learn the language properly. I didn't care for it at the time," she said, "but, as usual, he was right. And now I'm grateful that he did." Suddenly, the door across the hall from the study opened, and a man in evening dress with two bottles of wine tucked neatly under his arms walked in.

He nodded in the direction of the two women. "Hello, Frank," said Veronika casually. "Keeping the party oiled?" She leaned forward to peer at the partially obscured labels. "I hope that stuff isn't too good. The drinkers are at the point where they couldn't tell the difference. But there's no point in bringing it in here. Miss Jeffries and I are not that desperate for booze. Take it to the bartender." Harriet noticed his cheeks whiten as the girl continued to speak. "Have you met Frank Whitelaw, Miss Jeffries? He's my mother's man of business, as they used to say." Now the contempt in her voice was impossible to miss.

"Miss Jeffries and I met when she was photographing the house," said Whitelaw stiffly. Trying to lump me in with the servant class, thought Harriet with amusement. For company.

"How nice," said Nikki, and leapt to her feet. "But, Miss Jeffries, Klaus is dying to meet you, and here I am, keeping you to myself. Now, don't move. I'll be back with him in a second." She left the room without a glance at Frank Whitelaw.

"I'm afraid I should go as well," said Whitelaw. "To deliver the wine to the bartender." There was considerable irritation in his voice under the amiable half smile. Harriet wondered if he had been planning on opening one of those excellent bottles and drinking it peacefully by himself in the quiet of the study.

Veronika was true to her word. Before the atmosphere Whitelaw had brought with him had dissipated, she was back in the study, pulling a handsome young man after her. "Miss Jeffries," he said with flattering emphasis, clasping her hand in both of his. "I am overwhelmed. You must let me tell you how impressed I was by your show at city hall. Particularly that set of industrial buildings. What format were you working in?"

As he chattered on, it became clear that he had seen the show, probably more than once, and had examined her work with great care. He now looked just as intensely at her with large, soft brown eyes. Careful, Harriet, she said to herself as he talked on. Softly, softly. He is about to con you into giving him hours of free help and advice. You don't need that right now. In spite of herself, his infectious enthusiasm was chipping away at her automatic defenses, and she began to expound on some of her pet topics. As they drifted from 35mm to the merits of large-format photography— "Good or not," said Harriet cheerfully, "it impresses the hell out of clients"—to processing, she found herself being swept remorselessly down to his basement darkroom.

"I'm impressed," she said as she looked around the two rooms that Klaus had set aside for his work. "For an impromptu darkroom, it's well set up. You need a decent enlarger, though. That toy isn't going to get you anywhere. I got a new Beseler a while back, and I still have my first one tucked away in a corner. Come and see me. Bring a car." She pulled a small evening bag out from the pocket she had unceremoniously stuffed it into and extracted her wallet. After a certain amount of effort she pulled out her business card. "Call me first," she added. "I tend to be out a lot." She looked around her again. "What happens when the family charges in to use the washroom, though?"

He grinned and shook his head. "They don't. Not a chance. I don't think Aunt Clara's ever been down here. She doesn't concern herself with basements. And Bettl—have you seen Bettl?" Harriet nodded. "I think Bettl has problems getting down those stairs. She doesn't try very often. Anyway, the only other thing down here of any interest to anyone is the wine cellar," he said, leading the way out of the full bathroom where he washed prints and film. "Oh, and the freezer and some storage, I think."

As they moved toward the stairs, the basement door opened again. "Ah, Klaus," said a voice from the top. "Are you getting the wine? We have some complaints that— Oh, good evening," the man said to Harriet as she climbed the stairs with Klaus just behind her. "Down seeing our boy Klaus's etchings? I admire your taste, Klaus old man." The man stood where he was, half filling the doorway, expecting Harriet to press by him.

"Move, Milan, you son of a bitch," said Leitner, leaning forward and giving him a not-so-friendly push out into the hall. Milanovich staggered to regain his balance and then stayed where he was for a moment, glaring resentfully at the young man.

More time must have passed than Harriet had realized, because the crowd had thinned out to about fifteen hardy souls by the time she got back into the living room. She felt the first faint stirrings of hope that she might be able to slip away soon. She stifled a huge yawn and looked around for her hostess.

The party had broken up into three groups by now. Nikki and a lively-looking blond girl collected Klaus Leitner when he came back into the room. The wispy brown-haired one, now definitely identified from the baby pictures as the mother of the grandchildren, was leaning apathetically against the fireplace, talking to a group of three or four people. Clara was holding court in the front of the room, in apparently tireless conversation with a pleasant-looking middle-aged couple. Frank Whitelaw sat on the arm of the couch, leaning over her in a proprietary way. Harriet approached the group hesitantly, reluctant to break up the relaxed fag ends of the party but desperate to get away.

"Frau von—Clara—this has been delightful, but—"

"No, my dear. Do not say it. Here, you must sit down by me and chat for a few minutes before you go." She drew her down on the small couch beside her. "These are my neighbors, Bill and Lilian MacGregor"—she waved in the direction of the couple—"Harriet Jeffries, and perhaps you have already met my friend and business manager, Frank Whitelaw."

Once more they murmured acknowledgments of prior acquaintance. Bill MacGregor finished off the glass in his hand and looked around. "Miss Jeffries," he said in mock horror, "you have nothing to drink. Nor do you, dear lady," he said with a flourish in the direction of his hostess. "Let me suggest scotch and water, just this once. Very settling and soporific at this time of night."

Harriet nodded, helpless, but thinking that the last thing she needed now was something to put her to sleep. Clara von Hohenkammer, however, shook her head gently. "I really never touch alcohol, except a tiny bit of wine on ceremonial occasions." She turned to Harriet confidentially. "I follow a very strict regime, you know, of exercise and diet. Otherwise, I would not be able to work as much as I do. It gives one great energy. And I am never ill. You must let me tell you about it someday." She looked around her. "Bettl should have brought me my tea by now, in fact. Bill, while you're fetching Harriet her drink, do you think you could see if my tea is there? Or if Bettl is in the kitchen?"

"Would you like me to go and get it for you?" asked Whitelaw, slowly beginning to move as he spoke.

"It hardly needs two people to do it," she said tartly, and turned back to Harriet. "It really isn't a tea, actually, it's my tisane; you must let me get you the recipe." Harriet, who had once tried the mixture in question, smiled as bravely as she could. Her head was now pounding with exhaustion, and the sounds of conversation were hitting her ears, muffled, distorted, and unbearably loud. Just as she pulled herself together to leave again, a scotch glided into her hand, propelled by the smiling Mr. MacGregor.

"No sign of any tea," he said. "Someone said that she put it on the table, but I didn't see it there." They all began to look around the room, frantically eyeing the numberless little tables in it.

"There it is," said Clara in a silky tone. Harriet noticed the white spots on her temples and realized that she was very angry. "Sit still. I will get it myself." In the awkward silence that followed, the whole group watched her progress over to the drinks table, still set up, although the bartender had left long since, where her tea sat in the corner, probably cold and unappetizing by now. Harriet realized that everyone was settling in again and that if she were to get away, it was now or never. She started after her hostess at a brisk pace.

Halfway to the table she saw Clara von Hohenkammer pick up the cup, touch it experimentally to her lips, and then take a swallow. Almost immediately a gargling half cry bubbled out from between her lips. She clasped her hands to her chest and clutched it, letting the cup tumble to the floor, then took a step toward the table as if for support. She reeled against it and fell heavily to the ground.

CHAPTER 4

For a moment, everything froze. Harriet stopped, bewildered, and then ran toward the fallen actress. At the same time, Veronika von Hohenkammer shrieked, "Mamma," and launched herself across the room. She knelt down, grasping her mother by one shoulder and trying to turn her over in a futile effort to help her up. Just as Harriet reached them, a gray-haired man in evening dress materialized from somewhere, took Nikki firmly by the arms, pulled her to her feet, and without a word pushed her in the direction of a woman who had followed him. He crouched beside the actress, picked up her wrist, and then looked up at Harriet. "Here, give me a hand to get her turned over," he said sharply. "She's a big woman." Harriet knelt down beside him, and the two of them gently moved Clara onto her back. Her body shuddered with jerky convulsions and then was still. The man bent over her, his shoulders heaving with effort as he tried to bring breath back into her lungs. Finally, he sat back on his heels, exhausted. Harriet shivered. Clara's face, in a horrible parody of blooming health, was a brilliant pink. Her would-be rescuer shook his head and said, "Did you see what happened? I was on the other side of the room and didn't notice anything until she gasped."

"She drank the tea in that cup," said Harriet, pointing to the cup on the floor, "made a gasping noise, clutched her chest, and then fell." She shook her head in bewilderment. "That was all. It happened very fast."

He kept one hand on Clara's wrist as the other searched

her neck delicately for a pulse. "Well, there's not much I can do for her, I would say," he murmured half to himself. "And I don't particularly like the look of things." Then he spoke in a louder voice to the room in general. "Has anyone called for an ambulance?"

"I did," said a guest standing in the doorway. "They'll be right here, and the fire department rescue squad. Who's her doctor?" he added. A buzz of voices answered him; someone gestured at the man still bending over her.

"Was it her heart?" murmured Harriet softly.

"Not very likely. She was as healthy as a horse." His reply was as low pitched as her question. "Besides, that's not what a heart attack looks like, believe me." The doctor glanced around at the people who were standing about, awkward and silent, and said to Harriet, "Do you think you could find a sheet or something to put over her? And get everyone to move out of here? The dining room will do."

Harriet nodded. She headed out the door, not sure where she was going, and found herself beside Klaus Leitner. "Can I help?" he asked quietly.

"You can tell me where to find something to cover her with."

"How about a tablecloth? I think they're in this thing," he said, opening a massive antique linen press in the dining room and pulling out an enormous white linen tablecloth.

Harriet took the cloth. "And one more thing. Could you move everyone in here? The doctor wants them out of the way."

Before she had finished her last sentence, sirens screamed up to the house, and the fire department emergency resuscitation unit appeared. The last thing the guests saw as they meekly filed into the dining room was the doctor in quiet consultation with the rescuers, pointing at the cup and shaking his head.

There were seven people standing uneasily in the dining room, looking awkwardly at one another, wondering what to do. The lively blonde, now considerably more subdued, said, "I am Kirsten Müller, and I work at the Geothe Institute. Perhaps we could introduce ourselves to each other and all sit down. I know I am very tired."

At once there was a polite rush for the table. Harriet found herself in between Klaus Leitner and a man she hadn't met. Bill MacGregor leaned on the back of his chair and announced, "There's an urn of coffee on the sideboard. It smells done, and there are cups and things set out. Anyone else want coffee?" Six people rose and scrambled to get cups; Harriet sat and waited. Perhaps she had been the only person to notice exactly what had happened to Clara von Hohenkammer, but she was not anxious to try whether the coffee had the same effect on people that the herbal tea had. She smiled at the gentleman next to her and settled herself in to make small talk until something else happened.

John Sanders lay in bed, staring at the ceiling of his one-bedroom, concrete-walled, upper-floor, southern-exposure high-rise apartment and listened to the hum of the air conditioner. He didn't really need to have it on. The fierce temperatures of this unseasonable September heat wave had died rapidly with the sun, and the room was getting chilly. But the constant noise was soothing and cut out the clash and roar of sound that rose up from the street. And now, with four days off and no progress in the case and weeks and weeks of lack of sleep behind him, he lay in bed, staring at the ceiling, too tired to sleep. He tried to blank out his thoughts, concentrating on the hum of the air conditioner, until the shrill scream of the telephone dragged him back from the brink.

"John. It's Ed. You asleep? Sorry . . ." the voice on the other end was calm and not at all contrite.

"Jesus, Dubinsky, do you know what time it is? Yes, I was asleep—I think."

"Yeah, well, something came up." He paused a second. "Sinclair and Beech are supposed to be on, but Sinclair has food poisoning. One too many chicken-salad sandwiches. Anyway, he's not going anywhere tonight."

"So what's up?" Sanders was sitting on the side of the bed by now, yawning.

"Some woman died at a party. Her doctor called it in."

"Someone knife her?" he asked, yawning.

"It's not that kind of party. You know, respectable, all that crap."

"Don't bother. Tell me about it in the car. I'll see you downstairs in ten minutes." Like a zombie, he headed for the shower. By the time Dubinsky got there, he would be showered, dressed, awake, and mean as hell.

Sanders stood in the living room with Dr. Alexander and stared at the white bundle by his feet. The doctor gave him a second or two to take in the situation and then started his terse recital. "You see that cup lying on the floor? No one has moved it, by the way. It was supposed to be some kind of tea. She drank it, convulsed, and died rapidly." His eyes were glittering slightly with excitement, Sanders thought. Was he upset or merely enjoying the drama of it all? "I got to her pretty quickly, but she died as I was trying to resuscitate her. Do you want me to uncover her?"

"No, I'll do it," said Sanders, carefully avoiding the cup and delicately picking up the covering between thumb and forefinger. "What's this? The tablecloth?"

"Looks like it. It was all they could find, and I wanted to cover her up before people got hysterical." Sanders pulled back the cloth and noted the flushed face. "Smell her mouth," urged Dr. Alexander. "That was when I decided something was very wrong."

The sickly, bitter, almondlike smell lingered about the body, clear and unmistakable. "Christ," muttered Sanders. "Cyanide."

"That's exactly what I thought. I've never run into it before—my patients generally don't go in for poisoning themselves or each other—but it looked to me like a textbook case. So I left the cup exactly where it was, covered her up, and sent everyone into the dining room." He was rocking back on his heels now, looking animated and pleased with himself.

Sanders backed away and looked carefully around. Nothing in the immediate vicinity seemed to engage his attention except for a small piece of crumpled paper sitting under the table on the otherwise-pristine floor. Almost automatically he picked it up delicately between thumb and forefinger and slipped it into a plastic bag in his pocket. "What did you mean by everyone?" he asked, turning back to the doctor. "Who's in that dining room?" Sanders jerked his thumb back through the door.

"Six or seven people, I guess. The rest are upstairs."

"The rest?"

"Her two daughters are up there with my wife, I think. And maybe her son-in-law is there, too. Everyone else who was still at the party—and I don't know them all, by a long shot—is in the dining room. She had help, too. A housekeeper and maybe other people. You'd have to ask someone who knows the household better than I do." He paused for a second. "Actually, her nephew is in there. He should know."

"Thanks," said Sanders absently as he looked around the room, taking in the furnishings, the flowers, the candles, the well-stocked bar. "But maybe you could tell me what you know. The victim was a friend of yours?"

"Yes . . . well, more my wife's friend, and my patient."

"Was she suffering from some illness?"

"Good God, no. She was about the healthiest patient I've got."

"Her name?"

"Clara von Hohenkammer," said the doctor, and then began to spell it for him.

"And she lived here? This is her house?"

"Yes. But I'm not sure you'd say she exactly lived here. She spent at least half the year in Munich. She was here only for the spring and summer."

Sanders thought of the sticky, muggy heat of the day and commented that Toronto seemed to be an odd place to choose to spend your summers in.

"She also owned a summer place near Bala, and she spent the hottest part of the year there," said the doctor. "I suppose you'd have to say she didn't use this house much, really. May and June, I think, and then September and October. Or part of it."

"I take it Mrs. von Hohenkammer had money." Alexander nodded. "Anyone else live here? Did she have a husband?"

"No. She was a widow. She had two daughters. One lives in Toronto with her husband and kids, the other one lives at home, I think. There's a housekeeper, and a nephew. They all sort of live here, too. Her husband died three or four years ago, maybe longer. My wife would know. They were old friends from Clara's early days in Munich. I'm sorry. All I really know about her is that she wasn't sick and never took pills, but liked to get a physical checkup twice a year, once here and once in Munich. Insurance against something creeping up on you, I suppose."

Sanders nodded. "Did you see her drink the tea and collapse?"

The doctor shook his head. "No. One of the other guests saw it and told me about it. She was giving me a hand. Seemed to be a sensible young woman, but you can never tell." He jerked his head in the direction of the doorway. "She ought to be in the dining room right now."

"Perhaps you could point her out to me," said Sanders, and yawned. He looked down at the white-shrouded heap on the floor. "Is there somewhere in the house where I can talk to people?"

"Just a minute." Dr. Alexander walked across the hall to the dining room and opened one half of the big double doors. There was a murmur of voices, and Alexander returned. "The study is probably the best place." He led the way toward the back of the house and pointed Sanders toward the small book-lined room.

"And who was your eyewitness?" Sanders asked Alexander as the doctor turned back toward the staircase.

"Thin," said Alexander. "Long dark hair. There aren't that many women in there. . . . You shouldn't miss her. She's one of the better-looking ones." He leered at Sanders. "Now, if you'll excuse me, I think I'll go up and see how my wife is coping with the girls." He bounded up the stairs, two at a time, apparently unaffected by events or the hour.

Sanders walked into the study, noting with a doubtful frown the half-sized leather couch and matching chair, the big desk in the corner, and the round table on the other side. Entirely too cozy and comfortable. And cluttered. He shoved back the round table and heavy chairs, picked up the only straight-backed chair in the room, placed it in front of the desk, and nodded critically at his arrangements before moving back to the door. "Dubinsky!" he yelled impatiently. His partner's head appeared from the doorway of the dining room. "What in hell are you doing?"

"Getting statements from these people," said Dubinsky. He sounded profoundly bored.

"Get someone else to do that. Didn't I see Ryder around here somewhere?" Dubinsky nodded. "Let her do it, fast, so we can get rid of most of them." Dubinsky nodded again and headed for the living room.

Having effectively cleared the hall and study of distractions, Inspector Sanders stalked over to the dining room. He pushed open the door and stopped. There, dead in front of him on the other side of the table, sat Harriet Jeffries, looking characteristically poised and gravely interested, chatting to a prosperous-looking man in evening dress. Sanders scanned the crowd. No one else in the room remotely fitted Dr. Alexander's description; that put him in the impossible position of having as his principal eyewitness a woman who induced in him such a turmoil of conflicting emotions that he felt reduced to frozen immobility at the sight of her. He swore under his breath and seriously considered turning around and going home again. They could all stew in there in their black ties and expensive dresses until Sinclair stopped throwing up and came back on duty. Harriet glanced across the table, saw him, and colored slightly; she stood in response to his abrupt gesture beckoning her and walked, erect and almost stiff, over toward him. She closed the door carefully behind her. "For chrissake," he muttered, "what in hell are you doing here?"

"You don't have to look so horrified to see me," she said coldly. "I was invited. I do sometimes get invited to parties, you know. I'm considered quite an attractive addition to social occasions by some people."

He raised a hand in a gesture of truce. "Sorry. I didn't mean to put it that way. It was a shock seeing you, that's all."

"Well, at least I expected to run into you under the circumstances." He grabbed her by the arm and began to push her along the hall. "Where are you taking me?" She sounded distinctly irritated.

"To the study," he said grimly. "I want to talk to you." He steered her through the door with one hand on her waist, reached back with the other hand and shut it firmly, and then leaned back on the solid wooden panels to keep it from opening again. He released his hold on her, and she stepped back. "You look tired," he said. Her thin face was pale; her green eyes had dark smudges under them.

"Thanks," she said. "I needed that."

"If you want compliments, you can have them," he said. "You were described as one of the better-looking women here tonight. That's how I knew you were my eyewitness. But you still look tired."

"It's been a long day," she said, her voice sharp and hostile. "I just finished a rush job. And I got shanghaied by Clara to come here tonight—very much against my will, let me tell you."

"I wish you'd stayed home," said Sanders. "I'm not at my most gracious when I'm working."

"You couldn't be any less charming than when I first met you. Remember? And do you mind if I sit down? I'm tired."

Suddenly she looked even whiter and close to collapse. Sanders felt his heart lurch: he stepped forward and gathered her in his arms, holding her tightly. "I've thought about you," he said quietly. "A lot."

"Then why haven't you called me?" Her voice was muffled in the material of his suit.

"I did," he said indignantly, holding her out to allow him to look her in the face. "For weeks I called you. You were out or not answering your phone. God knows what."

"I was on assignment out of the city for a month! I have a machine. You could have left a message. I checked it every other day or so."

"I hate answering machines," he said fiercely. "I'm not going to pour my soul out to some goddamn piece of tape. When did you get back? You could have called me."

"I did," she said venomously. "You've obviously never tried to get in touch with you. It's easier to get through to the prime minister."

He slowly released his hold on her and then steered her toward one of the leather chairs. "Here, sit down." He began to pace back and forth around the cleared space in the study like a long-legged tiger in a very small cage. "What would you say," he said, and then stopped and took a deep breath, "if I suggested that we get the hell away from here for a couple of weeks? Maybe go down to the coast or somewhere where we won't run into anyone?"

"You're kidding, of course," said Harriet bitterly. She stretched out in the chair and yawned. "I won't even bother mentioning the work I have piled up waiting to be done. Since you probably don't find that important. But you also seem to have forgotten that you're tied up right now."

"What do you mean?" he asked suspiciously.

"What in hell do you think you're doing here? Isn't this your case? You can't just walk off and leave it, can you?"

"Oh, this." He looked around the study. "This'll be dead easy. Find out who gets all the money and there you have it. Might take a few days to nail down the proof, that's all." He sat down on the substantial arm of the chair and dropped a hand cautiously on her shoulder. "Just wait. One of them will have gone trotting off and bought some cyanide from somewhere a couple of days ago—it's amazing how stupid people can be—and he'll have been hanging around the kitchen ready to pop it in her drink. There you have it."

"Was it cyanide?" As Harriet spoke, she looked up at him, and her hair brushed softly against his wrist; he dug his fingers into her shoulder and bent closer over her.

"If your description was accurate, it probably was," said Sanders.

"Did that doctor tell you what I said?" Her voice had softened to a murmur.

"Briefly," he said, fighting to concentrate on something besides the feel of her shoulder under his hand and the scent of her hair and skin in his nostrils. "But I need the whole story." He moved his head even nearer and with his free hand gently pushed her hair away from her face.

At that moment, Dubinsky knocked once and thrust open the door. The sight of his partner sitting on the arm of a chair, leaning over a witness whose upturned face he seemed about to kiss, stopped him where he stood. His massive frame filled the doorway and injected an air of profound disapproval into the proceedings. "You need me?" he said finally. Sanders leapt to his feet, reddened, and nodded. Dubinsky settled himself at the table, watching sourly as Harriet moved with suspicious haste to the straight-backed chair. Sanders retreated behind the desk and began the interview.

When she had finished her recital, Sanders leaned forward and twirled a pencil around his fingers, as if getting the action right were the most important thing in the world. "That's all you know about the people here?" he said finally. "You didn't get to know her family?"

"If I had known she was going to get done in, I would have made a great effort to find something out about each one of them," she said, nettled. She felt that she had given a clear, lucid, and terribly useful account of the evening. "I had almost no sleep last night, and I spent most of the evening figuring out how to leave gracefully without offending her. I didn't have time to investigate her family. Or her friends."

"Her doctor seems to have had his eye on you, though," said Sanders. "I'd watch him if I were you."

She glared at him.

"Who was she, besides someone whose house you photographed? It's a nice picture, by the way," he added, glancing at the sixteen-by-twenty on the wall. "Where does all this ostentatious wealth come from?"

"What have you got against ostentatious wealth?" said Harriet sleepily. "No, forget it. She was an actress. Terribly famous in Germany, apparently. You know"—she yawned—"world-class on the legitimate stage. I saw her tonight doing a chunk of Shakespeare, and let me tell you, she was good." Harriet brooded for a minute over the thought. "In fact, fantastic. Anyway, she moved here to be with her daughter and her grandchildren, and if you want to know anything about them, there's a whole book of pictures of them on the table over by your sergeant there, and you can get bored out of your mind looking at them the way I had to. Her husband must have been rich as all get out and very upper class—she was a *von*, after all—but he died before she came over here. She was very charming, but overpowering. No one else could have dragged me out to a party tonight when all I wanted was to go to bed"—suddenly blushing and self-conscious, she glanced at Dubinsky and paused a second—"so I imagine she might have been difficult to live with. She seemed to squabble with her daughters, and they, I think, were squabbling with each other." She gave a brief account of what she had heard. "The only trouble is," she said, "that, naturally, they fight in German, and I lost some of it."

"Who was near the table that had the tea on it in the fifteen minutes before she died?" he said abruptly. "You must have seen that."

"For God's sake, John," she replied waspishly and familiarly, noticed Dubinsky's suspicious glance, and reddened again, "I wasn't keeping count of people. I didn't notice who was over there."

Dubinsky flipped back a couple of pages in his notebook. "The nephew was standing by the table," he said heavily. "Klaus Leitner. Also the daughter, Veronika. And the maid. And someone called Kirsten Müller, who really didn't seem to know anyone there. A lot of the people I talked to weren't certain about the times. Mrs. Theresa Milanovich never budged an inch from the fireplace that anyone noticed; her husband and Frank Whitelaw, the deceased's business manager, were at the other end of the room talking to the deceased."

"What did you get from the housekeeper? She must have had her eye on things."

"Nothing yet," he said, his voice still sour.

"You'd better watch out for her," said Harriet, looking over at Dubinsky's six-foot-four, 250-pound frame. "She's about five foot two by five foot two of solid muscle, and mean as hell."

"Why don't you go and tackle her, then," said Sanders to his partner. "Find out what you can about that damned tea and if anyone was in the kitchen. Yell for help if you need it." Dubinsky looked unamused, but got lightly to his feet and left the two of them alone.

"I'm not sure I can take having you around like this," said Sanders, standing up and moving closer to her. "Not if Ed is going to spend his time bursting through doors, looking morally outraged."

Harriet shook her head helplessly. "Is this going to take long, do you think?"

"Probably all night, if I'm lucky. But you don't have to stay." He placed his hands gently on her shoulders. "Why don't you go home and get some sleep?"

"No one has said I could go home yet. You've forgotten, I'm a witness. Maybe even a suspect." She yawned and stretched in her chair.

"Shit," he muttered. "I guess you'd better stay until the others have been seen." He looked critically at her. "And I suppose you should go back and join them. Look out for that doctor." Within seconds he was back at the desk, absorbed in his embryonic pile of notes.

Sanders stood as the woman entered the room. Her movements across the floor were jerky, as if each leg were uncertain about its destination and not at all sure it wasn't going to collapse when it got there. He preferred his women to have enough muscle to carry their height, he decided. This one would faint if you suggested taking her for a walk. Or even for a beer and a sandwich. She looked like an underfed greyhound, and a bad-tempered one at that. "Sit down, Mrs. Milanovich," he said perfunctorily. "I'm sorry to have to disturb you at a time like this, but—"

"How long is this going to take?" she interrupted. Her English wasn't quite sloppy enough to be native, but it was pretty damned good. Good enough to be extremely bitchy in.

"As brief a time as possible," he replied evenly. "But there are a few questions that I must ask—"

"Because I have to get home to my children—"

"Did you leave them alone?" He could interrupt as well.

"Certainly not." The words quivered with indignation at the suggestion. "They are with their nurse."

"Then, unless you believe she is likely to depart in the middle of the night, I hardly think that—"

"That is not the point. I feel uneasy if I am away from them too long." So, having established herself as a flawless mother and a certified "good person," she was settling down in the chair and preparing to be a daughter, thought Sanders. That is, she drew a tiny handkerchief out of the tiny gold bag she carried and dabbed at her eyes before looking up at him. "Do you know what happened to

Mamma? We have been going mad up there because no one will tell us anything. Except that it probably wasn't a heart attack. And why are the police here?"

"There isn't very much to tell, I'm afraid. At the moment, this is a routine investigation into a sudden death. Her doctor felt that it was possible that she did not die from natural causes and requested that we be called in." He paused in his recital for a reaction. She sat across from him, her long legs crossed, her elbow on the desk, her head to one side, listening with rapt attention. The pause lengthened.

Finally, she found the weight of the silence too much and played her side. "Not natural causes?" she said, her voice gently puzzled. Her eyes widened and filled with tears. It tugged the heartstrings until you remembered that she was the daughter of a famous actress; she was probably practicing inherited skills on him.

He declined the gambit. "That's right. Now, can you tell me what was happening when your mother collapsed? What you were doing at that moment?"

"No, I really can't," she said, sadly and sweetly. "I'm afraid I simply wasn't paying any attention to Mamma right then. I was talking to my husband and one of his friends, and to Dr. Alexander and his wife, as well, I think. I didn't notice—" Her voice broke, and the tiny handkerchief made its appearance once again. "I just heard that . . . that awful cry she made and saw her fall. It was terrible." She raised her eyes for one more expressive instant at him. "Do you think she could have . . . put something in her drink?"

"By 'she' do you mean your mother? Mrs. von Hohen-kammer? Are you saying that she deliberately administered a fatal dose of something to herself?"

Theresa's eyes widened again in confusion. "I don't know. If it wasn't a heart attack, though, how else could it have happened? And Dr. Alexander said it wasn't a heart attack."

"Why would she do such a thing?"

"It may not seem much to you, but . . . Mamma always had a reputation for being a very beautiful woman and a great actress, you know. And recently, well . . . she was pretty far into her fifties, although she pretended to be much younger," she added spitefully, "and the parts just weren't coming in. And after Papa's death—she felt terribly guilty about that. She wasn't living at home, you know, when he died, and that bothered her terribly."

"You mean that she had been separated from her husband?"

"Not precisely separated, but"—and she slid away from that topic—"perhaps she couldn't face the prospect of becoming old and helpless and unloved." Theresa's voice trembled with sincerity as she finished.

Sanders leaned back and considered her. There had been something else in that voice, too, and he was willing to bet a week's pay that it was hatred. "Thank you, Mrs. Milanovich," he said briskly. "We'll certainly take that into account. You have been most helpful." Two can lie as easily as one, after all. She smiled in sweet triumph, stood up with careful elegance, and walked out of the room. He was still repelled by the way she moved across the floor.

The door to the library snapped open before he could send for anyone else. A small, neat young woman with short dark hair and a white face stood in the doorway. "I am Veronika von Hohenkammer," she said crisply. "If you have finished talking to my sister, I'd like to get this over with." After the wispiness of the first one, this one's aggressiveness momentarily startled him. He could see why the two daughters might hate each other.

"Actually," he said, standing up and taking his brisk tone from her, "I had been planning on seeing her husband first so they could both go home. I gather they are concerned about leaving their children."

"What?" She looked genuinely surprised. "They pay for a lot of expensive nanny so they can leave them. And they're not going anywhere until they find out what's happening, either, if I know them." She walked in and sat down. "I'm sorry. That sounded very unpleasant. Even Milan and Theresa didn't deserve it. But thank you for seeing me now. It's very upsetting just sitting up there with only the two of them to talk to and not knowing what's happened. Obviously there is something very wrong, isn't there? I mean, what happened to Mamma." She gulped slightly and then gave her head a shake. "That wasn't anything normal, was it?"

"Probably not," he said. "Although we don't know. Can you tell us anything about what happened? For example, do you know what she may have eaten or drunk this evening? Besides the tea?"

Veronika's pallor intensified. "Besides the tea? No. No, I was talking to Klaus and a girl called Kirsten. I wasn't really noticing what anyone else was doing. Until . . . I did see the teacup in her hand, though. Was there something wrong with the tea?"

"It's a possibility. She collapsed shortly after drinking it, although that doesn't necessarily mean it was the tea that caused her to collapse." Then, speaking in a purely matter-of-fact tone, he dropped Theresa's theory into the conversation. "Your sister tells me that Mrs. von Hohenkammer was very depressed and that it seems probable that she took her own life. Had you noticed similar symptoms in her?"

"Depressed? Mamma? That's ridiculous!" She leaned back in amazement.

"You didn't observe that her recent behavior—say, since the death of her husband—had changed? That her mental state had deteriorated?"

"Nonsense!" said Nikki. She stood up and paced restlessly around the study as she spoke. "She was very upset when Papa died, of course. They had been very fond of each other, and she depended on him a great deal. I suppose she was depressed for several months after his death, but that's perfectly normal, I would think." She leaned against the wall opposite the desk and regarded Sanders steadily.

"Not if your parents were separated in the months before his death, I would have thought. Unless she suffered from guilt."

"Separated? Who have you been talking to?" she asked angrily. "Is this some of Frank Whitelaw's nonsense? Listen, I was there, and I know what went on. Mamma was away for a week or ten days in Cologne at an arts festival when Papa had his heart attack. She flew back at once, but it was too late. And yes, I think that had something to do with why she took his death so hard. But she would have been devastated anyway, even if she had been there." Tears sprang up in her eyes, and she shook her head impatiently again. "But that was four years ago. I can't imagine why Theresa said that Mamma committed suicide. Suicide! Mamma believed that suicide was a mortal sin. It's absolutely unthinkable that she would have done it."

"She didn't feel that she was getting old and unable to function—professionally or personally—the way she used to?"

"Mamma? Mamma was a tiger. Nobody could keep up with her. She certainly has—had—more energy than Theresa ever did." As she warmed to her subject, her face gained some color, and her eyes some of their normal snap. "She went off to dance class at least three times a week when she was in the city. And she usually got up very early in the morning and went for a long walk. I mean, really long, eight or ten kilometers. And she swam when we were in the country. She functioned better than most people in this house." Veronika glared at Sanders so that he didn't miss the point that he was included in her survey of the people in the house.

"Any problems with alcohol? Drugs?"

"Drugs? She hardly ever drank coffee or tea, even, except for those disgusting herbal mixtures of hers. She never touched alcohol except to be polite at dinner parties. She was practically a vegetarian. Lived on yogurt and whole grains and fruit and stuff like that. She was bounding with energy all summer." Veronika turned her head away for an instant. "She would never have done it. Never. If there was something in that tea, it got there by mistake or someone else put it in. Not Mamma. I know that." She shook her head and

looked soberly at him. "Not only that, but she was supposed to start rehearsals in October for a new play. She was
very excited about it. She wouldn't have missed that."

"Did you and your mother get along well?" he asked
casually.

"You have been talking to people, haven't you?" Her
cheeks reddened, and she raised her chin an inch or two.
"Well, we did. No matter what they say. I admit we used to
fight a lot. She didn't care for some of my, uh, friends in
Munich, and I felt that it wasn't any business of hers who
my friends were. That led to some disagreements. But even
so, we were very close to each other." She shrugged her
shoulders. "I can't prove that, but it's true." She stopped
and took a deep breath. "Is there anything else you want to
know?" Clearly, from her point of view, everything he had
asked so far had been an impertinent intrusion. Sanders
shook his head, and she walked out of the room. Every inch
of her radiated honesty and truth as she moved, but he
remembered that she, too, was the daughter of a great actress.

Sanders regarded the young man standing in front of him
with a gloomy and jaundiced eye. The evening clothes,
shrieking as they did of wealth and privilege, were enough
to arouse his dislike; the youthful athleticism and automatic
good manners merely strengthened it. But Sanders's expression was having its effect; the young man's elegance was
being undermined by worry. Sanders started with "Your
name is Klaus Leitner, and you are a nephew of the deceased?" in his coldest tones, when he was interrupted by a
distinctly official knock on the door. One of the small army
of men who were going over the house beckoned him into
the hall.

"Yes, Collins?"

"Sorry to disturb you, sir," said Collins with his usual
calm. "I found something in the cellar I thought I should
bring to your attention."

"It better be good," said Sanders irritably. "I'm busy."

"Oh, it is." There was a hint of smugness in his voice. "There's a photo lab down there. With a bottle marked 'Cyanide' in it."

"Well, I'll be damned," said Sanders. Collins stepped across the hallway to the closed door directly opposite the study. He flung it open and headed rapidly down the narrow stairs, across a clean and uncluttered concrete floor painted a shiny gray, to a set of four doors in the wall in front of him. They were all shut. The one at the far end was also padlocked. "What's in there?" asked Sanders.

"Don't know yet, sir," said Collins.

"Find out."

He nodded and headed for the two doors at the other end. "This is a darkroom. Nothing fancy or special about it," he said, pointing at the first door, "and this is where I found it." He opened the one at the end, turned on a light, and revealed a full-sized bathroom. It had been given over completely to photography. Stainless-steel developing tanks, graduated cylinders, and an expensive chemical balance were lined up on the countertop. Inside the bathtub was a plastic dishpan and a black plastic cylinder with a hose attached to it.

Sanders pointed at it.

"For washing film," explained Collins. He was the only member of the team at home in a lab; he had gone, in search of excitement, from photography to the bomb squad. After five years, in search of peace and quiet, he had transferred to Homicide. Now he stood behind Sanders, quietly waiting.

Finally, Sanders stepped inside the room, opened the cabinet doors, and contemplated a neat array of chemicals, all lined up in some sort of order, no doubt. Most of them were made by two or three prominent photographic supply companies—names even Sanders had heard of—but there were also glass and plastic containers of chemicals that were not standard enough to be sold by Ilford or Paterson or Kodak. Sitting in the midst of them was a brown glass bottle with a black plastic cap. The bottle was very neatly labeled "Potassium Cyanide. Poison. Handle with Care."

Sanders closed the cupboard door gently and stood upright again. "That seems to be it, Collins. Thank you." He headed back upstairs to finish his talk with Mr. Leitner.

"Who is the photographer in the house?" Sanders asked abruptly as he walked in.

Klaus Leitner had moved to the comfortable leather armchair and was apparently drifting off into semiconsciousness when Sanders asked the question. He sat up, wide awake. "I suppose if there is one, I'm it."

"You are responsible for the darkroom in the basement?"

"Yes. Aunt Clara let me have the space. No one else wanted it." He sounded defensive. "I'm the only person who ever uses the basement."

"Are you indeed?" murmured Sanders. "That's interesting."

"What do you mean by that?" Leitner asked. There was hostility in the charming voice, Sanders noted; one more jab and the smooth and polished exterior would crack apart.

"Only that down in the bathroom, which you apparently also use for photographic purposes— You do, don't you?"

"Yes. I need running water to wash film and prints, and the darkroom doesn't have any. I use both rooms." His manner was becoming stiff.

"In that bathroom," continued Sanders, ignoring the response, "we have found a glass bottle marked 'Potassium Cyanide.' Is that yours?"

"Yes, it is." Klaus grew distinctly pale. "I use it in processing."

"Really. Do all photographers have enough cyanide in their possession to wipe out several households full of people?"

"No." He had started to scrape nervously at his forefinger with his thumbnail; the action created a small but irritating noise. "It's used in a few specialized procedures. Most photographers wouldn't bother with it."

"Like what?" said Sanders nastily, trying to widen the crack.

"It's used for intensification of negatives." The thumbnail slowed.

"And that is?" With that question, Sanders lost him. Leitner gave him a thoughtful look; the anxiety ebbed away from his taut shoulders.

"I'd have to show you a print from a negative I'd processed. Otherwise, it's too complicated to explain." His voice suddenly became enthusiastic. "Just a minute." He bolted out of the room with such speed that Sanders was powerless to stop him. By the time he had yelled at someone to go after him, the basement door had opened, and hurrying feet on the stairs were the only trace left of him.

"Oh, Jesus," muttered Sanders. "He's probably down there swallowing the rest of the cyanide." But before he could get around the desk to rush after him, he heard footsteps racing back up the stairs.

"There should be some in here," said Klaus, breathlessly waving an orange box in one hand. "Come on. I'll spread them out here on the table." He pushed aside the photo albums and began to riffle through a pile of prints from the box. "There, that one worked fairly well. And so did that." He smiled.

Sanders looked down at the first print. It reminded him of an inkblot test. It was a collection of very black shapes against a very white ground and made no sense to him at all.

"If you want to see what goes on, look first at a print I made before I altered the negative." Beside the first one he put down a print of a reclining nude, small breasted, long legged, and round in the hips, with long hair that almost hid her face. Sanders was more impressed with the subject than with the technique. "Now what I did here . . . you see that the contours of the body are made up of alternating light and dark sections?" Sanders nodded. "Okay. I bathe the negative in Monckhoven's Intensifier—"

"What's that?"

"It's a bleach, a mercuric salt bleach. It alters the composition of the silver in the negative—you know, so it will behave differently. Then I plunge it in a bath of silver nitrate and potassium cyanide. Now, wherever the negative is thin—where there isn't much silver and so a lot of light will pass through it—the cyanide clears out the silver that's there, but more silver builds up in the denser section of the negative. So where there's no silver, you get a very dense black on the print because the light goes right through to the paper"—he was pointing to various sections of the print as he spoke—"and where there's a lot of silver, you get a very white white. In effect, you've wiped out all the middle tones, and you get this stark, contrasty print that has a rather surrealistic effect, I think. I was considering putting this one in a show—a better print of it, of course. This is just a work print." He stood back to let Sanders admire the results of his technical wizardry.

Sanders picked up the print, looked at it for a puzzled moment, and put it down again. "Very interesting effect." He preferred the girl before she had become a mass of black-and-white blotches but refrained from saying so. "Where do you usually keep the cyanide?"

"In the bathroom with the rest of my chemicals. That's where I mix up developer and so on. That counter around the sink is very handy."

"And you don't keep the cupboard or the room locked?"

Leitner shook his head. "It never occurred to me. I should have, because Theresa's children go down there sometimes." He gave a helpless shrug of his shoulders. "I'm not used to being around kids. I didn't think." He stacked up the prints again, his hands nervously tapping them together over and over again, and then put them back in the box. "I assume you believe that Aunt Clara was killed with my potassium cyanide," he said finally, and sat down beside the table, looking exhausted and miserable.

"I don't assume anything. I find it interesting that there is potassium cyanide in the house. Who knew that it was there?"

"I don't know." He looked up at Sanders and brushed his hair out of his eyes. "Anyone could have gone down into that bathroom. The cyanide was clearly labeled. And people go down there to get wine, and the freezer's down there. . . ." His voice trailed off helplessly.

"Later on I am going to ask you whether the level of crystals in the bottle seems to have gone down, but at the moment we are lifting fingerprints from the room and its contents. You could perhaps let Constable Collins have your fingerprints for elimination purposes. Did the housekeeper keep your darkroom clean?"

"No. Bettl disapproves of me and everything I do. She wouldn't volunteer to do anything she thought might help me. Besides, she only waddles down there when she has to get to the freezer."

"What's in the padlocked room?"

"I'm not sure. Old furniture and stuff like that, I think. Aunt Clara said it was padlocked because the kids used to go down there to play and Theresa didn't like it. Dirt, you know, and that sort of thing."

Sanders sat at the desk with the chair pushed back, stretching his cramped leg muscles in front of him. He looked around at the rows of books and wondered if Clara von Hohenkammer had chosen them. They were all in English and looked pragmatic and boring. Maybe an interior decorator had bought eight shelves of books for the study and the murdered woman kept whatever she actually read somewhere else. If she did read. He still had no impression of the woman beyond Harriet's clear but very sketchy portrait. Whatever anyone else said was canceled out by some other family member's contradictory account. And the brief, hostile, and unsatisfactory interview he had just had with her son-in-law hadn't helped much.

Milan Milanovich had presented himself as a hard-driving, successful businessman, a responsible corporate citizen, the president of the thriving Triple Saracen Development. That name rang a tiny bell in the back of Sanders's brain, but he wasn't sure whether it was a warning bell or simply one of recognition. According to him, his mother-in-law was a delightful woman, a devoted grandmother, gentle and affectionate, feminine, fragile and in need of protection, with no enemies. His wife had adored her mother; he himself had always been one of her greatest admirers; except for this unfortunate accident, their lives had all been perfect and harmonious. He dangled the accident hypothesis in front of Sanders as fetchingly as his wife had tried the suicide one. No doubt they had decided to present him with two safe theories he could choose between. Mr. Milanovich deplored the existence of cyanide in the basement, had had no idea before this evening that it was there, and opined that accidents will happen when people keep dangerous substances around the house. But he declined, his brown eyes cold, to offer any opinion on how the cyanide magically made its way from the darkroom to the kitchen and into the tea. He himself had not been near the kitchen. He had seen nothing; he knew nothing. He requested permission to return to his wife (also feminine, fragile, and in need of protection, clearly). Sanders shook his head and sent him away.

The inspector yawned and sent for the business manager. Perhaps he could present a more rational view, somewhere between Clara von Hohenkammer, tragic prima donna, and Grandma Clara, cozy but accident-prone.

When Frank Whitelaw arrived five minutes later, he was a study in bravery soldiering through trial. His face was red and puffy, his black tie askew, his hair damp and clinging thinly to his scalp. A powerful odor of brandy emanated from every pore. "My apologies, Inspector," he said, "for keeping you waiting. It's been . . . difficult. Still . . . nothing like cold water to sober a chap up."

Sanders stared in disbelief. Whitelaw sounded like a refugee from a British comedy series. The inspector waved him into a chair and tried to swallow his prejudices against the accent and the mannerisms. "You will have given us an account of your movements already."

Whitelaw nodded.

"I am interested in what you can tell me as Mrs. von Hohenkammer's business manager. About her financial affairs." Whitelaw developed a wary expression, as if information were something to be hoarded and doled out with great care. "Do you know, for example, who benefits from her death?"

"Benefits?" The business manager leaned back in his chair as if in shock. "How could anyone benefit from Clara's death?" He seemed to have picked up some of the family's acting techniques, thought Sanders. Any moment now he was going to launch into a soliloquy.

"Financially, Mr. Whitelaw. Who benefits financially from her death? All of this"—he waved his hand around him, taking in the house and all its expensive contents—"must go to someone, or did she leave it as a home for out-of-work actors?"

Sanders got a reproachful glare for that one. "Of course someone gets it," he said. "As far as I know, the estate will be divided up between her two daughters in some equitable fashion, but you'll have to ask the lawyers in Munich about that. There will be small individual amounts going to people like her housekeeper, Bettl. Bettl has been with her for twenty years or so—a very loyal servant." His tone was mournful.

"And you, Mr. Whitelaw. Do you qualify as a very loyal servant?"

"Servant?" he said coldly. "Clara certainly did not consider me a servant. I was a friend who happened to manage her business affairs for her. Her death represents a terrible loss to me, a personal loss that goes beyond description, and, I suppose, a loss in the business sense as well. No, I do not benefit from her death. Not at all."

"And so her estate," said Sanders, "except for individual amounts to loyal servants, and so on, will be divided equally between her two daughters."

"Not necessarily," said Whitelaw with a faint touch of glee in his voice. "I said equitably, not equally. Clara didn't feel that the two girls were equally capable of handling a large amount of capital or that each one deserved half of the estate."

"Which one gets cut out?" said Sanders abruptly.

"Oh, I don't suppose that either one gets cut out. But she battled a great deal with Veronika and certainly didn't think she was very stable." He glanced around as if he expected to see the young woman glowering in the corner, and then went on. "Veronika was—or is, I should say—mixed up with the Society for Peace and Justice in Munich. Do you know who they are?"

Sanders shook his head, although with that name, he thought he could guess how they generally planned to achieve peace and justice.

"They are the organization responsible for the bombing of a train station a couple of years ago in which twenty people were killed. Very dangerous people."

"She's been going around bombing people? And she isn't in jail?"

"Well, I don't think she's been an active member in that sense. But her mother worried that if she had money she would funnel it into the organization. They could become very dangerous if they had access to half the von Hohenkammer estate. I believe she was going to change her will in some way to prevent Nikki from being able to fund them significantly. You would have to check on that. I was her manager, not her solicitor," he said by way of justification. "I was responsible for the current state of her finances, not for their ultimate disposition."

"And so, as far as you know, most of the money goes to the other daughter?"

Whitelaw nodded.

"Did she know that?"

Whitelaw gave a judicious shrug of the shoulders. Now he began to look a financial man, rather than a brokenhearted old family friend. "I believe so. Theresa realized that Veronika was irresponsible and had discussed the problem with her mother. In fact, Clara forced Veronika to spend the summer in Canada because of her involvement with one of the members of the society."

"How did she manage that?" asked Sanders, incredulous.

Whitelaw smiled with pink and unctuous affability. "A combination of coercion and persuasion. Veronika is still— was still—entirely dependent on her mother. She gets a modest share of her father's personal estate when she reaches twenty-five." Sanders looked at him with distaste. He had a sudden very clear idea of who told Clara von Hohenkammer what kind of man her daughter was sleeping with.

"Had this change in her will taken place yet?" Whitelaw shrugged his shoulders again. "Did Veronika von Hohen- kammer know about it?"

"I don't know. You'd have to ask her that. If she'd be willing to discuss it with you." The sweetness of his tone invested his remarks with an extraordinary amount of malice.

"How does Klaus Leitner fit into the household, by the way? He lived with his aunt, did he?"

"Certainly not," said Whitelaw. Now his voice throbbed with open venom. "He's just another worthless drifter who's been sponging off her for the summer. He turned up in Toronto in June, before she left for the country, and talked her into letting him stay here, when he wasn't lolling around in Muskoka, and look what it has led to. A useless parasite, that's what he is, and the idea that he could ever make a living from playing around taking pictures is ludicrous. Clara would never have believed it." As his indignation level rose, Frank Whitelaw's plummy middle-class accent slipped here and there in a most interesting way.

"What had she to do with it?"

"Nothing at all," he said firmly. "Klaus merely announced to us that he was going to stay in the city and become a photographer. He was probably planning to sponge off Clara indefinitely, but it wouldn't have worked. She was too clear- headed for that."

"Did you notice that Mrs. von Hohenkammer had been depressed lately?"

Whitelaw paused a long time before answering. "I wouldn't have called it depression," he said at last. "But she was behaving in slightly odd ways, not dealing with her affairs in her usual manner. Nothing you could put your finger on."

"I see." What he saw was that Whitelaw was sitting on some fence or other. Waiting to find out what Theresa had said? "One last thing," he said. "Did Mrs. von Hohenkammer support both her children? Mrs. Milanovich seems to live very well," he added, thinking of the nanny. "Or is Triple Saracen a very prosperous concern?"

"I'm afraid I couldn't say," replied Whitelaw carefully. "You'd have to ask her husband. These development companies can be very deceptive." And with a slight bow of the head, he took his dismissal from the room.

Ed Dubinsky yawned his way into the study as soon as Whitelaw was gone. "I've done with the rest of them," he said. "That housekeeper is a pretty nasty piece of goods. By the way, the gardener is in there with her now."

"The gardener? What gardener? Where in hell did he come from?"

"He's been here all the time, only no one thought to mention him. His name is Paul Esteban, and he patrols the grounds at night, usually. With a pair of dogs, but he has them chained up right now because of the guests. He wants to know when he can let them loose."

"That's all we need," said Sanders. "Tell him to go to bed and take the goddamn dogs with him. I wish we could do the same," he added, getting to his feet.

CHAPTER 5

At nine-fifteen on Friday morning, John Sanders stalked into the office. It had been five o'clock when he had turned the von Hohenkammer house over to the specialists and tried to pick up his night's rest where he had left off. Now, with three hours of restless sleep behind him and the prospect of a hideously long day ahead, he could see little good in the morning. He set a container of coffee and a soggy Danish on the desk and looked blankly over at his partner. Dubinsky, as always, was in before him; the delicate but formidable Sally Dubinsky was ruthless about tossing him out of bed. "Autopsy report come in yet?" was the only question that percolated in Sanders's befogged and resentful brain. Dubinsky shook his head.

"Not as far as I know,' he said. "But I got in only a couple of minutes ago. I was out late last night," he pointed out in case Sanders had forgotten. His reward was a red-eyed glare.

Sanders pulled the phone over in front of him, narrowly missing his coffee, and dialed. After much holding and shunting and querying, someone finally put Dr. Braston on the other end of the line. "Melissa," he growled, "where in hell is that autopsy report?"

"Come on, John, who do you think I am?" said a cheerfully aggressive voice back at him. "I only got here a little before six. I know I'm brilliant and swift, but I'm not superwoman." She relented. "It's being typed. You'll get the prelim as soon as it's done."

"Give it to me over the phone," he said, yawning. "I need it now."

"Then meet me for breakfast." She sounded unbearably wide awake. "And I will tell all. I'm famished and haven't had a man to talk to over my orange juice for three days. Al's away."

Sanders swept his soggy Danish into the wastepaper basket. "Okay," he said, yawning again. "Jerry's? Five minutes?"

"Give me seven," she said. "I should wash the blood off."

"Melissa, you're disgusting," said Sanders, and hung up.

"So that's it," said Melissa Braston. "Cyanide. Very neat. Potassium cyanide, I imagine, and probably about three hundred milligrams at least, I would say. But lab techs sleep at night, and we won't have that for a while." She finished off her orange juice and began looking around for her bacon and eggs.

"That's a hell of a lot, isn't it?" asked Sanders.

"Oh, not really," she said, picking up the sugar. She poured about a quarter of a teaspoon into the palm of her hand. "About that much, more or less. Not a whole lot to have to carry around with you." She dropped it from her palm into her coffee and stirred it absentmindedly.

"Wouldn't she have noticed that the tea tasted funny?" said Sanders. "She tried it, to see if it was too hot, and then drank it."

"She wouldn't have. Most people can't taste cyanide." Melissa Braston shook her head. "Poor thing. She was in marvelous condition. You said she was fifty-five? Amazing. Beautifully muscled, lovely elastic fibers, liver in great shape . . . May the pathologist who carves me up find my remains so aesthetically pleasing." Sanders looked greenly at her.

"She didn't look so hot to me when I saw her," he muttered. "But I guess you're probably right. Didn't drink, didn't smoke, exercised, and lived on health food. I find it all very depressing."

"*You* do? What about me? Just once I'd like you to send me someone riddled with disease and foul living. Someone who if she hadn't been strangled or whatever would have died in six months anyway. In agony," she added, starting to butter her toast. "Then it wouldn't seem such a waste."

It wasn't like Melissa to take cadavers personally. "What's the matter with you?" asked Sanders. "You start getting gloomy over corpses, you'll have to take up another line of work."

"Nothing serious," she said, pushing aside her empty plate and waving her coffee cup pathetically in Jerry's direction. "It always happens to me during the cardiologists' convention. I get introspective when Al's away. No one to squabble with, I think, is the problem." She waited while Jerry gloomily filled her cup. "Maybe I should import my mother for the week. Except that it might be too much of a good thing."

Sanders managed a small laugh. Not much to start the day on.

When eleven o'clock came around that morning, Mr. Charles Britton was standing at the von Hohenkammers' imposing front door. He ought not to have been there at all. At nine-ten that morning the firm of Johnson and Carruthers, Chartered Accountants, had received a telephone call describing last night's tragic accident and canceling Mr. Britton's appointment. The receptionist commiserated politely with the caller and promised to relay a message to the absent Mr. Britton. And that should have been that, but just as Miss Christianson was flipping through her desk file to extract the name and number of the company where Mr. Britton could be found this morning, old Mr. Carruthers, at eighty-three the only surviving original partner in the firm, staggered out into the front office, complaining of slight discomfort. He asked for a glass of water and an aspirin and then collapsed onto the floor. The staff nurse, a doctor, an ambulance, all were summoned by the flustered receptionist.

By ten, Mr. Carruthers was grumbling in the hospital, the office had returned to normal, and Miss Christianson was heading out for her coffee break. As she reached for her purse, however, her eye fell on the message for Mr. Britton. "Damn," she muttered, and went back to looking for his current location.

"Oh," said the receptionist at Millven Industrial Products. "He just left. His team was here terribly early so they could finish up before we started, and he said he was off to get some breakfast. I haven't the faintest idea where he could be. Was it important?"

"Probably not," said Miss Christianson with a sigh. "I was only trying to save him a trip. It doesn't matter." She hung up the phone as her replacement walked in. "If Britton calls in, Alice, tell him not to bother going to the von Hohenkammer place, will you? It's too complicated to explain. See you." And off she went, conscious of having covered all her bases.

John Sanders and Ed Dubinsky had been in the conservatory when the front doorbell rang. It was exactly eleven o'clock. "Good morning," the man standing at the front door said briskly. "Charles Britton of Johnson and Carruthers. Are you Mr. Milanovich?"

"No," said Sanders. "Were you expecting him?"

"Why yes," he said. "Mrs. von Hohenkammer wanted us to go over the books with him this morning. Perhaps if I could have a word with her . . ." He was beginning to sound a trifle testy.

Sanders gave him a calculating look. "You haven't seen a paper this morning?"

"I was out of the house before the paper arrived," said Britton with definite irritation in his voice. "This is a very busy day."

"In that case," said Sanders, "come in. We have some explaining to do to each other." He led the way into the study. Briefly and economically, he outlined the events of the previous night.

Mr. Britton paused a moment to register shock. "A terrible thing," he said, "to happen to a charming and gracious lady. With some awkward implications for Mr. Milanovich," he added after a longer pause. "Mrs. von Hohenkammer called yesterday and insisted that I see her today. She was so insistent, in fact, that I arranged to finish up early this morning so I could fit in this visit. Not that it matters," he added. "Accountants often work strange hours. Like policemen, I suppose. But my impression was that they were in urgent need of financial advice."

"Was this common?" asked Sanders. "I mean, for her to call and ask you to drop everything and dash over?"

"Not at all," said Britton. "We do have wealthy clients who feel that every utility bill is a potential financial crisis, but Mrs. von Hohenkammer was not like that. She was a wealthy woman, with large holdings in Canada, and elsewhere, and a complex tax situation. Generally, though, she went at things rationally, took excellent advice, and never panicked. This is the first time in three or four years that she has asked to see me right away, and so I made a great effort to comply." He nodded soberly. "She was the sort of person you enjoyed working with. Very pleasant and reasonable."

"Didn't her business manager handle her financial affairs?" asked Sanders.

Charles Britton shook his head thoughtfully. "I wouldn't say so." He paused to consider his next sentence. "She may have called him a business manager, but basically she employed him as a personal secretary. I think that is the best way to put it. He made appointments and wrote letters and so on. And paid bills or looked after minor accounts. But he didn't make the day-to-day decisions, except as her theatrical agent."

"Who called you yesterday and asked for the appointment?"

"That was rather odd," said Britton. "First of all, Whitelaw

called and set up an appointment at eleven A.M. today. I was
to examine the books of a firm called Triple Saracen
Development with Milanovich, its principal, who is Mrs.
von Hohenkammer's son-in-law, and with Whitelaw. Then
Mrs. von Hohenkammer called me herself later in the day
and said that she wanted to discuss the results of this appointment and to go over some other matters with me
alone. She suggested that it be over lunch. I was looking
forward to this with some interest." As he paused for breath,
his eyes narrowed, and his normally imperturbable face
betrayed signs of excitement. "Triple Saracen is rather noto-
rious at the moment. One hears that the bottom is about to
fall out of it, although people connected with it still insist
that it has the capacity to become extremely profitable."

"What do you think?"

"Since I don't suppose I will get to look at the books, I
couldn't really hazard an opinion." He cocked his head
slightly to one side. "I wouldn't advise you to sink much
money into it right now, though, if you were to ask me."

That seemed to be a joke, and Sanders smiled.

"If there is nothing else I can help you gentlemen with,
however, I suppose I should be going. It doesn't seem likely
that there will be a meeting today, does it?" Mr. Britton
eased himself out of his chair.

Sanders shook his head. "Where did she keep her financial
records?"

"Not in here," said Britton, "although you'd think this
would be the logical place for her office. She worked either
in the conservatory or up in her sitting room. I generally
saw her in the sitting room. You should find everything you
need in the filing cabinets and drawers up there." He picked
up his briefcase. "It was quite a promotion to get to do
business with her upstairs, by the way. For the first couple
of years I came here, she had all her records and statements
brought downstairs." He shook his head in mild wonder at
human peculiarities. "She had her oddities, I suppose, but
they were fairly mild ones. I can see myself out, gentlemen.

If you need any information, just get in touch with me through the office. I left my card on the desk." Mr. Britton smiled. "Oh," he said, turning back, "do you think anyone would mind if I used this phone to call in? Don't go, gentlemen—nothing private."

Sanders shook his head and pushed the telephone across the desk.

"No, no, don't worry about it," Charles Britton was saying firmly into the mouthpiece a moment later. "It's just as well that I came over here. Thank you." He hung up and pushed the phone back toward Sanders. "Someone called in this morning and canceled this appointment. Didn't give his name. It was just by chance that the office didn't reach me. Good-bye, gentlemen."

"Must remember to ask Mr. Milanovich about that canceled appointment," said Sanders, watching Mr. Britton's retreating back. "I wonder if he was afraid we'd find out about the meeting. Interesting."

"Or why he was afraid," Dubinsky said. "Isn't Fraud doing a thing on Triple Saracen?"

"Fraud? How in hell do you find out about all these things?" asked Sanders. "Because I haven't the faintest idea. Better give them a call before we have a go at the sitting room. Then maybe someone in the family will tell us about this meeting. Where are they, anyway? This place is like a morgue."

"The housekeeper is sulking in the kitchen," said Dubinsky. "And I think the daughter and the nephew are still upstairs. I don't suppose they're used to getting up in the morning."

In fact, Dubinsky was maligning the entire family by assuming that they were all sleeping the long morning sleep of the rich and idle. While he and his partner were standing in the middle of Clara von Hohenkammer's bright and sunny sitting room, trying to decide where to start, all of that lady's closest relatives had been awake for hours.

Theresa Milanovich was sitting in the dining room of her sprawling suburban-style house, staring out into the back garden, her attention apparently entirely absorbed by a pair of squirrels chasing each other up and down trees. It would have been more tactful of her to have devoted some of that attention to her husband, who was pacing up and down the room and addressing her in vehement tones, but if the expression on her face was anything to judge by, she was not concerned with trying to please him. "I don't see why you're being so bloody unpleasant about it," he was saying. "Or were you just waiting for the chance to see me in jail?"

"For God's sake, Milan, don't be so stupid. What good would it do me to have you in jail?" She whirled around from her contemplation of nature and looked at him. "If I had wanted to get rid of you, it would have been easy enough the ordinary way. I didn't need to try to get you arrested." Her eyes narrowed to thin cracks in her face. "You certainly have given me enough grounds to ditch you. And if I haven't chosen to get rid of you up until now, I'm not going to start while the whole world is watching us."

"What do you mean?"

"I mean that there was cyanide in Mamma's tea, and it sure as hell didn't get there by mistake, did it? Somebody went down to Klaus's little lab in the basement, took it out, and put it in that cup. When did you get it from the basement? While we were at the reading? Because you were in and out of the kitchen all night. I saw you. Wandering around like a restless cow. Did you poison Mamma?"

"Jesus, woman, watch what you're saying!" he gasped, looking at her in horror. "How can you even think that?"

"It's easy." Her voice was calm. "You're in a hell of a hole. You hated my mother, and you knew perfectly well that the second anyone with any brains looked at your books, you hadn't a chance of getting a penny out of her. This way you don't have to. You figure you can always get it out of dumb little Theresa, don't you? The way you got all my father's money out of me. Well, don't count on it."

"When did you come up with all this crap?" he asked heavily.

"Last night. I was thinking. I got up and had a drink and sat in the living room and thought. I had some interesting ideas." She turned again to contemplate the squirrels. "But if you did poison Mamma, you'd better tell me about it and we'll figure out what to do. With your brains, they'll catch you in a minute."

"Hold on there," he said. "I didn't kill your mother. You're trying to push me into something, aren't you? I mean, maybe you could've killed her just as easy. You'd love to get your hands on all that money." He resumed his walking up and down . "Anyway, I didn't have a thing to worry about today. You must really think I'm stupid if you think that accountant was going to get anything but a lovely, clean set of books. We were all set," he said, and flashed a confident smile at his wife. "This is a real bind." He stopped and placed himself directly in front of her. "I'd have been better off if she'd still been alive."

She looked up wearily. "You always did underestimate all of us, didn't you? Must be because we're women and you can't believe that we could have any brains." Suddenly she yawned, an enormous, exhausted yawn. "Well, if you didn't do it"—she sounded as though she had not quite accepted that proposition—"then it must have been Nikki. Nobody else had any reason to kill her."

"You'd like that, wouldn't you?" said her husband in an oddly flat voice.

"Somebody had to do it," she said, and picked up a magazine.

"No, you don't," he said, yanking it out of her hands. "You don't turn off like that until you call that lawyer in Munich." He looked at his watch. "Eleven—just in time for a nice late-afternoon chat. Come on, Theresa. I have to know what's in that will before I face the bankers on Monday morning. It's the only way."

"No." She picked up another magazine. "Can't you see how that would look? Murdered woman's grieving daughter phones lawyer in Munich to find out how much she's worth?

We're supposed to be rich, Milan. Remember? We're not supposed to be worried about money. It has never occurred to us that the bank won't extend your loan on Monday. We don't need an extra penny!" She glared at him. "You have to remember that. We don't need an extra penny. Mother's money is of no interest to us at all."

Her husband returned her glare for a moment and then sat down in a large chair and took up his wife's vigil over the squirrels.

Sanders looked around Clara's bright and cheerful sitting room for a good couple of minutes before he turned to Dubinsky, who was leaning in the doorway, watching him. "I think we'll get further talking to people, don't you?" he said, trying to sound as if he believed it. "Instead of plough-ing through a lot of paper here." His tired brain shied away from the enormous amount of work the four-drawer filing cabinet and the three-drawer desk seemed to represent. "What about the housekeeper? Did you manage to get anything from her last night?" He yawned, sat back in an overstuffed chair, closed his eyes, and appeared to go to sleep.

Dubinsky pulled out his notebook and read rapidly, in a flat, bored voice. "She said that at eleven the women from the catering service put the coffee urn, cups, and plates of cakes and cookies in the dining room. The bartender was supposed to be on duty until eleven-thirty, but at twenty after he put clean glasses, ice, and mix on the table, col-lected the dirty glasses, and left. She seemed to feel he was cheating on his time," he said, looking up. "In fact, she seems to be convinced that everyone is cheating, including us. So after that, no one was noticing what was going on with food and drink. It was a help-yourself situation."

Sanders spoke without opening his eyes. "Did she go around the living room and pick up dirty dishes and things like that? Or was she in the kitchen all the time?"

"I asked her if she stayed in the kitchen, and her answer

was 'Where else would I be?' Which doesn't really help, does it? Then Mrs. von Hohenkammer told her to have tea ready for her at midnight. She got it ready and took it out, and since Mrs. von Hohenkammer was talking to a lot of people and she didn't want to interrupt her, she put it down where her employer could see it and left. And that's all she knows. Except that no one was in the kitchen but the gardener. Who came in two or three times."

"Why?"

"Supposedly to check on the progress of the party, but probably to cadge food and drink. And that's all I got. I've met hit men who were more cooperative witnesses."

"Okay," said Sanders, pushing himself slowly to his feet. "We'd better talk to her again. But first, call the business manager and get him over here so we can start in on the filing cabinets." Dubinsky shrugged and headed for the telephone.

"When do you want to see him?"

"When? Now, of course. Where does he live?"

Dubinsky dropped the receiver back down and shook his head. "On Woodlawn. In what he calls a small flat. And I'm not facing that little fart-face until I've had some lunch. Two o'clock," he said mutinously.

"Big," said Sanders. "He's really quite a big fart-face. Two o'clock it is."

Bettl Kotzmeier was standing precariously on a kitchen stool in front of a row of cabinets. Her head was in the cabinet, and her strong arms were scrubbing the middle shelf as if she were trying to purify it. "Miss Kotzmeier," said Sanders. There was no response. "Miss Kotzmeier!" This time his voice reverberated through the room. "Inspector Sanders, Homicide. I have some questions about your statement to Sergeant Dubinsky last night. I would appreciate it if you would come down here so we can talk." The shoulders continued to rotate as her arms scrubbed in circular motion.

"Or, if you prefer, we can conduct this interview down-town." The movement slowed and stopped. Her head and shoulders emerged from the cupboard. She dropped her sponge into the brown plastic bucket beside her on the counter and climbed heavily down off the stool. She folded her arms in a gesture that he hadn't believed anyone used off the stage and said, "Yes?"

The interview inched its painful way through a recalcitrant hour. Sanders started with all the questions that Dubinsky had asked and got answers that were, if anything, briefer and less helpful this time. Yes, she had stayed all evening in the kitchen. That was where she was supposed to stay, wasn't it? "Except when you brought in the tea? You didn't stay in the kitchen then."

"No." Grudgingly. "I brought in the tea."

"At twelve?"

She nodded.

"At exactly twelve?"

"That was when she wanted it."

"It must have been pretty cold by the time she drank it. Did your employer like her tea cold?"

She glowered and then finally shook her head. "No. Frau von Hohenkammer was . . ." She waved her hand while searching for the word.

"Then it is very odd that she drank the tea without complaint."

No response.

"I said it's odd that she drank the tea cold, Miss Kotzmeier, isn't it? Or don't you think so?"

"She didn't drink it cold."

Sanders stared at her, irritation building up to higher and higher levels.

Her gaze dropped, and she muttered, "Somebody got her more from the pot. The pot was still hot. It was in the tea basket."

"What?" Sanders stared at her. "You mean somebody came into the kitchen and refilled her cup from the teapot?"

She shrugged. "That's where the pot was."

"Who?"

"I didn't see."

"Then how do you know somebody got her a fresh cup?"

"Because when I made the tea, I poured a cup and put the pot in the tea basket. Frau von Hohenkammer often had more before she went to bed. When I looked over at the counter, the pot was out of the basket, and it was almost empty. I had to put on another kettle for when she would want more tea." There was bitterness in her voice.

"What did you do with the teapot?"

"I washed it, of course, because when she would want fresh tea, I would need to use it again soon."

"Where is this pot?" he asked.

"They took it away." Her shoulders twitched with resentment.

"I don't understand," he said softly, "how you failed to notice someone come in, look for the teapot—where was it, by the way?" She pointed wordlessly to the counter beside the stove. "Find it, dump out the cold tea in the sink, refill the cup, and walk out again. That just isn't very likely, is it? That says to me that either you replaced the tea yourself or you're trying to protect some member of the family. It won't work, you know. We'll find out, anyway."

"I tell you, I didn't see who it was. I don't know. I just know that someone moved the teapot out of its basket." Her mouth closed in a narrow line. "I wasn't in the kitchen then."

"Where were you? I thought you said you had been in here all night."

She glared. "People left glasses and dirty plates everywhere. Those maids were supposed to clean up, but there were glasses in the dining room and dirty plates in the study, and glasses. I couldn't leave them there. They would mark the furniture. I took them away and polished off the marks with a cloth." Dubinsky grinned and shook his head in disbelief. Even Sally's *mother* didn't polish furniture during a party.

"So between twelve and twelve-thirty, you were polishing the furniture in the study and the dining room?"

She glowered. "Not twelve-thirty. Twelve twenty-five. I checked the time. I figured when she'd had her tea, they'd be going soon."

"Especially with you polishing the furniture all around them. And so at 12:25 you came into the kitchen, put on the kettle, and washed the teapot. What else did you do?"

"Nothing. There was nothing to do until people left." She turned her back on them and reached into the bucket for her sponge once again.

Sanders turned on his heel. "We'll need to talk to you again, Miss Kotzmeier," he threw back at her, with menace in his voice, as he walked rapidly toward the living room. He stopped in the doorway. "Let's see," he said, "she's sitting there," and he pointed to a couch and two chairs to his left. "She sees the tea." He sat down on the small couch and looked at his watch. "Which is on the corner of that table. It's been there for a little while, because she doesn't see anyone bring it out—long enough for someone to empty the cyanide into the cup from the paper and throw it under the table."

"Was there cyanide in that paper?"

"Don't know yet. There's some discussion about it, she says she'll get it—I suppose someone else offered to fetch it for her—and she gets up." Here he got to his feet again. "She walks over there, tastes the tea, which is not too hot to drink, or too cold, since she's fussy," and as he was saying this, he was walking over to the table and then miming the drinking of a cup of tea, "and then she has a fit of some sort, which takes a little time, the doctor has to notice it, and he runs over." Sanders paused a second. "And then he glances at his watch and it is twelve twenty-nine. "Sanders looked at his watch again. "And that whole thing couldn't have taken more than two minutes unless there was a lot more conversation than people claimed. Which means that the poisoned tea was on the table by twelve twenty-seven. How long does it take a cup of tea to cool down?"

"Christ almighty," muttered Dubinsky, "how in hell would I know? Depends on the kind of cup it's in, how hot it was, all that sort of crap. Are we sure the poison was in the tea?"

"Had to be," said Sanders uneasily. "Where else could it be? But we'll know by this afternoon; the lab should be through by then. I wonder if they got anything from the pot. Anyway, if we know how long it took to cool down, we'd know roughly when it was poured. But it has to be before twelve twenty-five if she"—he pointed at the kitchen—"isn't lying."

"And how do we know that when Big Bertha says twelve twenty-five she means just that? What clock was she going by? For all these calculations to mean anything, it had to be the same as the doctor's watch."

"Shut up, Dubinsky. That doesn't help. Naw, you're right. Let's go get some lunch. This place is getting to me."

As Sanders was trekking back and forth in the living room with his watch in his hand, Veronika von Hohenkammer, in jeans and a sweatshirt, was padding down the carpeted hallway between her room and her cousin's. She knocked, emphatically. "Klaus, you awake in there?" There was a muffled sound that she assumed to be an invitation to enter.

He was lying on his stomach in a tangle of bedclothes and opened the eye that was visible to her. "What time is it?"

"Almost noon," she said. "I couldn't stand being in my room all alone or sitting in the kitchen with Bettl. The police are still poking around in Mamma's room and downstairs."

Klaus rolled over and groaned. "That's all right," he said, yawning. "Do you think you can get us some coffee? And do you mind if I take a shower before trying to talk?" She shook her head. "Then why don't you try to find us some coffee and rolls and we'll have them in the little back room.

It seems sunny out. It'll be more cheerful than this." His wave included the unmade bed, the clothes on the floor, and the general air of dissolution and decay in the room.

"Go and take a shower." She left him there and slipped quietly down the back stairs to see what she could produce. The sight of Bettl scrubbing the already-clean kitchen cabinets evoked a response in the girl somewhere between irritation and compassion; but Nikki decided that if she had to run the house for the next few days, she would have to quell the compassion and establish some ground rules. "Bettl," she snapped. "We'll have a pitcher of orange juice, a large pot of coffee, and some rolls with jam and butter for breakfast. In the sewing room, please, since the police seem to be everywhere else. As soon as possible." She turned rapidly and went back up the stairs to the sewing room.

Klaus strolled into the sunny little room, clean, wet headed, and relatively clear-eyed. "And where is our coffee, may I ask?" he said in mock horror. "I thought you'd be down in the kitchen opening a jar and boiling a kettle, not sitting here doing nothing."

Nikki silenced him with a gesture and pointed wordlessly at the door. He heard heavy footsteps on the stairs, and then Bettl entered with a large tray. On it were glasses, cups, plates, napkins, cutlery, a pitcher of orange juice, sugar, three kinds of jam, and butter, along with a basket covered neatly with a white napkin. "I'll bring the milk and coffee in a minute," she said in a neutral tone, then put down the tray and left.

"No flowers?" asked Klaus. "My God, Nikki, how did you do it?"

"I screamed," said Nikki. "It's the only form of communication she understands. But it never worked when Mamma was around. It just made her mad. Shhh. Here she comes again." And this time she had a small heating element with a china jug filled with coffee and one of hot milk on it. She plugged it in and turned. "Thank you, Bettl," said Nikki crisply. "You had better order in groceries for the weekend.

Theresa and her husband might be here a great deal. We will need to have plenty." Bettl nodded and left. "I may be about to get arrested, but until that happens, I don't intend to starve to death." Her eyes were wet, and her chin quivered, but she turned resolutely to the array of food and drink on the large table. "Orange juice?"

"Please," he said, taking the proffered glass. "And what do you mean, you may be about to get arrested?"

"Breakfast first, and then we can talk. I've been thinking."

Fifteen minutes later, Klaus helped himself to another large cup of café au lait, leaned back comfortably on the chintz chesterfield, and said: "Right. Now what in hell are you talking about?"

"Klaus, darling, you can't be as stupid as you're pretending to be. You must realize what's going on." She put down her half-eaten roll and curled up with her feet tucked under her, shivering in spite of the warm sun. "No matter what Theresa says, I can't believe that Mamma killed herself."

"Killed herself! That's preposterous." Klaus shook his head in amazement. "How could anyone, even Theresa, believe that?"

"It's easy. Either you believe that, or you believe that one of us killed her. Who could have wanted her dead?" Nikki's eyes swam with tears again, she blinked and went on. "Only someone who was going to benefit from her death. And that's either me or Theresa. And Theresa didn't move from the fireplace all night. I thought she had turned into a statue."

"Except when the two of you were in the hall," said Klaus slowly. "What were you fighting about?"

"Who?"

"You and Theresa."

"Oh, that. That was nothing." Nikki shrugged and turned away in embarrassment. "I was just teasing her a little, that's all."

"Teasing her? What about?"

"Well, she had the idea that you and I were going to get

hundreds of thousands of marks—well, fifty thousand dollars—out of Mamma for this business of yours and that this would cut into her precious children's inheritance, and so on." Nikki looked up and shrugged, the ghost of a smile on her face. "I'm not sure where she got the amount from."

"I think I mentioned it in a theoretical way as the cost of setting up a first-class studio from scratch."

"That's it, then. Anyway, she said we'd never get away with it."

"Maybe she—"

"No. If there had been cyanide in *my* drink, maybe, but why Mamma? She couldn't do anything like that. Not Theresa."

"Maybe Milan did it for her?"

"Him! That lecherous little worm. He's scared of his own shadow. He'd do it only if you could guarantee he wouldn't get caught." She clutched her knees tightly to her chest to keep them from trembling. "And that leaves just—"

"You. I don't see why. If you know you didn't do it, then somebody else must have. All we have to do is figure out who it is."

"I'm just trying to think the way the police will. Either someone had a reason to want Mamma dead, or there's a maniac running around dumping cyanide in drinks and anyone at the party could have been killed."

"Be reasonable, Veronika," said her cousin sharply. "If you're talking about motive, Theresa stands to inherit as much, or . . . in fact . . ."

"Yes. I've thought of that. I may be out searching for a job once the will is read. I knew I should be learning a trade of some sort."

"Do you know if your mother left you anything?"

"All I know is that she was mad as hell at me last spring and she was thinking of changing her will. I wouldn't be surprised if I'm featured in it in an unpromising way. You know, 'And to my daughter, Veronika, I leave one hundred marks and the wish that she may learn to change her life for the better.' "

"But you see," said Klaus, checking to see if there was any more coffee, "if that's true, then no one will suspect you."

"That's a wonderful choice, Klaus. Impoverished and free or rich and in jail. Do you think I should get a lawyer?"

"Whatever for?"

"We really don't know the police around here, do we? They're not all like that nice man up at the lake. He probably works up there to get away from real criminals in the city. Murderers and so on."

Klaus shook his head. "Not even the same kind of police. But if you think you should get a lawyer, why not ask Frank? He seems to know everyone in the city." He glanced sideways at her. "But isn't running for a lawyer going to make you look guilty? Maybe you should just be straightforward and honest and tell them everything that happend and assume they'll catch whoever did it."

Nikki looked at him steadily. "And if they don't? Then what do I do?"

"We'll worry about that when it happens."

The lunchtime crowd had already thinned out when the buru walked quickly into the little Portuguese restaurant on College Street and sat down in a booth close to the kitchen. He ordered coffee and a pastry before asking casually whether the chef was available. The waiter nodded amiably. "He'll be out in a moment," he said. "He just has one order to finish, and it's time for his break."

Before his friend had finished his pastry, Manu pushed through the swinging doors that led from the kitchen, carrying a plate of chicken and rice in one hand and a coffee in the other. He put them down, walked over and picked up a napkin and cutlery, set a place carefully on the other side of the table, and finally eased himself down onto the bench.

"What's happening?" he asked casually. "I thought we had decided you should not come here."

"We have reached a crisis point," he said. "It is time to decide whether to go on or give up. Can they understand?" he added softly, nodding in the direction of the two waiters who were lounging by the coffee machine, waiting for the last of the lunch crowd to finish.

"Not a word," said Manu. "A Columbian and a Chilean. I don't like the idea of giving up," he added in his mournfully gentle voice. "Not after we've done all the dirty work. And I don't leave without the money. That's what we came here for, isn't it?"

"Yes, of course," said the buru. "I didn't mean that. We'll get the money all right. We'll get the money for everything that has already crossed the border."

"How much has he sold?"

"A lot. Almost half of what has been taken across. At decent prices, too. The other half could take up to a year to dispose of, but that doesn't matter, does it? We have time. That is not what worries me."

Manu smiled gravely and went over to get the coffee-pot, refilled both cups, and sat down again. "What is it that worries you, then?" he asked, bending over his coffee.

"It's obvious, isn't it? We have to make our move now, before it's too late." He pushed his coffee cup away, the worried frown on his face making him look like a fifteen-year-old, and ran his hands through his light brown curls. "I hate this," he said with passion in his voice. "I wish there was some other way to raise the money."

"There isn't," said his friend. "You were the one to realize that. This isn't '36. There aren't crowds of helpful foreigners out there to pity us, to send us money for guns and rice. And the better things get, the harder it is to get money. So here we are, two paces along the road to freedom and independence, and we cannot move a single step farther. Unless we do what we are doing. What I hate is having to use a pig like Carlos. Or his friend."

"Once you accept the necessity of subverting honesty to achieve your goals, you accept the necessity of a Carlos. That is why they exist," said the buru mournfully. "That is why they exist." He shook his head. "But it is too late now to worry about that. I have worked out the only way to do it and keep us safe. Because that is what is important. It is complex, perhaps too complex, but it should enable us to get clear. The others appear in their proper roles," he said, all of a sudden grinning angelically, "as mules, bearing their burdens patiently and stupidly." He pulled out a sheet of paper and a pencil and once more began to jot down the beginnings of a plan.

CHAPTER 6

At precisely two, Frank Whitelaw walked into the sitting room without bothering to knock. He was a very different creature from the red-faced and brandy-soaked buffoon in the crumpled dinner jacket of the night before. He was now dressed with casual nonchalance in velvet corduroy and Irish tweed; his silvery gold hair billowed in richly shaped clouds around his elegant head. Sanders did some rapid mental revisions in his estimate of Whitelaw's possible function in Clara von Hohenkammer's household.

"Was it you who tried to call off the meeting this morning?" asked Sanders.

"Meeting?" said Whitelaw in apparent astonishment. "What meeting?"

"The meeting with"—and Sanders drew out his notebook, which he consulted ostentatiously—"Mr. Charles Britton, an accountant." He looked up again. "The one Mrs. von Hohenkammer asked you to arrange. To discuss her finances, I assume. Only she died before he got here."

"Oh, no," said Whitelaw easily. "That meeting was to look into Triple Saracen Development, Milanovich's company. Clara was considering helping her son-in-law out of his current disastrous mess. She wasn't worried about her own financial situation. I would have known if she had been. As for who canceled it, I don't know." He cocked his head charmingly to one side. "I should have, I admit. But in the stress of the last twelve hours, I forgot about it. Mr.

Milanovich must have called and canceled. A thoughtful gesture."

"Did your employer have any enemies that you know of? She was a famous woman. Had she received any threats, by telephone or in the mail? Who opened her mail, Mr. Whitelaw? You?" asked Sanders.

"Enemies?" Whitelaw stood up and walked over to the other side of the room, where he paused to straighten a pen-and-ink drawing that had drooped a millimeter out of true; he turned and slowly shook his head. "No, I don't think so. And yes, I usually opened and answered her business correspondence. There were no threats that I knew of. Who could possibly have—" He suddenly sat down on a small damask love seat. "This has been a great blow to me. She was a great lady, a very great lady."

Sanders regarded him thoughtfully for a moment. "That's an interesting sketch over there," he said, nodding at the one that Whitelaw had just straightened. "Is it valuable?"

Whitelaw nodded. "Clara didn't bother hanging things that aren't valuable. By and large. And except for the Mondrian in the living room, her best pieces are all in here. For security, really. She never let strangers in this room."

"What else is in here," said Sanders, "besides a fortune in art?"

"Her business records," said Whitelaw, nodding at the filing cabinet set against the wall. "All the ones that aren't in Munich, that is."

"Perhaps you could give me a quick run-through on her filing system," said Sanders gloomily. "Before we start going through them."

"Certainly," said Whitelaw in tones of the gravest courtesy. "How's your German?"

"German?"

"All of her financial records except for a few Canadian bank statements are in German, of course." Sanders could hear the deep belly laughter that Frank Whitelaw was suppressing as he stood there and looked solemnly in their direction.

By the time John Sanders had recovered his equanimity sufficiently to check through the filing cabinet to see if Whitelaw was telling the truth—he was—and to come back downstairs, the von Hohenkammer family had gathered in the dining room. Theresa was in a black skirt and white blouse and carefully, but not garishly, made up. The perfect grief-stricken daughter, thought Sanders. Her sister was in jeans and bare feet, looking white faced and miserable. Sorrow? Guilt? Maybe both.

"Do you think," said Theresa, "that we could sit somewhere more comfortable than this room?"

"Just a minute," said Sanders. "I'll check the state of things." In the conservatory, Collins was standing by the table, holding several sheets of paper in his hand. "Did you find anything?" asked Sanders.

"Nothing significant, as far as I can tell." Collins shook his head gloomily. "There's nothing here but writing paper and airmail envelopes and stamps and things like that."

"Then leave it and start in on the upstairs sitting room."

Collins gave him a mutinous look. "Give us a break. We've been working down here all morning. O'Connor just went out for sandwiches; we thought it'd be nice to eat for a change. If you don't mind."

"Yeah, go on," Sanders muttered, looking down at the desk. "You didn't find anything else in the room?" he asked. "This is it?"

"That's it. I checked everywhere: in the plant pots, under the furniture, behind the radiators, everywhere except under the tiles. I didn't have a chisel. You want to go over the room again?"

Sanders chose to ignore the implied insubordination and went back to the crowd in the dining room. "The conservatory is free," he said from the hallway. "If you'd rather be in there. We'll be out of the upstairs rooms by the end of the day, I imagine; the living room may take longer." He turned to Klaus. "Don't try to use your photo lab until further notice."

Klaus nodded somberly. "I don't think I'd feel much like using it right now, anyway," he said. "Feel free."

Sanders sat grimly in the study once more. Mrs. Theresa Milanovich had just stalked out the door, filled with righteous indignation. She had certainly not been in the kitchen, had not exchanged any cross words with her sister or any other person in the house, and was devastated that Sanders could suggest such things. And now Veronika von Hohenkammer was huddled in the leather armchair, her feet tucked under her, shivering.

"When did you take your mother's tea out into the kitchen and pour it out?" said Sanders, looking up from his page of notes.

"Who told you that?" she said quickly. He could see that her hands were trembling; when she noticed the direction of his eyes, she thrust them quickly down around her knees.

"And then you replaced the tea you poured out with more from the pot, didn't you? And what did you put in that tea, Miss von Hohenkammer?"

"Nothing," she said, her voice slightly hoarse. "I didn't put anything into the tea. I just poured more from the pot and put the cup back where it was on the table."

"Why?"

Veronika stared at him, confused. "It was cold," she said at last. "No other reason."

He looked back down at his notes. "What were you and your sister quarreling about last night?"

Veronika pulled herself upright in her chair and looked steadily at him. "I believe that even in this country I don't have to answer your questions unless I have a lawyer present to advise me. Is this not true?"

Sanders was suddenly overwhelmed by a wave of exhausted irritability and stood up. "Yes, Miss von Hohenkammer, it is. But it's a privilege innocent people don't invoke," he said, his voice heavy with threat. "In my experience. I'll see you later. With or without your lawyer." He turned to Dubinsky. "Let's get the hell out of here before I fall asleep," he muttered. "Don't go anywhere, Miss von Hohenkammer," he added, yawning.

Veronika headed straight for her bedroom. She sat down on the bed, reached under the night table, and took out the telephone book. After looking up a number, she picked up the receiver and began to dial.

Harriet Jeffries was sprawled in a comfortable chair, clutching a mug of coffee and staring out at the deck. When she had finally reached home that morning, the sky was graying in the east, and the first birds were chirping and grumbling themselves awake. Grimly, she had showered, changed, and set about finishing off the work that had to be delivered by morning. At seven-thirty, she had driven over to the architect's office and dropped it all off. The rest of the morning she had spent in bed, in and out of sleep, dreaming lurid dreams of people dying in agony, spewing brilliantly colored poison from their lips and clutching accusingly at her. It hadn't seemed worth staying in bed, and now she was staring out the French door, the unread morning paper in her lap and the foulest cup of coffee she had ever tasted becoming tepid in her hand. The telephone rang.

As she set the receiver down again, she cursed softly. Stupid, stupid Harriet. Overwhelmed with work, sick and tired of other people's problems, yet she had just promised to drop everything in order to solve all of Nikki von Hohenkammer's life crises. Why, with a city filled with relations, with a downtown bursting with lawyers, and plenty of money to spend on them, did she decide she needed to confide in Harriet Jeffries? Because her Mamma trusted her, she had said. Bullshit! She was simply fastening herself on the first convenient object she found, like any other leech.

No, that was unfair. Her sister was a bitch, her brother-in-law a jackal, and she wouldn't trust that business manager unless she had him right under her nose. But why me? was Harriet's silent wail. Why not someone who enjoys collecting waifs and strays? Another shower, another change of clothes, and she would go over to comfort the oppressed.

With fifteen minutes' sleep, more coffee, and another shower behind him, John Sanders was sitting at his desk considering the probability that Clara von Hohenkammer had been killed by one of her daughters. It was not beyond the realm of possibility that the woman had had a lover who, enraged with jealousy, had done her in, but if that was the case, who was he? The business manager? Could a woman really take that posturing fool seriously? The doctor? Improbable, in spite of his lascivious air. And jealous of whom? Perhaps they should dig a bit. He stared at the pile of material in front of him, too tired to decide where to start. When Dubinsky came back into the office, he found him still staring, this time out the window at the hazy sky.

"I got them," he said loudly.

Sanders dragged his head around from the window. "Got what?"

"The lab reports. Here." He threw them down in front of him.

"You read them?"

Dubinsky nodded.

"Then how about just giving me the high points." Sanders yawned.

"Sure. In simple English, it was potassium cyanide, a dose of probably 250 to 300 milligrams. There were traces of cyanide in the teacup and in that paper you found, but nowhere else. Her stomach was almost empty, consistent with a light supper six or seven hours before she died and nothing else but the tea. So the cyanide must have been carried up from the basement in that piece of paper and dumped into the tea."

"Unless she had a cyanide pellet in her lower left molar," said Sanders.

"Yeah, sure," said Dubinsky sourly. "You want any more?"

"I'll look at it later," he said. He had just picked up the notes he had been going over when the door to their office opened again.

"Excuse me, Inspector." The intruder looked vaguely familiar. "A reply on your call to Munich. You want it now?"

"You the translator?"

"Not a professional translator, sir, but I speak German."

"This from that lawyer?"

The translator nodded.

"Well, get on with it, then," said Sanders irritably.

He took out a sheaf of notes from his pocket and began to read from them in the awkward manner of someone who is half-reading, half-translating. "Peter Lohr, the lawyer for the deceased, telephoned to say that the estate is being divided more or less equally between the two daughters, with individual bequests of between thirty and a hundred thousand marks going to her sister, her nephew, her housekeeper, and her business manager. He will be arriving in Toronto on Monday and staying at the Plaza II until he has settled the most pressing affairs connected with her estate over here. He would like to meet you and requests that you leave a message at the hotel naming a convenient hour. He speaks perfectly good English. And he is sorry to take such a long time to reply, but he was out for the evening. It's near midnight in Munich, sir," added the translator, just in case.

"I realize that, Constable—"

"Bauer, sir."

"Bauer. And we went to the trouble of finding an interpreter and having him do the calling when I could have just picked up the phone and talked to him. He didn't give you any more details?"

"He said they were complicated and that he would prefer to discuss them in person with you."

"Wonderful," said Sanders with a prodigious yawn.

"Well," said Dubinsky. "That does it, doesn't it?"

"Does what?"

"All that crap about not knowing what's in the will and being sure that she had been left without a nickel to her name. She never got cut out of the will. So, do we pick her up?"

"Hang on," said Sanders wearily. "She isn't going anywhere. Wait till the lawyer gets here. But let's ask her a few more questions."

Whatever John Sanders had expected to see when he walked into Clara von Hohenkammer's conservatory that afternoon, it had not been Harriet Jeffries, in jeans and a sweatshirt, curled up on one end of the elegant little couch talking cozily to his chief suspect.

"Ah, Miss Jeffries," he said, glaring at her. "Could I have a word with you?" His tones were clear and precise. And hostile.

"Certainly," said Harriet coolly. "Why not? We could go—"

"No," said Nikki. "Use this room. I have to talk to Bettl, anyway, about dinner and things like that. And I should call my sister."

Sanders looked around the room and with heavy-footed deliberation sat down as far from Harriet as possible. She gave him an inquiring look and then waited, silent. He remembered her formidable capacity for unembarrassed silence. "What in hell are you doing here?" he asked finally.

"I should have thought that was obvious enough," she said. "I'm visiting a friend. Veronika von Hohenkammer. I believe you've met her."

"You're damned right I've met her!" he exploded. "Since when was she a friend? And what are you doing messing around with my investigation?"

"And I could just as well ask why you're messing around

with my life. What difference does it make to you what friends I have and when I visit them? What right do you have to interfere in what I choose to do?"

Sanders gritted his teeth. It was time to bring reason into the discussion. "Look, Harriet, I'm sorry about last night."

"Whatever for? You didn't do anything. Not that I can recall, anyway." She drawled these last few words, and he winced.

He rubbed his hands over his temples in a gesture of despair, took a deep breath, and stared down at the rough tiles of the floor. "What I'm sorry about," he said carefully, "is that last night we didn't get a chance to talk about anything that I think . . . that I was hoping we might be able to say." He looked up. "What are you doing tonight?"

"Nikki has asked me to dinner. I have accepted." Her voice was still chilly. "She is twenty-two, and her mother has just died. It seemed a humane thing to do."

"Shit," he muttered. "No, don't get me wrong. Of course you're doing the right thing, except . . ."

"Except that you think she poisoned her mother. Deliberately and, as they say, with malice aforethought. Right? Using her cousin's generous supply of potassium cyanide. Well, she tells me she didn't. I think you should at least entertain that possibility. There must have been other people who wanted a crack at poor Clara's money. Haven't you even considered them?"

"They didn't have a chance to put cyanide in Clara's cup. Nikki did," said Sanders flatly.

"But maybe—"

Sanders held up a hand. "Just a minute. I'm not trying to steer you away from who could have done what when, but . . . about that cyanide. One question. How reasonable is Klaus Leitner's explanation for having all that cyanide downstairs?"

"I don't know," said Harriet. "You didn't tell me what his explanation was." In spite of the coldness of the words, he thought he could detect a slight liveliness behind her wide green eyes and deadpan expression. And that meant there was still hope for him.

"He said he used it in developing—"

"Not terribly likely," she interrupted.

"—negatives," finished Sanders.

"Possible. Just possible. Did he say why? Or did he just throw it in, as if everyone used cyanide? I certainly don't use it myself. Or own any. And I assure you, I know what I'm doing."

Sanders frowned. "Just a minute," he said. "I think those pictures are still in the study." He stalked out, returning in a moment with Klaus Leitner's orange box. "It was these two prints on top," he said, dragging a small table over in front of Harriet and spreading the two prints out in front of her. "This is what he took a picture of," said Sanders, pointing to the long-legged nude, "and this is what it turned into after he dumped cyanide and God knows what else on the negative. Dubinsky has the explanation written down. I could find him for you if that would help."

Harriet looked at the two prints and shook her head. "No, don't bother. My God, what pretentious bullshit these kids turn out. But it's all right. He was using it to intensify the negative, and yes, you use cyanide for that. As a process I think it's garbage, but a lot of very respected people would disagree with me. Artistic, you know," she added, her tone heavy with sarcasm. He was relieved; he had developed a profound respect for her abilities, and he was afraid she would like that picture. "Anyway, he didn't buy the cyanide just to poison Clara." She stacked up the two prints and dropped them back in the box. "He's not a bad photographer, by the way. That nude was good before he started screwing around with the processing. He still could have done it, though."

"Look, Harriet. Nikki poured fresh tea for her mother shortly before she drank it. As far as I can find out, she was the only person who went anywhere near that cup. Everyone else is accounted for."

"But why did the poison have to be in the cup? Why not in the pot?"

"Think about it, Harriet," he said reasonably. "If you make a pot of tea or coffee at a party and fill it full of cyanide, then God only knows who you're going to poison. I mean, the person you're after might decide to have another drink instead, or someone else might see the fresh pot of tea and think, Oh, goody, that's just what I need right now. And old Auntie Maude pours herself a cup. Not only do you do in someone you're not after, but you won't get the right person. Who's going to want tea after watching Auntie Maude writhing on the carpet? For chrissake, Harriet, *you* could have drunk that tea," he said with some irritation.

"Not a chance," said Harriet. "She drank the most godawful muck—some foul-tasting weed or other from the Alps. She was forever trying to foist it on people; she said it calmed the nerves and cleaned the bloodstream and helped you sleep and I don't know what else. It might have worked for her, but no one else would even try it." She yawned and stretched, completely unaware of the effect of her words.

He was sitting bolt upright now, staring at her. "Are you sure?"

"Sure of what?"

"That no one else would drink her tea? No one else at the party?"

"Well, I don't know everyone who was at the party, but they all knew Clara, and if they knew her, they'd met that tea. She carried it around with her and used to get restaurants to make it for her. I tried it once, and that was enough. And I suppose everyone else did, too. If you dumped cyanide in the teapot, no one but poor Clara would drink it. Except maybe someone who didn't know her." She considered that for a moment. "Not even that. It smelled very strange. You'd have trouble getting it close to your face without noticing that it was very peculiar stuff. So, of course, the poison could have been in the pot, couldn't it?" She sat up straighter. "And that lets out Nikki."

"No," he said. "But it does let in a few more people, like anyone else who could have been in the kitchen after the tea was made. Damn. That means going back over everyone's movements. . . ." His voice drifted off, and he stood up. "I'm still talking to your friend before I leave. And you can tell her she's under surveillance, in case she decides to bolt."

Harriet yawned and picked up a magazine. "You tell her," she said in a bored voice. "But go ahead. Talk to her all you like."

CHAPTER 7

At precisely midnight, Constable Peter Franklin drove up the circular drive in front of Clara von Hohenkammer's house and parked behind another cruiser. He slid quietly out of the car and walked over to the drowsy occupant of the other cruiser. "Everything quiet?"

"Yeah, sure," said Constable Strong. "It's about time you turned up," he went on, yawning. "This is boring as hell. The girl has gone to bed, I think. That's her bedroom up there"—he pointed to the front right set of windows on the second floor—"and she turned the light out about ten o'clock. The doors are all locked; the gardener is around. He's supposed to look after security, so you might see something of him. If you stick around here, you'll be able to keep an eye on everything well enough. Have fun." And with this vain wish, he drove gently off.

Franklin was resigned as he settled back in the car. Not that he enjoyed surveillance, but tonight looked easy. All he had to do was stay awake. The crickets chirped; the trees rustled occasionally. In this law-abiding neighborhood there was no other noise. Then, suddenly, the sound of a door closing reverberated like a gunshot in the silence. Franklin tensed, turned his head in the direction of the noise, and waited, alert to every whisper in the air. Soon he heard footsteps, loud and steady, on a gravel surface. He reached for the door handle and peered into the darkness to see what he was dealing with. Without warning, he was blinded by a bright light in his eyes. A soft voice said, "Evening, Officer." The beam of light moved down, and he blinked.

"Who are you?" Franklin barked, opening the door and stepping out. The man was almost as tall as he was, but young and slighter in build. His English was accented, and his face was mild and conciliatory.

"Sorry . . . Paul Esteban. I'm gardener here, and in charge of security. Or I was, before Doña Clara was killed." He shrugged. "I suppose I still am, until things are finished up. I was just making my last round. I didn't mean to frighten you." It was difficult to tell if he spoke with a sardonic edge to his voice or if, perhaps, he meant what he said.

"Everything quiet tonight?" asked Franklin, who, after a brief and heartfelt struggle between revenge for the scare and desire for a peaceful shift, elected peace.

"Very quiet," said the gardener. "I came out to say— I don't know if you're permitted to do this, but Bettl, the housekeeper, she always leaves me a big thermos of coffee. If you want to come in, you're welcome to some. I can't drink it all—never do. She makes good coffee." He sounded diffident, embarrassed, as if never in his life could he have imagined offering an invitation to someone in authority.

"Thanks," said Franklin stiffly, although with some deeply hidden reluctance. He could taste hot, strong coffee. "Couldn't possibly come inside. I'm on duty. But I'm fine out here."

"I'll bring the thermos out to you, then," said Esteban. "Just leave it on the step before you go."

"Well . . ." said Franklin, uneasy but not quite sure what was wrong with the suggestion. "I guess—" The gardener was gone before the constable could frame his next sentence.

In less than a minute Esteban was back, holding a large thermos. "I'm going to bed," he said lightly. "How many security people do you need around the place in one night? I've left the dogs locked up." The gardener laughed and headed around the house.

Franklin waited until Esteban's footsteps disappeared in

the distance before opening the thermos and trying the coffee with a certain amount of caution. It was strong and bitter, just what he needed on a night like this; he blew on it to cool it down and drank most of it.

The police officer stared up at the windows of the house, passing the time by counting how many there were. It was a strangely taxing occupation. The windows kept shifting sideways, not really wanting to be counted, and he had to open his eyes very wide to enable them to concentrate on each one long enough to number it off. Still, life seemed very pleasant and slow and relaxed, with nothing to worry about . . . nothing at all to worry about . . . worry . . .

The noises filtered through to him at an enormous distance. People talking. A metallic screech. A door? A door . . . He struggled to raise his head and open his eyes. There shouldn't be doors opening. His eyelids were fastened shut, and he fought to force them open. Footsteps and more voices. He tried to lurch to his feet and was stopped by something smooth and round. A steering wheel, his fingers told him at last. Have to get out of the car, said one small part of his brain. Have to look. The car door was swinging open beside him, and he fell out onto the gravel. He blinked. Once, then twice. It was dark. He pushed his hands against the gravel and somehow was on his feet again, moving toward the house, his legs folding and buckling and growing fantastically long and unwieldy under him. He looked up at the front door and blinked. Locked, said his brain. Back door. He fell against the side of the house and let it carry him around. He wasn't surprised to find the back door swinging open. He grabbed the doorframe; it swayed and swelled in his grasp, bringing him dangerously close to the floor. A stove floated over to his right. A kitchen. If only he could lie down on the nice soft floor for just a moment. . . . Footsteps echoed in front of him, and he pushed himself forward again, leaning on the walls with his long, rubbery arms. He threw himself in the direction of the door to the central hall.

Just then the door next to it opened up. He blinked again and turned his head with painful slowness in the direction of the sudden light. Someone made a noise. He raised an arm in a gesture of menace or self-defense, but too late to protect him from the slashing blow to the side of his head. He crumpled onto the floor and lay still.

By nine o'clock that evening Veronika von Hohenkammer had been dazed. She felt exhausted, ill, achy, utterly wretched. Sanders had abandoned her in the study after ten hostile minutes of questions, during which he went over the same material one more time, rarely pausing long enough for answers. Left alone with Harriet at last, she had poured out her tale and the background to her tale and finally her life history. Harriet had listened silent and stony faced, the least sympathetic looking confidante that Nikki had ever run into. At nine o'clock, over the remains of dinner, Harriet had finally poured herself a cup of coffee and decided she was too tired to listen anymore. She told Nikki brusquely that it was time for bed. Nikki had sworn that she wouldn't sleep—she hadn't slept the night before at all—and Harriet had stood up abruptly and walked into the kitchen.

When Veronika followed her in, she found her engaged in heating up a small saucepan of milk. "If that's for me," she said, "I hate milk, and warm milk is disgusting."

"Shut up," said Harriet, her last dregs of amiability gone long since. She stalked back into the dining room and began to open doors: to the sideboard, to the linen press, to the small teak cabinet. "Bingo," she said. "Scotch. I knew there'd be some in the house."

"What are you doing?" asked Nikki, following her back into the kitchen. By now the milk was boiling over onto the stove, and Harriet moved the saucepan off the burner.

"Preparing an ancient native remedy, known only to a few million North Americans," she said curtly, grabbing a glass. She poured in a dollop of scotch, added the scalded milk, found some nutmeg, and grated it in. "There, take that upstairs, get ready for bed, open up a really boring book, and drink it. You will find staying awake impossible. I'm going home. I'm so tired I can't keep my eyes open."

Only now Veronika was wide awake. Her mouth felt thick and woolly; her eyes throbbed, her stomach fluttered unhappily, but she was thoroughly awake. Her ears rang with the memory of some alarming sound. Something must have awakened her, then. She sat up in bed and reached for her watch: one-fifteen. She was never going to get back to sleep. A door slammed. A car engine started up, very close. She heard voices, voices she could not quite understand, say something brief and then be quiet again. The car must be in the driveway that ran up beside the west side of the house, right under her window. Doors slammed shut. The car moved away in a burst of engine noise and squeal of tires. The police, thought Nikki. Checking up on her. Prowling through the house as if they owned it, hoping to rattle her and trick her into running away. She pulled the sheet over her head; tears oozed into her freshly laundered pillowcase.

The ringing telephone caught Sanders just as he was about to go home. Dubinsky had left hours ago, grumbling that he wasn't crazy enough to spend the night there, and Sanders had no choice but to pick up the receiver. It was the sergeant on night duty, with worry in his voice. "Inspector? Franklin hasn't reported," he said. "He's fifteen minutes late, and they can't raise him. They want to send in a team—"

"For chrissake, that's all we need," grumbled Sanders. "Six cars charging up there, lights flashing, all the neighbors screaming bloody murder. No. He's probably in the kitchen, cozying up to the housekeeper, eating bacon and eggs. I'll drop by on my way home. If there's anything wrong, I'll call in." He picked up his jacket and left.

Sanders parked the car in front of the house, behind Franklin's cruiser, grabbed a flashlight, and jumped impatiently out. The night was cool and still, the neighborhood silent except for the frantic call of a cricket and the faraway hum of traffic. He shone his light into the cruiser, half-expecting to find a tired constable deep in slumber. Nothing— just Franklin's private thermos of coffee on the passenger seat. He listened for the muted crashing of someone doing a tour of the property. Not a sound. Unless he was bare-foot and very agile, Franklin wasn't walking around out there. The silence of the night seemed to grow in intensity as he strained to listen. He turned off his flashlight. The house was still and dark, and he was beginning to like the situation less and less. It occurred to him that he had been crazy to come out here alone. Tell me, Inspector Sanders, he muttered to himself, exactly how much does lack of sleep impair your judgment. A little? Somewhat? A lot?

As he started a slow circuit of the house, the spot between his shoulder blades twitched. He was brave enough when occasion demanded it, he supposed. But tonight we're talk-ing about stupidity, not bravery, he thought. And stupidity got people killed. He thought of Underhill, the cheerful kid from the Thirty-third Division, who ended up with a bullet in his back on a night like this, and stopped to listen hard behind him. He rounded the back corner of the house onto the patio and walked over to the French doors that led into the conservatory. Suddenly the leg of a chair materialized under him, and he stumbled, smashed his shin, almost fell, and cursed. He turned on his flashlight, picked his way through the garden furniture over to the door, and shone the light through the glass.

The little conservatory was tranquil in its emptiness. He raised his arm to break through the panel of glass in front of him and then stopped. There was a red light glowing from beside the door inside. A burglar alarm. "My God, Sanders," he muttered. He had been about to break into a substantial house on the insubstantial evidence of an empty car. He shook his head. Time to raise the inhabitants and get let in legally. In the meantime, he could use a little backup in case something had gone wrong.

Moments later, he was standing on the front doorstep, leaning on the bell, having already called in a bad-tempered demand that they get the security system turned off and send help. He could hear the expensive gongs reverberate, to no effect. No lights going on, no noises of irritable sleepers. He rang again. And again. He stood back and looked up at the windows for some sign of movement. Nothing. He moved back around the house as fast as he could and peered once more through the glass. To hell with the alarm, he thought, picking up a metal chair and using it to smash a hole through the glass in the door. He reached in carefully and turned the knob. No sirens, no bells, no red lights. Nothing disturbed the silence of the night. He flicked on the overhead light. The room was empty. As he reached the door into the hall, he heard the faint, irregular gasps of someone struggling for breath. One sweep of his light answered his questions. Franklin was lying on his stomach in the open doorway to the basement. Blood was pouring down the constable's face and onto the floor from an indefinable mess on the side of his head.

Sanders looked at the wound helplessly. None of his emergency training had covered hemorrhaging through a mass of shattered bone. And even if he knew what to do, he didn't think he could bring himself to touch that battered head. In the distance he heard the approaching ruckus from the emergency call and ran toward the front door, bumping against furniture, cursing and moving his light around until he found the round knob of a rheostat. With an impatient twist he turned it up to full power; the entire central portion of the house blazed with light from the enormous chandelier hanging above him.

The first uniformed man was already running up to the house as he opened the door. He charged up the steps, his pistol in his hand, ready to shoot anything that moved. "Put that goddamn thing away before you hurt somebody. Where in hell's the ambulance?" snapped Sanders.

"What ambulance? You hurt?"

"Christ almighty!" he snarled. "No, you idiot, he is—the one lying on the floor."

"My God, who's that?"

"Franklin. He was supposed to be watching this place." Mumbling incoherently, the constable shoved his weapon away and turned to go back and radio for further aid when the next carload of help pulled up and disgorged two officers. Within moments there were five men in the front hall looking expectantly at Sanders. "Could one of you clowns go back there and see to Franklin?" he asked, his voice heavy with sarcasm. A figure hastily detached itself from the group. "And upstairs there should be three more people. God knows how they slept through all this, so maybe someone had better just tiptoe up there and see what's up." The two men closest to the stairs looked at each other and, taking him at his word, began to move gingerly up the stairs.

That left two men. Sanders turned to them and pointed in the direction of the open basement door. "I want to know what's down there, or rather, who. Move carefully. Then check this floor. There's supposed to be a gardener responsible for security. He lives on top of the garage. When you're through with the house, see if you can raise anyone over there. His name is Esteban—Paul Esteban. And look out for the dogs."

"What dogs?" said one of them suspiciously.

"Guard dogs," he said. "The house is protected by guard dogs. Why aren't they barking? Or don't you think they've noticed us yet?" He suppressed the further remarks that sprang to his lips. "Don't worry. They didn't take a piece out of me, so they must be chained up."

Not much more than thirty minutes later, five police officers, three cruisers, an ambulance, and the injured man had all left the premises, leaving Sanders sitting in the kitchen with one healthy replacement for Franklin, Veronika von Hohenkammer, Klaus Leitner, and Bettl Kotzmeier. It would be hard to say which of the people in the room looked the worst, with the exception of Franklin's replacement, who was in fine shape. Out in back, two more men were still dealing with the problem of the gardener. The five of them were sitting around the kitchen table; Klaus had his head cradled in his arms and was apparently unconscious. Bettl sat bolt upright, but her eyelids drooped, and her eyes kept unfocusing, while her head sank down from time to time, then jerked rapidly back up again. Nikki sat very still, her dark eyes enormous in her white face.

"Listen," said Klaus, opening an eye and cautiously raising his head an inch or two, "I have one hell of a headache, and I feel like death. Do you think you could tell me why we were dragged out of bed in the middle of the night like this?"

"Gestapo!" Bettl muttered.

Sanders looked at her with interest, did a few mental calculations, and then figured that she would have been prepubescent at the time the Gestapo had been disbanded. He turned back to Klaus. "Just a few questions . . . We'd like to know exactly what happened here tonight, if you don't mind. You must have heard something going on."

"I didn't hear a thing until I woke up and this gorilla in uniform was shaking me, with another one leaning over his shoulder, watching. They dragged me out of bed." He had raised his head a little higher to speak and then let it drop cautiously down again to where it had been.

"When did you go to bed?"

"Oh," he said, raising his head once more, "that. You want to know when I went to bed. I can't remember." His eyes fogged over. "It's so damned hard to think." He grasped his head in both hands. "I remember. It was early, very early. I finished dinner, and suddenly I was so tired I couldn't stand it, and I went to bed. That's all I can remember."

"And what about you, Miss von Hohenkammer? What did you hear?"

She jumped, startled, glanced at him, and then turned her head away. "Nothing much, I guess. I heard your men in the house. Downstairs."

"My men?" asked Sanders, puzzled.

"Yes," she replied coldly.

"Did you hear me ring the doorbell?"

She nodded.

"Then why didn't you answer?" he asked.

"I assumed one of you would answer it."

"I see," said Sanders. "You assumed one of us would . . ."

She nodded again.

He shook his head and filed this away for future consideration. "And you, Miss Kotzmeier?"

"No."

"No, what?"

"No, I know nothing, I hear nothing, I clear the table and go to bed, and that's all I know."

"What time was that?"

"I don't know. I don't watch the hour every minute that I work." She managed to invest this remark with moral force, as though even asking her the time betrayed a slack attitude toward one's employment.

"Was anyone else in the house?"

"That photographer person was talking to Miss Veronika," said Bettl. She made the word "photographer" sound like a species of vermin. "And she stayed for dinner." She obviously felt that photographers had no business eating at the same table as honest folk.

"No one else? What about Mr. Whitelaw?"

"Yes, of course. When did he ever miss a meal here?" At that moment there was a mild commotion at the door that led outside from the kitchen. After a certain amount of stamping about, three men came in from the utility room behind the kitchen: two neatly uniformed police officers and one bedraggled gardener. His clothing was rumpled and twisted, as if he had been sleeping in it, and his hair was wet and tousled. His eyes were red, and he yawned enormously as he staggered into the room.

"Esteban, the gardener," said one of them. "Sorry we took so long, but he was kinda hard to wake up." He looked up above their heads as he spoke. "While we were knocking, we noticed that the door was unlocked, and we entered in order to ascertain if Mr. Esteban was in any difficulties. On account of him not answering," he added. "We thought something might have happened to him. From the difficulty we had in arousing him, we thought he might have been drugged, or something." Sanders looked at the red face and wet hair and wondered what methods they had tried.

"Thanks," he muttered, and turned his attention to Esteban. One thing was clear: He hadn't been in a drunken stupor. If he had consumed enough alcohol to do that to him, the whole room would have reeked of it. He smelled as if he had gone to bed cold sober. "Okay, Esteban, what happened tonight?" His voice was crisp and unsympathetic. "And you two, keep him on his feet. We don't want him passing out again."

"Nothing happened tonight." His consonants were thick and indistinct. "Nothing. I did what I always do. Nothing different."

"What do you always do, then?"

"I had my supper over here with Bettl. She always keeps me something from their dinner."

"Did you eat together?"

He glanced over at her uneasily. "No, she eats early. She had coffee while I ate my supper. Then I went out and did the rounds. I took the dogs for a run, because I was going to have to keep them locked up."

"Why?"

"There were all those policemen out there."

Sanders nodded.

"Then I chained them up and went over to the house to

make sure the doors were locked and the burglar alarm set. It wasn't, either. Bettl must have left some doors open." At the sound of her name, that woman jerked her head upright again and gave him a fierce glare. "Anyway, I locked up."

"What's happened to the dogs?" asked Sanders suddenly.

"They're asleep," said one of the constables. "In a kennel behind the garage. Can't budge 'em. But they're breathing okay. I checked."

"My God," said Sanders. "It's like one of those fairy tales. And then what, Esteban? After you locked up."

"Oh, before I locked up, I took some coffee out to the policeman on duty. Bettl always leaves me a thermos full of coffee. Then I must have gone back to the apartment, I guess, because that's where I was, but I don't remember anything else."

"Why this generosity toward the police, Esteban? Are you in the habit of playing host to police officers?"

The gardener flushed, looking at the moment like a tousled little boy caught doing something naughty. "Not really. But Doña Clara's daughter—Miss Veronika—she told me to ask him in and give him coffee."

"Is that true, Miss von Hohenkammer? Did you tell Esteban to ask Constable Franklin in?"

She nodded.

"Why did you do that?"

"Because that man was going to have to sit there all night," she said with a flash of anger. "It seemed a gracious thing to do. It wasn't his fault you were making him spy on us."

Sanders looked steadily at her for a moment or two, as if considering challenging her statement, and then turned away. "Did you have coffee, Mr. Leitner?" he asked.

Klaus Leitner raised his head, a little more confidently this time. "Yes. I always have coffee after dinner. I must have. Yes, I did."

"Did you have coffee, Miss von Hohenkammer?"

She shook her head. "No. I was too tired to want coffee."

"How about Miss Jeffries?"

"Miss Jeffries?" Klaus looked baffled.

"The photographer," said Sanders dryly.

"Oh, Harriet." Sanders clenched his teeth. "No, I don't think so."

"Yes, she did," said Veronika. "I'm sure she did. Because she was so sleepy when she left. . . ."

Sanders made an incoherent noise, jumped up, and turned to the constable. "Round up some more cars and get these people down to the General. And Whitelaw as well. I'll take care of Miss Jeffries."

"What for?" he asked.

"For chrissake, for blood tests. They've all been doped, you idiot. And stay with them until we're sure they're all right," he added grudgingly. He bolted from the house and drove through the quiet streets like a man possessed.

Sanders pulled up to the curb with a squeal of brakes that sliced through the quiet of the night and startled a prowling cat in the bushes belonging to Harriet's landlord. He ran up the walk, up her brief flight of steps, reached for the doorbell, and stopped. There were keys dangling from the lock. Door keys, car keys, the lot. When he grasped them to open up, the door swung in. He yanked out the keys, slammed the door shut behind him, and turned and ran to Harriet's bedroom. She was sprawled on top of the covers, facedown, fully dressed, her feet dangling over the edge of the bed. His stomach contracted with a cold thud. "Harriet?" he said tentatively, reaching over to touch her neck. It was warm, with a lovely strong pulse beating in it. She didn't move. "Harriet," he said, louder this time, grabbing her by the shoulder and shaking her.

She mumbled vaguely and rolled over on her side.

"Harriet! For chrissake, wake up!" He shook her harder.

She flopped over on her back.

He grabbed her by both shoulders and yanked her to a sitting position. Her head dropped down and straightened up. Her eyelids fluttered and then opened. She blinked twice and focused on his face. "What in hell are you doing, John?" she asked thickly. "What time is it?"

"Time to get up," he said.

"Uh-uh," she muttered. "Gotta sleep . . . just a minute."

"No! We're getting up!" He dragged her, mumbling protests, up the stairs and into the bathroom, filled up the basin with cold water, and pushed her face into it.

"Christ almighty," she said with a certain clarity that had been lacking before. "Did you have to do that?"

"Yes," he said. "How do you feel?"

"Like hell. My head aches and—"

"Did you drink the coffee tonight?"

"Did I what? John, are you crazy? You came over here to wake me up and ask me if I had coffee? What is this?"

"Did you?"

"I can't remember," she said. "God, but my head hurts. Where was I tonight? Was I with you?"

He shook his head.

"No, I was at Clara's house, wasn't I? Did I stay for dinner?"

He nodded.

"Then I probably had coffee, if there was any. I always do." He took her by the arm and began pulling her toward the door. "Hey, where are you going with me?"

"Off to the hospital," he said. "Your bloodstream is evidence."

It was noon before Sanders dragged himself back to his desk. An interested little crew of medical personnel had checked Harriet over, taken blood samples, and pronounced her undoubtedly drugged. "Like most of the rest of them," said the resident cheerfully. "But she'll be all right."

He had asked after Franklin, and the resident shook his head. "I don't know," he said. "He didn't look too good when he came through here. They've taken him upstairs."

With that, he had taken Harriet home again, tucked her

into bed, and fallen asleep upstairs on her couch, reluctant
to move too far away from her and unwilling to crawl into
her bed when her brain was too fogged to know he was
there. She had seemed unsurprised to find him in the morning and had quietly thrown together a sketchy breakfast for
the two of them.

"Are you all right?" he asked as he finished his coffee.

"I think so," she said doubtfully. "Except that my head
aches and I haven't the faintest idea how I got home last
night."

"You drove," said Sanders grimly. "Doped to the eyeballs
and you drove back here and put the car in the garage. I
don't know how you did it, but you did."

"Automatic pilot," she said. "Did I hit anything?" He
shook his head. "And listen—I had one small glass of wine
at dinner. I was so tired I didn't even have a beer, in case it
put me under. And I sure wasn't popping any dope."

"I never said you were. Somebody doped everyone in the
house."

"Why?" asked Harriet. "What was the point? Not to
speak of how."

"I don't know," said Sanders. "Although it will be interesting to explore that question. And how? Probably in the
coffee. I don't know any more about it because I brought
you back here instead of sticking around to find out. You're
an evil influence on me, Harriet Jeffries."

She looked gravely at him. "Perhaps I am," she said.
"You should consider that. Is everyone else all right?"

"I don't know," he said. "It's one of the other things I
should be finding out. Which means I ought to be going."
He paused for a moment, searching for the best tone to
strike, and then said lightly, "I could always come back
tonight, though. If that doesn't sound too grim."

"What's today?" she asked. "Saturday?"

He nodded.

"I have to be downtown at six tomorrow to do the north

side of a building. If you're here, you'll have to come along to guard my stuff."

"Six? In the morning?"

She grinned.

"Sure," he said. "I'll call you."

Dubinsky had been there for hours going through stacks of reports with his usual air of bored efficiency. "I hear there was some excitement last night," he said, looking up.

"I hope Sally appreciated your presence," Sanders remarked sourly. His partner grinned and didn't answer. "Any reports in on it yet?"

"Yeah. Franklin's in pretty bad shape. What in hell happened?"

"Someone doped them."

"I know that," he said, picking up another piece of paper and waving it at Sanders. "The report from the lab. All of them but little Miss Veronika. Nothing in her bloodstream but small amounts of alcohol. And only trace amounts in Whitelaw. How'd they do it?"

"It must have been the coffee. After dinner. It's the only thing that figures. Whitelaw said he ate everything but only had a mouthful of coffee. He claims that after Thursday night he has trouble drinking coffee made by Bettl. Veronika didn't drink any. Everyone else did. So that's what it looks like. Do we have an analysis of the coffee?"

Dubinsky shook his head. "It's still over at forensic."

"I guess we'll know soon enough," said Sanders with a yawn, "once they get off their asses and start doing something."

"How in hell did they get to Franklin? He didn't go on duty until midnight. You're not telling me they were having dinner at midnight and invited him in to join them."

"Uh-uh." Sanders shook his head. "As far as I could get out of them, the housekeeper made a huge pot of coffee and handed out some of it at dinner. And zap! They're all out. She had some after she cleaned up the kitchen, and that was the end of her for the night. Before she passed out, she put the rest into a thermos for the gardener. And the gardener—under instructions from our Miss Nikki, by the way—drank one cup and gave the rest to Franklin. The thermos was in his car."

"Who doped the coffee?" said Dubinsky innocently.

"Someone who didn't drink it," said Sanders. "Which leaves us—"

"Whitelaw or the girl. She didn't touch the coffee; he had just enough not to look suspicious."

"The question is, why was Franklin in the house? He must have been damned groggy if he drank from that thermos. And how in hell did he get in? When I got there, the house was locked, and the alarm was on. Someone in the house must have let him in and then smashed him on the head."

"And that makes it Veronika. She was the only person in the house who was awake enough to do it."

"Aggravated assault," said Sanders. "Maybe attempted murder. To start with, anyway."

The telephone rang, and Dubinsky picked it up. "How about murder?" he said grimly as he put it down again. "That was the hospital. Franklin died ten minutes ago."

"Bring her in," said Sanders.

"It's ridiculous to think that someone Nikki's size could smash a full-grown man on the head hard enough to kill him," said Harriet.

"Not entirely," said Sanders defensively. "He was too heavily doped to resist. If she grabbed something heavy enough and just dropped it in the right place, she might have—"

"If she could reach that high," Harriet interrupted.

"Come on, Harriet. We don't know what position he was in when he was hit. He'd have been damned near unconscious, anyway. He could have fallen to his knees."

"If you're so convinced, why did you let her go, then?"

"Not enough evidence," he said curtly. "No matter what you may think, we don't arrest people without evidence."

"Sure," she jeered. "I believe you. I'm used to believing impossible things. If there ever was anyone you thought was guilty, John Sanders, it's that poor girl." The night was growing cool, and Harriet slipped on her coat. "Where are we going?" They had been walking along King Street West, past the theater, toward a pastiche of restaurants, some good, some bad, but most of them expensive.

"We're almost there," said Sanders, looking up at the signs dangling over the sidewalk. He stopped. "Here it is. I know you wanted the corner pizzeria, but you'll just have to lump it, sweetheart. I made reservations, and I have a reputation to keep up in the city."

Harriet looked up at the name. "Are you sure you're not on the take, John? Or are you just addicted to eating in places you can't afford?"

"Actually," he said as soon as they were seated and had ordered a bottle of wine, "I was planning on marrying this incredibly rich girl I met a few days ago and living off her immorally gotten gains. I released her this afternoon in return for an ironclad agreement to support me for the rest of my life. Wine, madam?"

"I still can't see why you had enough evidence to arrest her at two and not enough to keep her past six."

"A couple of things," he said. "The pathologist thinks Franklin was killed by a blow administered with considerable force—her words, not mine. When I asked her if a woman could have done it, she muttered something nasty about a female shot-putter, maybe. In other words, no. And then someone found out there were several keys that disabled the alarm system," he said simply. "We thought there were only two—the gardener's and Nikki's. Anyone with a key could have turned off the alarm, entered the house, and attacked Franklin. And besides, why dope the dogs if it was someone from inside? Although why anyone would want to put the entire house and the dogs to sleep," he added bitterly, "just to kill Franklin, who was as harmless a guy as you'll ever meet, I don't know. And that's another thing. Why? If it was Nikki, it would have been so she could run, wouldn't it? And she didn't. The mystery is why it happened at all. It's absolutely insane." The waiter intruded his inquiring face into Sanders's speech. "The antipasto and grilled fish for both of us," he said.

"But wouldn't you like to choose your fish, sir?" asked the waiter, shocked. "If you'll wait a moment—"

"No. I prefer not to meet my fish before I eat it. You choose." And the waiter hastily backed away under the force of Sanders's glare.

"Aren't we getting a little masterful?" said Harriet. "What if I had wanted soup and spaghetti?"

"Then we'll come back and eat soup and spaghetti and you can pay for your own meal. This time we're eating antipasto and grilled fish."

"You were right," said Harriet as she pushed away her coffee cup. "Although it pains me to say it. It would have been a waste to have soup and spaghetti, wouldn't it?" She looked at her watch. "I think you've forgotten that I have to be back on King Street at seven A.M. tomorrow."

"It was six last time." His tone was accusing.

"I couldn't possibly have said six. The sun doesn't rise until way after six these days."

"You lie, Harriet. Repeatedly and with intent," he said, standing up. "Let's go," he added, looking at his watch.

"I can get home on my own without any trouble," she remarked as soon as they were outside. "The streetcar stops two blocks from my apartment." She stepped up to the curb and began looking up the street.

He grabbed her by the arm. "Harriet, I'm taking you home. My car stops right outside your door." He paused. "If you don't want to invite me in, you don't have to. But women have been attacked in your neighborhood. I'd much prefer it didn't happen to you." He spoke in a loud enough voice to attract the attention of several passersby, who paused, interested, to see what would happen.

"For God's sake, John, stop being so goddamn protective," she whispered, suddenly embarrassed. "How do you think I survive when you're not around? And anyway, you live just over there, don't you?" she asked.

"Would you rather come to my place?"

"Don't be stupid. I have to get going at dawn. I'm only trying to save you from driving halfway across the city." Her voice lost its edge, showing signs of capitulating. "I'm not trying to make a thing about it."

He wound one arm around her waist to propel her across the street. Under the soft material of her coat and dress, he could feel the configuration of her spine and hips and found himself pulling her closer to him as he scanned the road for a break in the Saturday night traffic.

He almost wished that traffic had been heavier as he pulled up to Harriet's front door; this seemed to him to be a moment charged with too much significance, one that he would gladly put off. He let the engine idle for a moment, then turned it off. "Harriet . . ." he began.

"You don't believe me, do you?" she said. "I have an assignment that has to be done tomorrow morning. This weather could change any day. If we have a rainy spell, it could take three weeks before I get out there again, and by then the sun will be too far to the south to be any use."

"Oh, I believe you," said Sanders. "But you could wait— just once in a while, anyway—to hear what I had to say before biting my head off."

"Sorry. I should stop assuming—" She stopped and shook her head, tired and confused. "It's been a lousy couple of days. Actually, it's been a lousy week. What were you going to say?"

He reached over and took the hand that wasn't poised on top of the door handle. "Something else that's going to make you bite my head off. I . . ." He was about to say he couldn't bear the thought of going home alone tonight and clamped his mouth shut on the words. Harriet looked at him, waiting for him to finish. "I thought we might prolong the evening for five minutes or so," he said casually.

"Five minutes, indeed," she said. "All right. Only you'd better pull the car into the driveway. You'll get a ticket there."

He doubted that, but without a word he turned on the engine and pulled up in front of the garage.

Carlos was standing with the refrigerator door open, shoving things around and swearing. The buru was sitting at a corner of the table, reading a newspaper; Manu sat at the end, beside him, watching Carlos with a calculating, interested, but not especially friendly look on his face. Finally, Carlos emerged with a summer sausage in one hand and a bottle of red wine in the other. He put these down on the kitchen table beside a large Italian loaf, a bowl of peaches, and a plastic container of black olives. He grabbed a pile of plates and a couple of knives from the counter and set them on the table as well. As an afterthought, he reached back into the cupboard behind him and brought out a bag of chips.

"That's it?" said Don.

"It's what there is," said Carlos.

"Jesus," said Don. "You call that crap dinner? I'm sending out for a pizza. You guys want some pizza?"

Manu's soft eyes swiveled over briefly in Don's direction; he shook his head. The others shrugged.

"I'll get a large, then."

As soon as Don left the room, the conversation switched from English. Manu turned his pale, gloomy face back to concentrate on Carlos; he leaned his long body forward in his chair, his hands grasping his knees tightly, as if to prevent them from lashing out and hitting someone. Carlos was trying desperately to explain something, stumbling over his words. Twelve years as a child and adolescent in North America had lost him facility in his native tongue, a facility that a few months of working with the two other men had not fully restored to him. When his search for a way to end his sentence turned into a lengthy pause, Manu began to speak in a low but emphatic voice. Whatever it was he wanted to get through to Carlos, however, was interrupted by Don's noisy reentry into the big kitchen.

"Christ, I wish you sons of bitches would talk in something I can understand. You make me nervous, and I don't like being nervous." The threat hung in the air for a second or two before dissolving. "The pizza'll be here in thirty minutes," he added, sitting down beside Manu and cutting himself a large chunk of sausage with one of the communal knives.

Manu waited until he finished. "I was pointing out to Carlos your great stupidity, yours and his." The gentleness of his voice almost belied his words.

"What's that?" said Don, past a mouthful of hard sausage.

Carlos leaned back in a relaxed stretch and yawned. "All I said was, why don't we just leave the rest of it where it is. Nothing's happened to it before. It's a lot more dangerous trying to move it, especially with an asshole like Don around. There are cops looking for us everywhere these days. Jesus, there's one walking two feet behind him at work every time he goes to the can, and he's stupid enough to trip over them with a box in his hands."

"Watch who you're calling stupid," said Don resentfully.

"Sure," said Carlos. "Anyway, we were lucky to get half a truckload out. Just remember, you wouldn't have any of it if it hadn't been for Don and me. But Manu here, he wants—" he paused to jerk his thumb in the direction of Manu, whose eyes widened into clouded, unhappy pools.

"I want to be able to go back home with enough money to help the fight for independence," Manu said. "That's all. And if we sell the rest of the stuff, we can. But before we can sell it, we have to get it out. And besides, as long as it's there, it is a danger."

Carlos leaned forward and turned to the buru, who was

still deep in his paper. "Poor Manu. He thinks it isn't safe anymore," Carlos sneered. "And he's afraid. He's good with cars, but he gets scared, eh, Manu?"

Manu turned a steady gaze on the other man. "Scared? A man who shoots helpless women shouldn't talk about scared. I'm not scared. I just don't want to lose everything."

Angry red blotches spread across Carlos's cheeks. His fingers curled around the edge of the table and whitened. There was a long silence. He seemed at last to decide that Manu's comments could be taken for rough joking, sat back, and forced out a laugh. "Trying to get it all out now, that's even more dangerous. It's crazy." He flicked his expressive thumb across his throat.

"It's safer than your idea," said Manu doggedly. "Any day they could investigate that house, maybe even Monday. And then what happens to us?"

"Screw the fucking war for fucking independence," said Don. "But I sure as hell could use my share of the money. I say we think about Manu's plan, whatever it is." Manu froze as Don's words sank in. His hand moved almost imperceptibly toward his ankle and then appeared at table level with a hunting knife not quite concealed under his downward-pointing fingers. He slowly rose to his feet and flipped the knife so that he was grasping it lightly, palm and fingers up, pointing it upward and moving it in the direction of Don's belly. Sweat appeared on Don's upper lip, and Carlos leaned forward, his eyes bright with interest. Suddenly, Manu changed grip on the knife again, brought his hand down with one rapid motion, and slashed a two-inch piece off the summer sausage.

The buru looked up from his paper. "Nothing will happen before Wednesday at the earliest." Authority rang in his voice. "And besides that, New York can't handle any more goods right now. It takes a long time to get a good price for those things, and he doesn't want any more identifiable stuff around than is necessary, you understand?"

Manu turned to him with a jerk. "So . . . it doesn't matter

that we're not safe, eh? Or that we lose everything we've worked for here, does it? All that matters is that he is safe and rich. Bastard!" he hissed, and muttered something in his native tongue, something that sounded unpleasant in the extreme. "Now what do we do, eh, Buru?"

The boss, for it was he who was being addressed, looked at the other three men's impassive faces. "We wait," he said at last.

Sanders walked out to the deck and leaned on the railing, looking down into the garden. It was a cool and melancholy night, neither summer nor fall, smelling neither of dying leaves nor of heat-ripened decay. A bastard of a night, caught unacknowledged between seasons, reminding him of how little he belonged, leaning here, between the pots of basil and the flowering plants that Harriet nursed intermittently when she wasn't too busy. In fact, she probably regarded him in much the same light, something to be taken up when she wasn't too busy, looked after for a while, and put back where it belonged. He turned to go.

He hadn't heard Harriet's footsteps behind him. She had kicked off her high-heeled sandals and was standing in her stocking feet, looking at him with her head tilted slightly, her face expressionless in the dark. "Look, Harriet—" he started, but she had begun to speak at the same time.

"It's a strange night, isn't it?" she said, gliding silently up beside him and leaning over the rail. "Not like September at all. I can't decide if I'm cold or not."

He was startled that her thoughts should have echoed his own so clearly and yet that she seemed completely unaware of his unhappiness. It was in some obscure way unfair. "I'd better go, Harriet," he said. "You're home, safe. You don't need a cop around anymore." He had tried to sound lightly ironic and managed only a bitter whine.

"Go?" she said, leaning farther over the rail. "I thought you had allowed yourself at least three more minutes."

"For chrissake," he exploded, clutching the rail as if it were her throat, "do you have to?"

"Have to what?" she said. "Oh, this. Maybe I do. I prefer you irritable, I think. Instead of looking as if you were considering pitching yourself over the railing. It's not very far, by the way. And you'd land in the bushes. They're a bit prickly, but too soft for you to do any real damage."

"Harriet," he said in a warning voice, and turned toward her. Angry, he grabbed her by the shoulders, digging his hands into her taut muscles. She flinched automatically and then, controlling herself, looked up at him, her eyes steady; he shuddered at his own rage and pulled her toward him until she was tightly enfolded in his grasp. To his horror he could feel his eyes beginning to sting with the hint of tears, and he buried his face in her hair. Time trickled by until his arms began to ache and relaxed their hold; she slipped from his embrace and led him into the living room.

"Sit down," she said. He sat and watched her walk across the room, passing over the invisible line into the kitchen, open the refrigerator, and take out two bottles of beer. She took clean glasses out of the dishwasher, picked up a bottle opener, and carried the lot over to the table in front of him. "Now, what in hell is wrong with you?" she asked. Her tone was inquisitive rather than sympathetic, and he bridled at it.

"There's nothing wrong with me," he snapped. "I'm fine. What's wrong with you?"

She sat down, one foot under her, relaxed and casual, neither close to him nor far away. The distance a sister might choose. "You first. The way you were looking at Derek's garden out there, I thought it must be filled with green slimy things out of a horror movie. Assuming that it isn't, what's wrong? It's not like you to go around looking haunted. I don't think it is, anyway," she added dubiously, acknowledging that there was much that she did not know about him.

"You can't take anything seriously, can you, Harriet?" he

said bitterly. "Except your goddamn work and your own goddamn little problems. Everyone else is some kind of joke. No one else deserves consideration or understanding or even sympathy."

"You don't need sympathy," she said. "You need sleep, and someone to chase besides my friend Nikki. And you probably need a couple of weeks' vacation as well. And maybe a few other things, but you'd hate me if I were sympathetic. Social workers are sympathetic."

"And what does that make you?" he asked.

"I don't know," she replied slowly. "I don't know. A woman . . ."

"Oh, God, yes," he said painfully. "You are a woman. Agonizingly a woman."

Color flooded her pale cheeks. Abruptly, as if she had only just then become aware of his presence. Her arm, which had been lying carelessly over the back of the couch, suddenly seemed to be stretching itself toward him. "Harriet," he said tentatively, and then sat still. She put down her glass slowly and turned toward him; then, with a slither of pale green silk, she was right against him, her face looking upward. He bent and kissed her, lightly at first, then with a ferocity that was out of his control. Her body seemed as fluid as the silk of her dress, blending into his in spite of the awkwardness of the position. The scent rising from her skin, her hair, her clothes, obliterated awareness of anything but his intense need.

He applied himself with all the skill at his disposal to getting rid of her panty hose; she twisted under his fingers so that the awkward things slipped down to her ankles, and she kicked them off. At the same time, she had undone his belt and his trousers and was now working at having them join her underwear on the floor. "Just a minute, Harriet," he murmured. "Your dress—"

"Screw my dress," she whispered huskily.

"No," he said, pushing her back onto the couch. "Not the dress, lady." He buried his face in the skin bared as the silk slipped from her shoulder and half-exposed her breast. "You."

He knew and yet had forgotten in the intervening months how her body responded to the slightest touch. The crumpled silk tormented every nerve as he pushed it out of the way, and with a cry Harriet flung her legs around him and pulled him close.

"A gentleman—" said Sanders, leaning on one disheveled elbow and looking down at her.

"Always makes love on his elbows," said Harriet, reaching up and kissing him on the chin. "You damn near smothered me," she added, and giggled huskily.

"That wasn't what I was going to say. Smothering you was intentional, even though it wasn't successful. I'll do better next time. What I was going to say is that a gentleman never makes love in his socks. Everyone knows that. Or his watch. Much less his shirt and tie, I suppose," he added ruefully. "I am going to look rather rumpled tomorrow." He sat up, picking up her legs and moving them behind him. "And speaking of tomorrow . . ." He reached over, picked up the telephone, and punched in some numbers. "Sanders," he said into the receiver as he picked up his untasted beer and took a swallow. "Anything new? . . . Good . . . My number here is—" He reeled off the number with the assurance of one who has been dialing it every day for weeks. "That's what I said. Yes, until tomorrow morning," he added after a pause, and hung up, pulling off his tie as he did.

"Planning on spending the night, are we?" said Harriet. "Aren't you rather taking me for granted?"

"Of course I'm spending the night," he said lightly. "Anything else would be an insult to someone as . . ." Suddenly his voice hoarsened, and he pushed the hair out of his eyes. "My God, Harriet," he said with a fierceness that startled her, "I almost forgot what it was like with you." He lowered himself down gently until he was almost on top of her and leaned forward to kiss her. "Now take that damned dress off before I ruin it completely."

CHAPTER 8

Sanders paused in front of the recently completed office tower. The low morning sun was burning through a slight haze and pouring golden light onto the great commercial tombs erected in the last ten years over every square inch of the financial district. There was silence—stunning and bizarre silence—except for the chirping of a sparrow perched in a small tree that grew wanly in its concrete prison. He looked back at Harriet, her face pale and clean of makeup, dressed in scruffy jeans and a long jacket filled with bulging pockets, and was awestruck by her beauty in that rich morning light. She was looking in every direction except at the building or toward him, unaware of the cloying sentimentality of his thoughts. "Here?" he called at last.

"Sure. That's fine," she said. "Put them down there. Carefully," she added with a touch of sharpness in her voice. He raised an ironic eyebrow at her, but it was wasted effort. She was deep in calculations. He set down the large aluminum camera case, the almost-as-large lens case, the tripod that had been squashing his fingers as it balanced on the camera case, and finally shrugged carefully out of the green knapsack whose exclusive purpose was to hold objects with very sharp edges.

"Is all this necessary?" he asked suspiciously when she finally walked up to him and set down the orange cooler filled with sheet-film holders.

"I would have carried half of it," she said. "Only you had to go all gallant on me and insist."

"You've got more stuff than you were carrying around in Ottawa," he complained. "I wouldn't have believed it possible."

"Sinar," she said laconically. "Four by five. Bigger camera."

"Does a bigger camera take as much time as a little one?"

"As the Olympus? Oh, no, that's a speedy little thing. This *is* more cumbersome, but the customer expects four-by-five transparencies." Despair struck as he absorbed her meaning. This was going to take a hell of a long time. As she talked, she was setting a bar on top of the tripod. Onto the bar she slipped a lens mount and a film back and then carefully joined them with a bellows. "There. Instant camera. Make your own. I hope you're impressed." She looked around, picked up the tripod, walked with calm deliberation into the middle of the road—not busy at this hour, but not blocked off, either—and set it down. From around her neck she took a large square of double cloth, dark blue corduroy on one side, white cotton on the other, and used it to cover both her head and the film back. "This'll do," she said finally. "Do you think you could keep the cars from killing me? You must remember how to do that, don't you?"

"When I got a call to investigate a suspicious death on Friday, the last thing I expected to end up doing was this," he said, walking over to the lane she was occupying. "Standing in the middle of King Street directing traffic." But Harriet, of course, was paying no attention.

An hour and a half later, Harriet, who was now set up on the top of the stairs of the building opposite—much to the distress of that building's security guard, who felt she was doing something obscurely wrong but was not quite sure what—turned to Sanders, gave him a dazzling smile, and pushed the cable release. "That's it," she said. "Last exposure. I've got four terrific shots: three color, three black and white in each one, twenty-four in all. And unless something goes horribly wrong, we eat next week." Suddenly, she hurled the focusing cloth at him. As he reached to pluck it expertly out of the air, he was hit, twice, by the weights concealed in the corners. He gave her a reproachful look and folded it up. "Now let's get some breakfast," she said. "I'm absolutely starved."

Twenty minutes later, they were sitting in a Swiss restaurant, with coffee and fresh orange juice in front of them, having ordered, without a qualm, muesli and a farmer's breakfast each.

"Why did you say I needed someone to chase besides Veronika von Hohenkammer?" asked Sanders suddenly.

Harriet set down her orange-juice glass and looked directly at him. "Because you know how unlikely it is that she killed her mother," she said calmly. "Your conscience is bothering you."

"My conscience? What do you know about my conscience?"

"A lot," said Harriet. "Not only do you have a very complicated conscience, but you appear to be completely unaware of its existence."

"You mean I make love like a man with a tormented conscience?" he asked grimly.

She shook her head and waited until the bowls of fresh raspberry and cream-filled muesli were placed in front of them. "No," she said, her tone matter-of-fact. "You don't. You have lots of hang-ups, but they don't seem to be about sex. Or at least not sex with me." She picked up a spoon and looked at him sharply. "I'd like to know what would happen if a whore tried to pick you up, though."

"If?" he said. "You're kidding. When you're on Vice, you fight them off nightly. That's how they pay off. It's cheaper than cash."

"Did you?"

"Did I what?"

"Fight them off."

"Oh, yes. I have more hang-ups about sex than you realize. I can't make love to a woman who doesn't want me. And whores by definition don't want you." His face went blank, and he turned his attention to the muesli until he was almost finished. When he spoke again, the topic was dead.

"Why are you trying to con me into believing that Nikki couldn't have done in her mother? She has as good a motive as any of the others. Why are you so sure? You don't know her that well, do you?"

Harriet shook her head. "Hardly at all. I just met her Thursday. But it's so unlikely. When you consider how many people were wandering in and out of that basement all evening . . . Any one of them could have helped himself to the cyanide. The murderer didn't have to live in the house."

Sanders set down his coffee cup very carefully and stared at Harriet. "How in hell do you know who was down in the basement?" he asked. "Or did someone tell you? Because that doesn't count, you know."

"I was down there . . . for quite a long time, really. Looking at Klaus's darkroom, telling him what was missing, where to store various chemicals, in general being very officious and overbearing. He was terribly polite about it. I'm sure he only wanted me to say how wonderful it all was, but when you ask my opinion about something technical, you have to be prepared to get it." She noticed his expression and paused irritably. "Why are you staring at me like that?" she asked. "He's just a kid. I don't go in for cradle snatching, if that's what's bothering you. Anyway, lots of people came down: the housekeeper and the ghastly brother-in-law and the business manager; just about everyone. I remember wondering how he could possibly work down there. It was like Union Station on a Friday afternoon. In fact, Nikki was one of the few people who didn't come down."

Sanders waited until the muesli bowls disappeared and the heaping frying pans filled with scrambled eggs, rösti potatoes, bacon, ham, and sausages were put in their place. "Did it ever occur to you, Harriet, that what you saw just might fall into the category of what we like to call, for lack of a better word, evidence?"

"You're annoyed," she said flatly. "Well, I guess you have some justification. But actually, I had completely forgotten about Klaus's darkroom. It must have been getting down to routine again that brought it back to me. But anyway, I did go down there, and I forgot, and I'm sorry."

"Sorry," Sanders muttered with heavy sarcasm. He reached into his pocket, extracted his notebook and a pen, and looked up at her. "Now," he said, "let's go over this again. When were you down there? Who did you see? Who came up before you or down after you left? Have some more coffee."

Once more he stood in Clara von Hohenkammer's sitting room and felt a powerful reluctance to start in on it. He had dropped Harriet off after breakfast, written up his notes on what she had seen, routed out Dubinsky, and the two men were back. A team was coming in on Monday to look at her files—a team who could understand both financial statements and the German language. Now they were looking for anything that Collins and his team might have missed. But drawn by the warm September sunshine, he wandered over to the French doors, opened them, and stepped onto the balcony. The prospect was utterly wild. Behind the garden was a tangle of trees and shrubs, falling away into a ravine; on the east side was a utilitarian fence half-hidden by lush plantings. The only building visible was the garage, with its upstairs apartment that belonged to the gardener and his dogs. That was what money bought you around here. Privacy.

He ran an impatient hand through his hair and walked into the bedroom. The room was light and uncluttered, with a large, comfortable-looking bed, a love seat and chair, a couple of small tables, and in one corner, a triangular-shaped dressing table with mirrors. He drifted around, looking without anything much in mind, and finally sat on the edge of the bed. He hoped she hadn't been the sort of person who objected too strongly to people sitting on beds. The table beside him was almost bare. A clock, a lamp, and a copy of a paperback novel. He picked it up. The title meant nothing, but Günter Grass, the author's name, acted like a bell, immersing him in nostalgia. And the illustration on the battered cover told him what the German title, *Die Blechtrommel*, did not. What mood had she been in that made her want to reread *The Tin Drum*?

He began to turn the pages, mildly regretful that he'd never bothered to learn German. Here and there, in the sea of meaningless black symbols, only a few names leaped out at him. He was jeering silently at his own sentimentality, watching himself sit there, staring at a book he couldn't read because it reminded him of university days, when a folded sheet of airmail-weight paper fluttered out and fell on his lap.

It was neatly and closely written over in black ink, and, of course, in German. "Meine liebe Clara," it started, and it ended, "Peter." The rest was mystery. The chances were excellent that it was a chatty letter from a friend that she had picked up and used as a bookmark and that after he had gone to great efforts to have it translated, he would discover that the weather had been good and little Hans had had a bad cold. Nevertheless, something had to be done with it. He stood up again, regretfully. He liked this room. What he would really like to do would be to slip off his shoes and stretch out on the big bed and stare up at the wide, cool ceiling. "Dubinsky," he roared.

"Yeah?" Dubinsky's voice floated through from the sitting room.

"Find Bauer."

Constable Bauer was, in fact, at home, enjoying a rare Sunday off duty, standing in the driveway of his neat brick house, supervising two small children who were washing the family car. The air was filled with shrieks, giggles, soapsuds, and water. Bauer was not pleased at the sight of Sanders and Dubinsky drawing up to the curb in front of his house. "Hi, Martin," said Dubinsky, getting out and leaning his elbows on the roof of the car as though there were no reason Bauer would not be delighted to see them. "Sorry to bother you, but—"

Sanders unfolded himself from the front seat. "I need you to read this letter and tell me what's in it," he interrupted. "Now."

Bauer dried his wet hands on his jeans, took the letter, and started in on it, squinting from time to time at peculiarities in the handwriting. He shook his head slowly and started to reread it. "It's weird. It came in another envelope because he didn't want someone to read it."

"What?"

"He doesn't want her to sell some . . . uh . . ." He looked up. "It'll be faster if I just type up a translation, instead of trying to explain it to you. Just a minute. Jan!" he yelled.

A dark-haired young woman came to the door. "What do you want?"

"Could you keep an eye on the kids for five minutes while I do this?"

She sighed and nodded. "I knew it was too good to be true," she said, frowning. "Remember . . ." On that note she came down the steps, grasped one slippery child in each hand, and headed for the backyard.

Dubinsky remained draped across the car in an attitude of total relaxation; Sanders paced irritably back and forth on the sidewalk.

"I translated it as literally as I could," said Bauer when he finally emerged a few minutes later. "Here it is, for what it's worth."

Sanders took the two pages out of his hand, thanked him perfunctorily, and started reading as he walked back to the car. Dubinsky winked at one of the Bauer children, shrugged his shoulders at their father, and followed after. The letter was not terribly long.

Munich, Sept. 7

My dear Clara,

Such an old friend will excuse the childish trick I have played with the envelopes. I know when you open this you will be expecting a letter from your sister, but Friedl assures me that she will send you a real letter of her own next week. She is well.

Because of what I wish to say, I did not want this to be opened by another, perhaps by a secretary, believing it to be just another dull business communication, and so I have dressed it for a masked ball, as it were, for your eyes only.

Your latest request to sell, among other things, AMZ Gmbh. alarms me greatly, especially after what you sold in the spring. It is unwise to let your holdings in assets that are easily liquidated drop to such a low level. If I sell this now—and I have risked your anger by ignoring your request—not only would most of your European holdings be in real estate and other assets difficult to realize, but because of the current value of the mark vis-à-vis the U.S. dollar and a certain amount of reorganization in the company itself, its shares are temporarily at an artificially low level. This is a disastrous time to sell.

If you are in difficulties of some sort, Marthe and I would much rather advance the cash ourselves than have you placed in such a position.

I am coming to Toronto as soon as I can arrange it; probably the week of September 17th. You have often invited me; I now accept. As an old friend, I must insist that you permit me to talk these things over with you in person.

Please do not be too angry with me. Until next week, then,

Peter

Sanders read it again, then read it aloud to Dubinsky, who was weaving through the Sunday traffic. "Now what?" he said gloomily. "Peter, of course, is the lawyer. And that means this trip isn't something he just laid on. What do we know about who opens her mail?"

Dubinsky shrugged. "Whitelaw does," said the long-suffering sergeant. "When he's around. But why is she selling all her stock?"

"Broke suddenly? Transferring cash into some other project? Blackmail? A boyfriend? Someone could be conning her out of it. Although she didn't sound easily conned."

"And whatever was going on, she was being secretive about it, because we haven't heard anything. Not even from the accountant."

"If whatever she was doing was so drastic that her lawyer was going to fly out from Germany, there must be a whiff of it somewhere."

"You want me to go back for Bauer? Put him to work on the files?"

"No good," said Sanders morosely. "I tried him yesterday. He can understand the German, all right, but it's all financial stuff, doesn't mean a thing to him. Back to our own files, then."

Ed Dubinsky was working steadily and unhurriedly through the file on Frank Whitelaw, making his usual precise jottings on the material as he worked. Sanders had collected everything on Clara's family and was flipping erratically through it, occasionally stopping to read something that seemed to be of interest and otherwise apparently paying little attention to the material in front of him. Finally, he piled all the folders up again, pushed his chair back, and slouched down in an attitude of total collapse.

"Find anything?" said Dubinsky.

"Hard to say," said Sanders. "Did you?"

"Whitelaw keeps claiming that he ran all her business affairs," said Dubinsky, "but I don't see how he could have had anything to do with all this." He nodded at the letter from the Munich lawyer lying on the desk in front of him. "He wasn't even in the city most of the summer. Off visiting friends in New York and Cape Cod, even went to Paris for a week."

"There are such things as telephones," said Sanders repressively.

"Yeah, but if he had been the one helping her raise all that cash, or whatever she was doing, then why would the lawyer worry about .him opening the mail when he wasn't around? If you see what I mean. I mean if he's an accomplice— Dammit!" he said, and scratched his head. "The lawyer addresses the letter that way because someone is helping her do whatever she's doing, and that person opens her mail for her, and he doesn't want that person to open this letter."

Sanders was staring at him as if he were the family dog, suddenly endowed with the gift of speech. "What in hell are you talking about?" he said finally.

Dubinsky took a deep breath. "I'm trying to figure out who he didn't want to open the letter, that's all."

"Could be anyone," said Sanders. "She could have told anyone to open the business mail and sort it and to send on the personal mail unopened."

"Like who?"

"Mrs. Milanovich," said Sanders. "Mr. Milanovich. Her neighbor. Her nephew. Wasn't he around part of the summer?"

Dubinsky nodded. "Maybe the other daughter was, too."

Sanders yawned and nodded. "Sure. She was back and forth. Between Toronto and Muskoka. It's in there somewhere."

"What I can't see is how that could have anything to do with why she got killed. Suppose someone was helping her raise cash. Why kill her? And why does she need someone to help her, anyway?"

"You've got it backwards, Ed," said Sanders coolly. "She was doing it on her own, and someone killed her to stop her from throwing all her money away. Like her daughter. Like both her daughters."

"So why the crazy letter?"

"Just because this Peter doesn't want Whitelaw or whoever reading a letter where he's rapping her knuckles? It's tact, Dubinsky. That's all. Just tact. Or is that a concept you've never run into?"

"So it doesn't matter why she was spending all that money."

"Or whatever," said Sanders. "Probably not. Just that she was. We've got to get those damned files read," he added in a mutter, running his hands impatiently through his hair.

"Maybe we should call the lawyer," suggested Dubinsky, "and find out what he knows."

"No point," said Sanders. "He left yesterday. He's in London, and no one knows exactly where. Or if they do, they're not telling us."

"Hell," said Dubinsky. "Why should they? Nobody tells us anything over here."

"Quit bitching, Ed. You can drop me off on your way home. I need some sleep," he added without specifying the reason. "We should be able to get a line on things tomorrow. Nothing's going to happen tonight."

Which, as it happened, was true enough. But the consideration of what tomorrow might reveal was causing the drafting of some interesting, or even drastic, contingency plans here and there about the city.

CHAPTER 9

At nine-thirty Monday morning, in a state of extreme irritation, Harriet Jeffries walked up to the front door of Clara von Hohenkammer's house. She had sleep to catch up on, work to get finished, and some profound disruptions in her life that needed time and thought. Simple humanity and ordinary charity had been battling with her own selfish interests ever since Nikki had telephoned her an hour and a half ago, but with guilt on their side, humanity and charity had won hands down. They hadn't been able to make her feel happy about this mercy visit, though.

Nikki was sitting in the conservatory in the full morning sun, still looking white with exhaustion, the morning paper spread out, unread, in her lap. She struggled to her feet when Harriet walked in and smiled a pale smile. "I'll get you some coffee," she murmured, and pressed the bell on the desk. When Bettl appeared, however, her voice lost its languor; she snapped something too rapid for Harriet to catch, and the housekeeper hustled out again as fast as she had arrived. Nikki was getting very like her mother, thought Harriet, very quickly.

"I won't ask you how you are," said Harriet as soon as the coffee had arrived. "But tell me if there's anything I can do." As soon as the words fell out of her mouth, she realized she had made a horrible mistake. She was right.

Nikki took the opening at a dead gallop. "Could you stay here with me for a few days?" she said. Her eyes filled with tears as she spoke. "I know it's a lot to ask, but . . ."

Harriet stared at her in amazement, wondering if this child had any idea just how much she was asking. "I need someone. I am so tired and miserable; I can't cope with people, and they seem to be turning up all the time, asking me to make decisions about everything."

"Isn't your cousin staying here?" asked Harriet. "Can't he help?"

"Oh, Klaus," she said with just a touch of amused contempt in her voice. "He's not very good at that sort of thing. For one thing, he doesn't understand how to deal with staff. If Bettl asked him what we wanted for dinner, he'd tell her not to worry about cooking, we could all go out to eat."

"I'm not sure that I'd do any better," Harriet said cautiously. She paused to think. "I wouldn't mind staying here, really," she said, lying furiously, "but I have to work this afternoon, out of town. An overnight assignment. I won't be back until tomorrow morning. If then."

"Can't you put it off for a few days?"

"No. It's the way the business works. If I can't do a job when it's wanted, it goes to another firm." She felt a twinge—very small—of guilt as she said this, since although what she was saying was true enough, it certainly didn't apply to this particular project. It was a small condominium development, and when she had told the architect ten days ago that she wouldn't be able to start until this week at the earliest, he hadn't cared at all. "Just get it done before the snow hits the landscaping," he had said briskly. She had no intention of telling Nikki that.

"I'm sorry, Harriet," said Nikki, with a stricken look. "But it's so lonely here. I don't know anyone who isn't involved day and night in some important project or other, and I can't occupy myself for two consecutive hours," she added bitterly. "I'm worse than Theresa. She at least has the children, even if she lets other people clean up after them." She looked out the window to hide the tears that had welled up as she spoke. "I lead a completely useless life. I have no occupation, no interests, nothing I can do well. Not like

Mamma," she said in a very low voice. "Mamma was so good at what she did, and loved it so much. She never had time to sit around and feel sorry for herself."

"Well, dammit, Nikki, if that's how you feel, then do something," said Harriet, exasperated. "Get a job, go to university, start a business, I don't know. What you need is a little hard work. When did you last work hard at something?"

Veronika's head swiveled back to Harriet in surprise. "What?" She had to think for a minute. "Four years ago. Greek. That was hard work."

"Well, do something like that again. Have you been to university?"

"I started," she said brightly. "Then I got mixed up with all kinds of people and sort of didn't get finished."

"There you go," said Harriet. "Go back to university." She paused. "Is there anything you'd want to do in university?"

Veronika leaned forward in excitement. "Archaeology. I want to do archaeology. That's why I took Greek. Only Mamma thought—"

Harriet held up her hand. "You're twenty-two, Nikki, and you can do what you want to do. Within reason. If it's archaeology, then why not? It's respectable, and a great career for someone with money," she added with slight malice.

"If I have any money," Nikki replied uneasily. "Mamma may not have left me anything. Still, my share of Papa's estate will keep me while I go to university if I'm not too extravagant." She shook her head in mock sorrow. "It won't buy me red sports cars, though."

"Believe it or not, Nikki, my child, it's possible to live without a red sports car," said Harriet. "Since you're stuck in Toronto, anyway"—this was the most tactful way she could find to refer to the police investigation—"why don't you spend a few days down at the museum? They have a good Middle Eastern collection. Maybe the curator won't mind talking to you about, uh, pots and things. I mean, archaeology."

Nikki jumped up. "What a great idea! Let's go to the museum. You don't mind coming with me, do you? Damn," she said, and sat down again. "I forgot."

"Yes," said Harriet. "The memorial service."

Harriet felt as if she had just kicked a puppy. A tiresome but lovable puppy. "We'll have to put it off to tomorrow," said Veronika. "When shall we go?"

"Later on," said Harriet. "Call me." She put down her coffee cup and stood up. "Take care, Nikki. I'll see you later," she murmured, and fled from the house.

At ten minutes past ten the smallest boardroom at the bank gave the appearance of being sufficiently filled to contain a meeting of consequence. A half-dozen soberly attired men and one equally drably clad woman were chatting amicably. A certain distance separated Milan Milanovich from them—a distance you couldn't measure with a tape, but it was there, a clear, obvious, and almost-palpable barrier. Beside him, within the invisibly fenced off area that he occupied, was his lawyer, briskly cultivating an air of professional boredom.

"Good morning, gentlemen," said one of the beautifully tailored crowd, the one at the head of the table, and he evoked a hush of impressive dimensions. "We are waiting for Charles Britton, are we not?" He raised a questioning eyebrow about the table. "Who requested permission to attend as a representative of a major investor in the firm in question; major new investor, that is."

Milanovich's lawyer straightened out the papers in front of him and addressed the middle of the table, speaking to a tray holding a carafe of water and eight glasses. "Mr. Britton was to have represented the late Mrs. Clara von Hohenkammer, who was prepared to inject a sizable amount of new capital into the firm. Not sizable in your terms, gentlemen"—and here everyone smiled politely—"but sizable in terms of the present capitalization of Triple Saracen." He paused to allow an appreciative murmur to run through the group, should anyone care to start one. "This would, of course, have materially changed the position of the company in relation to its present obligations."

"Does this mean that Triple Saracen will, or would, have enough to pay back the monies loaned it by this and other banks, then?" The question came from the woman, whose face was deadpan and voice sardonic and whose relative power was indicated by her seat on the chairman's right.

"Bloody bitch of an accountant," the lawyer whispered into Milanovich's ear. "Not quite," he replied. "It certainly would have been enough to enable the company to navigate successfully through this temporarily difficult period, to satisfy suppliers, meet payroll and interest obligations, and generally to convince you, gentlemen"—he stumbled slightly and looked up—"and, uh, lady, that this is a viable corporation."

"This money, however, is not now forthcoming?" This was the smooth, rich voice from the head of the table, a chairman-of-the-board voice. "Because of Mrs. von Hohenkammer's tragic and unexpected death?"

"Yes." The lawyer nodded in agreement, and shuffled through the papers in front of him. "That is correct, but only in a manner of speaking. Mr. Milanovich informs me that he will shortly have access"—and here he moved a few more papers—"again in a manner of speaking, that is, through his wife, to half of the von Hohenkammer estate." His eyes remained glued to the material in front of him until he finished. At last, he raised his head and smiled. "Which is, as I'm sure you realize, a considerable sum."

"Are you sure?" asked the chairman. The woman frowned, clearly wondering whether *Mrs.* Milanovich knew what was being said on her behalf. Milanovich's lawyer moved over to the other side of the table and began to lay out their position to the chairman and the accountant. Milan sat where he had been put when he first walked into the room thirty-five minutes before, sweat beading in the creases of his forehead and trickling down his collar. Finally, the chair-man raised his hand and voice once again. "In that case, perhaps we should adjourn this meeting for two weeks, and at that time, if Mrs. Milanovich would be so kind as to attend, and, if possible, the lawyer for the estate, perhaps we can work out a satisfactory solution to the present difficulty. Gentlemen? Madam?" Everyone murmured and smiled and began to gather up papers and briefcases. Milanovich sat as he had been sitting, until his lawyer grasped him under the arm and steered him out of the room.

One of the gray-suited types collared the chairman deftly before he could get away; he engaged him in two minutes of intense discussion and then strolled out of the meeting room. He walked casually over to a window where a tall man with his back to the crowd was studying a large dark green, menacing-looking plant. "Hello, John," he said. "Enjoying yourself? Our boy is off the hook for two weeks. Stay of execution granted by the executive vice-president. Which is just as well. I'd like to do a bit more digging before the roof falls in on him."

Sanders turned and nodded. "Bloody well time you turned up, Doug. You sure the roof is going to fall in on him?"

Douglas McMeans of the fraud squad smiled serenely. "As sure as God made little green apples," he murmured. "A week next Monday the receivers go in. Even if his wife comes through with a promise of all the money from Mummy's estate, it won't help. He's into two different pension funds, paying off two different sets of officials, and they're both scared shitless. Anyway, the estate won't get through pro-bate for months and months. And when it does, it won't be enough. No matter how much it is, it won't be enough. By the way, you didn't need to worry about him noticing you. He wouldn't have noticed you if you'd climbed into his lap."

Sanders paused at the top of the stone stairs that led into St. Peter's Church on St. Clair Avenue. He was even later than he thought, and the memorial service was well on its way to

being over. He slipped into a side pew at the rear and
looked cautiously around him. In spite of Clara's wealth
and fame there were few people in the church, most of them
familiar. Front and center he picked out the pale brown of
Theresa's hair and the darker brown of her husband's.
Veronika sat beside them, looking small and insignificant. In
a well-organized world, unbearable guilt should be forcing
one of them to rush over to the coffin and scream, "Mamma!"
or maybe, "Clara!" or even, "Aunt Clara! Sorry about the
cyanide." Or words to that effect. But things like that never
happened on his cases.

Twenty minutes later, the small crowd was milling about
aimlessly on the church steps. A proper funeral mass, with
all its attendant pomp and circumstance, would be held in
Munich. Under the circumstances, there would be no
postfunereal festivities here, and people seemed uncertain of
what to do with themselves. Except for John Sanders, who
was scanning the crowd carefully in the approved manner.
But not for a murderer. He caught sight of slender, squared
shoulders and medium-length straight hair under a dark
beret moving quickly down the outside edge of the broad
stairs. His heart lurched. He raised an arm in a futile gesture
to catch her attention and started to run at a diagonal down
the steps to reach her before she got away. A hand fell on
his shoulder as he was darting around a tightly knit group.
"Inspector, I'm pleased to have caught you." He recognized
the voice of Klaus Leitner and turned in fury. "Mr. Peter
Lohr would like to speak to you. He is the family lawyer; he
just got in from Munich."

Sanders stopped where he was, pale with anger. As soon as
he had let his eyes wander from her, Harriet had disappeared.
There went his only chance to talk to her. Suddenly and
frustratingly, she had made herself completely unavailable. She
had turned on her answering machine last night and, as far as
he could judge, simply left it on. He could not bear to lose her
again so soon after rediscovering her, and lost she must certainly be, he felt profoundly, if he didn't see her again for weeks.

A man in a dark gray suit was standing quietly on the church steps, studying the landscaping with apparent concentration. "Inspector Sanders? I am Peter Lohr," he said, and held out his hand. He was fiftyish, tanned, lean, and fit, and he had the pleasantly relaxed manner that often seems to accompany an enormous bank balance. The rigors of intercontinental travel had failed to destroy the effect of his exquisitely tailored suit or understated silk tie. But then, reflected Sanders, you couldn't expect Clara's lawyer to look as if he spent his life bailing whores out of jail in the middle of the night. "I am most anxious to speak to you about this business, Inspector," said Lohr. "Perhaps you would accompany me to the house. I understand it is only a brief walk."

Sanders nodded and followed him down the steps.

"I'm afraid that we have things to discuss," Lohr added as soon as they had crossed the wide and busy street. "I haven't even had time yet to see how Clara's poor children are," he said as a gentle reminder to Sanders that he represented them as well.

"Yes," said Sanders curtly. "There are also certain things that we need to know from you, such as the terms of Mrs. von Hohenkammer's will."

"The will that is presently in effect?" asked Lohr.

"Yes," said Sanders curiously. "Was there . . ."

"She had asked me to prepare a new will for her. But she did not have time to have it signed. According to the old will, the estate is split between the two daughters, but Theresa's half is largely tied up in trust for the children. Two-thirds of it."

"And in the new will?"

"In the new will, it is completely tied up. She doesn't get a mark in capital."

"But why . . ."

"Clara thought her a fool married to a fool and a thief. Is this the house, Inspector?"

*   *   *

The huge living room made the small group look very small. Klaus Leitner was leaning against the cold hearth, one elbow on the mantelpiece, a study in elegance. Sanders saw him shoot his arm out from his sleeve and glance quickly at his wrist. Trying to figure out how long he had to stay there. He sympathized a little. Theresa was sitting in one of the large chairs, at its edge, perched upright and looking intensely at her husband. A look of wifely concern and affection? Not bloody likely, thought Sanders, taking in the rhythmic sideways swish of her foot. It reminded him of the tail of an angry cat, lashing slowly back and forth. Her husband stood for a while beside Leitner, then paced up and down, and then sat down on the large couch beside Veronika. She was the only one who was absolutely still, very pale, concentrating hard on Herr Lohr as he read the document in front of him. Frank Whitelaw leaned slightly over the back of the couch, but whether the attitude was protective or predatory, Sanders could not tell. Bettl stood in the doorway with the air of a waitress anxious to clear away the coffee cups and go home. Sanders was finding it interesting to sit in the background, watching their actions and expressions, unable to understand what anyone was saying, yet knowing to some extent, from Lohr's brief summary, what was being said. Only the Milanoviches and Whitelaw conversed in English, since Milan's German didn't seem to be good enough for this sort of occasion. Milan's voice provided an annoying tenor counterpoint to Lohr's steady baritone as he bobbed back and forth, asking his wife what was being said. She frowned and shook her head and refused to translate.

Lohr finished his preamble to the will and started in on the specific provisions. Klaus Leitner looked surprised; he hadn't expected as much as he got, then. Maybe. Bettl—that is, Elisabeth—Kotzmeier looked impassive, her face a closed mask. Annoyed. She had expected a larger slice of the pie. Whitelaw looked as if he had known all along what to expect. Perhaps he had, or perhaps he was as good an actor as his former employer. There was a jumble of strange names—friends and relations in Munich—and then a quick summary of the disposal of the residual estate. The inclusion of "Veronika, my daughter," drew a sideways glance, bright-eyed and heightened in color, from wife to husband, but not until Lohr came to Theresa's name did the real reaction come. Even her husband grasped that part. Milan Milanovich leaned back and stared at the lawyer, his cheeks splashed with scarlet rounds of color; his wife slowly turned an ashen gray.

"So that's that, Nikki dear. I'm so glad that Mamma didn't carry out her threat. It would have been awkward for us if she had. Or perhaps you already knew?" Theresa's tone was carrying; she spoke in English, making sure Inspector Sanders had not missed her speech. Veronika von Hohenkammer shook her head in bewilderment and then began to sob.

Sanders looked at his watch: seven twenty-three. Lohr, whom he had to talk to, was tied up with the von Hohenkammer children and assorted hangers-on tonight. He would see the inspector in the morning, he had said firmly, in a voice that invited no argument. And now he was alone. Whatever she was doing, wherever she had been, she ought to be home by now. He dialed the number, very carefully. The telephone rang, once, twice, started to ring a third time, and clicked. "Hi, there," said a slightly tinny version of Harriet's voice, "you've managed to dial Harriet Jeffries/Parallax Productions. I'm in the darkroom and too covered with chemicals to take your call right now. Wait until that funny little noise sounds and then leave your name and number. I'll get back to you as soon as humanly possible. Thanks."

"Goddamn it, Harriet," he roared into the phone, "I hate answering machines. I especially hate cute answering machines that lie. You can't still be in the darkroom. If you are sitting there listening to this and you don't call me back, I am going to come over to your place and drown you in the fucking darkroom. And thank you, too. I'm at the apartment," he added in a slightly more normal tone. "And it's bloody Monday at bloody seven twenty-five." After he hung up, it occurred to him that he hadn't thought to leave his name. She'd know who it was. How many irascible, unpleasant, obscene, and overbearing male friends could she possibly have?

CHAPTER 10

Nikki von Hohenkammer woke up in a state of acute physical discomfort. After a little groggy thought, it occurred to her that she was cold. Very cold. Her feet, covered only by a sheet, were aching with cold. And there was no remedy for it where she was. She ran across the icy floor, pulled back the curtains, and slammed the window shut. A new and hostile world looked back at her from the other side of the pane. The sky outside was gray; the tree branches shivered restlessly in the wind. The summer's heat, which had stretched so unseasonably into September, had come to an abrupt end. She continued her survey of the premises, nagged by a sense that something else was wrong. After a minute, it came to her: The omnipresent police car no longer sat in the gravel drive in front of the house, and as bitterly as she had resented its presence, its absence now made her feel unprotected and alone. She shivered and headed for the shower.

While she stood under the biting spray, letting the hot water run through her hair, she considered her various problems. The first one needed little thought. If she were arrested before her plane left for Munich on Thursday afternoon, there would be no decisions to be made. Herr Lohr would stay in the country until he was sure she had a good lawyer. If she weren't arrested, though, there would be things she had to come to terms with. She needed to talk to someone about the money. She had been so convinced that she would get nothing—as convinced as Theresa had been that *she* would get everything—that she was totally unprepared to face undisputed possession of all that wealth. Not that her mother's will was out of character: Veronika, who had always been careful with money—that extravagant red car had been a present—received her just half; Theresa, who had always thrown money away with abandon, had her just half tied up to protect her from herself and her husband. No matter what threats she made, Mamma had always acted rationally. Nikki stepped out of the shower and toweled herself dry as fiercely as if she were trying to remove her old skin. She wrapped a towel around her head and went back into the bedroom.

Last night's dinner had been appalling; she had no intention of going through anything like that again. Theresa's voice had become softer and sweeter with every sentence, the way it always did when she was in a homicidal rage. Nikki shuddered. And Milan. Halfway through the schnitzel, one of Bettl's more successful efforts, he had put down his knife and fork, smiled wordlessly, and walked out. They had all looked at Theresa, whose expression did not change, and then pretended that nothing had happened. Through the delicate clatter of knife and fork on china, they heard the crash of the front door, the metallic slam of the car door, and a grinding of the ignition as the Porsche started up. It was followed by a screech of tires scrabbling to make contact on gravel, and Milan was gone.

For the rest of the evening Theresa sat like an infuriated Roman matron, toying with her food and drink until Frank Whitelaw offered to drive her home.

Throughout the whole hideous meal Whitelaw had tried valiantly to pretend that nothing had happened; he had done his best to maintain a witty dinner-table discourse with Nikki and Herr Lohr, being amusing about art and the oddities of the colonial cultural scene. Paradoxically, he made everything worse. She was grateful for his efforts, but they reminded her that she didn't really want him, oozing tact and charm, around forever. How was she going to dismantle her mother's network of dependents without being totally coldhearted and ruthless? She shook her head. She would have breakfast, talk to Klaus about his business, ask Herr Lohr about the estate, and make some decisions. Throwing on some jeans and a sweatshirt, she headed out to face the world.

The smell of coffee drifted in through a silent house. She walked down the hall and pounded on Klaus's door. She was rewarded by a low moan. "It's past nine," she called. "Breakfast is now."

The table was neatly laid with a basket of rolls and several pots of jam. Veronika walked into the empty kitchen. It was spotlessly clean. A large china pot of coffee sat on a warming plate, and on the stove was a pan filled with milk. She reached over and turned on the burner under it. Inside the refrigerator she found freshly cut butter and a pitcher of orange juice. She carried them all into the dining room, considered the ambient gloom, piled everything on a large tray, and carried it into the conservatory. "Bring the coffee," she called to Klaus, whose footfalls were echoing on the stairs.

"What about the milk?" he asked. "It's boiling."

"Bring it, too, of course," she answered impatiently.

"Where's the omnipresent Bettl?" asked her cousin as he came into the conservatory with two china pots.

"She must be out shopping," said Nikki. "I came down and found everything laid out. Like the magic castle in 'Beauty and the Beast.' "

"Well, we've got Beauty," he said, "and Bettl makes a good Beast, but I don't know quite where I fit into this plot." His ramblings were interrupted by the ringing of the phone. "I'll get it," he said. "Pour me some coffee, will you?"

He listened for a long time, looking slightly glazed, and finally spoke. "Look, Theresa, just let me finish my coffee and I'll be right over. Have you called the police?" The phone sputtered hysterically back at him. "All right, sweetheart, we won't do that. Just hang on until I get there." He dropped the receiver back in its cradle. "That's all we need right now," he said gloomily.

"For God's sake, what has happened?" snapped Nikki. "What do you mean, police?"

"Your esteemed brother-in-law has disappeared, taking two suitcases, the Porsche, all the cash in the house; a considerable amount."

"How much?" interrupted Nikki.

"Over seven thousand dollars," Klaus continued. "Kept around for buying milk with after the banks close, I suppose. Anyway, he vanished during the night like the snows of yesteryear."

Nikki giggled. "You aren't very sympathetic. Is Theresa upset?"

"She appeared to me to be furious rather than upset, although she did use words like 'worried out of her mind' and 'what if something has happened to him.' But it struck me that she'd be even more upset if nothing had. Anyway, I'll go over there and see what I can do to calm her down. Unless you need me here?"

Nikki shook her head. "I have lots to do, if I can only get around to it. I might have lunch with Harriet. Don't worry about me."

Veronika shut the door thoughtfully behind her cousin and walked back to the conservatory. The room was gray and gloomy, like the day, and she shivered with the cold. She had to get out of the house, but first she had to find some warmer clothes. Her mother must have had sweaters over here. After all, she always came in early spring. As soon as she put socks on her icy feet, she would look for something she could wear.

Her mother's sitting room was still locked and sealed off, but the police had removed their seals from the bedroom. She went over to the dressing room and threw open the huge closets. They were almost empty. Damn! What had happened to all the clothes? There were some thin wool dresses, not warm enough, too long, and much too conservative in cut. There should also have been warm wool pants. She began to open the large drawers that filled one wall. They were empty. Goddamn Theresa must have been in here as soon as the police left and swiped everything she could get into. Or Bettl, in which case it would be everything any member of her large and unpleasant family could get into. She slammed the drawers shut. Unless . . . of course. Mamma might have had her woolens packed away in the basement, not cluttering up her closets during the hot weather.

Veronika put on a pair of running shoes and headed for the basement stairs. Where would she have kept everything? Not in Klaus's darkroom. She opened the wine cellar, looked around, and shut it again. The next room was a storage room, usually locked, but of course the police had removed the padlock. It contained four wooden packing cases and an assortment of empty cartons. She glanced at the wooden crates, which were filled but not yet nailed down. Surely even her mother didn't ship all her clothes back and forth across the Atlantic in wooden crates, but you never knew. Poor dear Mamma—her eyes filled with tears—had had some rather pre-jet travel notions. She pushed open the partially closed box nearest to her. It was filled with shredded paper and objects carefully enveloped in bubble packing. She took out one and unwrapped it. It was a silver teapot, in need of polishing, but, to her inexpert eye, very pretty. A box filled with antiques she had picked up over here? Odd when you thought of the house in Munich and the house in the country both stuffed full of this sort of thing. She set the teapot down on another crate.

She opened the next wrapped package. It was a silver teapot, in need of polishing. She stared at it for a long time. She opened the next one. It was a silver teapot, in need of polishing. She began to giggle. Mamma must have been going berserk. She kept pushing away the material and finding more parcels. When she had extracted the fourth silver teapot, three sugar bowls, six sets of tongs, a tray, and four cream jugs, she had a demented vision of her mother opening an antique shop in the house in Munich. Her impulse to laugh was suddenly displaced by cold fear. What in hell was going on?

She tried to remember when Mamma had started insisting that this room be locked. This summer? Last summer? Or was it Mamma? Maybe it had been Theresa. She could see herself, as clearly as if she were still there, sitting on the dock in the sun, dangling her feet in the water, reading the Toronto papers, which were filled with articles about a wave of large-scale thefts in the city. Thefts of art, jewelry, and silver. Good, expensive silver. And Mamma had become worried about money, hadn't she, in the last year. Worried about Theresa being left penniless, about Milan's shady dealings. And, she suddenly remembered, worried about running afoul of the law. Mamma would scarcely have been breaking into houses, but she could have been helping someone, for a share in the profits. . . . Veronika shook her head. It was mad. Her mother would never do something like that. Would she? But how much did she really know about her mother? And what other explanation could there be for all this? And whom, of all the people in this city, would Mamma have bent the law to help? She felt a sick sense of dread as she thought of her sister and her husband, in prison, and her niece and nephew . . .

Meanwhile, she was getting colder and colder. She left the room, flung open the door of Klaus's darkroom, and grabbed a heavy sweater he had left hanging there on the hook. She ran upstairs to her bedroom, put on a T-shirt, pulled on the sweater, reached for the phone, and dialed 911. But as soon as she heard herself asking for the police, she broke out into a sweat. This was crazy. Whatever it was that Mamma had been mixed up in, she couldn't call the police. She hung up and redialed. She listened impatiently to Harriet's answering machine and then poured out her dilemma in incoherent bursts. "Harriet, it's Nikki. I've found some things . . . in the house. I'm sure they shouldn't be there, and I have to talk to someone. I'll meet you at noon . . ." Suddenly she remembered that Harriet was out of town for the morning. "No, four o'clock would be better for you, wouldn't it? I'll see you there at four. By the front entrance."

As she dropped the receiver down in its cradle, another telephone in the house disconnected as well.

When the telephone rang, Carlos was just patting cologne onto his newly shaved cheeks. He listened to the steady voice, grunted, and slammed the receiver down. In less than a minute, he had changed into more respectable clothes, stuffed his pockets with wallet, cash, and keys, and was out the door. In another ten, he was heading east along St. Clair, confident that the girl would be moving west, toward shopping and restaurants. In fact, there she was, walking across the bridge, in the direction of the subway station. The car would be a distinct liability. He turned at the first corner, parked under a No Parking at Any Time sign, and set out after her.

He thought briefly about what he had been asked to do and rejected it as too complicated and dangerous. Never leave loose ends was the credo he lived by. Much better to deal with her permanently. The subway station would be the best place. As he mulled over the problem, his longer legs eating up the distance between them, he fished in his pocket for change. He paused at the first newspaper box he came to, indifferent to its contents, shoved in his money, and took out a paper, useful for hiding busy hands. Up ahead, the girl slowed as she approached the subway station, and he reached into his pocket for bills to buy tokens with. She paused in front of it and peered into her big shoulder bag. She looked up at the sky, dropped the flap of her bag shut, and headed toward Yonge Street.

"What the hell?" he muttered as he tucked his paper under his arm and followed, adjusting his pace to hers as they moved. Wherever she was going, she was dead easy to follow. In her red-and-blue heavy sweater that reached almost to the knees of her disreputable blue jeans, she offered a striking contrast to the neat dark suits and skirts of the working women striding purposefully along the street.

She turned at the corner and headed briskly down Yonge Street.

Manu put down his burden and knocked peremptorily at the door of the apartment. He heard leisurely footsteps inside; the door opened halfway, and there was a split second of frozen movement as the fence took in the sight in front of him.

"For chrissake, man," he hissed, "get that stuff out of the hall." Manu leaned down lazily and picked up the box again; as soon as he had a grip on it, the fence grabbed him by the arm and yanked him into the apartment. "I thought I told you not to bring it here. Not now."

"Don't bother to close the door," said Manu. "The buru will be here in a second with the rest. It's all downstairs. He's bringing it up."

"You idiots!" said the fence as an ominous bump from the hall outside testified to the probability that Manu meant exactly what he said. He flung open the door and began to haul the boxes into his apartment. The buru sauntered in, carrying the last box.

"Something wrong?" asked the buru.

"Something wrong?" he reiterated. "You're bloody right there's something wrong. You can't leave this stuff here. Look, you arrogant son of a bitch, I said I'd move it for you, but I never wanted to see you or it anywhere near this place. Remember? A helluva lot of good I'll be to you if I'm in jail. And that's where I'll be if they find all this in here. I'm moving it out again if you don't. I'm putting it out on the street, and they can haul it away with the rubbish."

The buru sat down and stretched his legs out in front of him comfortably. "You do that, my friend, and I call the police and tell them where these boxes came from. You want me to do that?" He smiled. "You see, we're already in big trouble, Manu and I, aren't we, Manu?" The gloomy-looking man standing beside him nodded. "And Manu thought—Manu's very smart, my friend, more than you think—Manu thought it was time you shared just a little of the danger. In case you were planning to pull out and leave us. From now on, we're going to visit you every day—and many people will see us here, won't they?—until you pay us our share of the profits. And don't tell me there haven't been any profits. I know. I have friends in New York, and they've checked the galleries for me. We've sold a lot. So if your friend in New York—if he exists—hasn't paid out, you'd better start getting some money from him."

The fence looked at him for a long time, as if trying to assess with absolute accuracy the likelihood that the buru knew what he was talking about and would carry out his threat. At last, he turned and opened a closet door containing shelves piled high with towels, sheets, and various oddments. He removed a stack of towels and handed them to Manu, who dropped them contemptuously on the ground, revealing a small gray safe. He leaned in to dial in the combination, shielding the workings of his fingers with his body.

In less than thirty seconds the gray door swung open, and he reached into the cavity. In a few more seconds, he slammed the door shut, backed out, and closed the cupboard door. He was holding several packages of bills. "Right," he said, staring steadily at the buru and avoiding Manu's more ambiguous gaze. "This is roughly what the first two lots brought in." He handed it over. "Minus my commission. But I'll have you know I haven't seen that money yet. It's being held in the States. You move it in here, and people start asking questions. This is my own money I'm giving you. The other two can take their share out of this."

The buru looked at the money in his hand as if it were covered with some strange and vile growth. He opened his mouth to speak, thought better of it, and leaned back on the wall.

"And as for getting this lot over the border," continued the fence, "for chrissake, two cops and a harmless old lady! You don't make it easy."

"Us!" said Manu suddenly. "We didn't touch them. It was Don, and Carlos. Crazy bastard. Your crazy bastard, too. Not one of my people. He speaks our language like a child. What does he know about the fight for independence?" He shrugged. "Don't blame us."

"How in hell was I supposed to know he was crazy?" muttered the fence. "You fools needed help. You were damned lucky I got someone who used to be in the antiques business. You look at that money in your hand. If you hadn't had Carlos, you'd have been picking up worthless trash, netting a few hundred a time for all that work. And Carlos wanted Don."

"Well," said the buru casually, "they can have their money when the next shipment pays out." And with that he began carefully splitting up the contents of the packets between himself and Manu.

"Can I drive you somewhere?" asked the buru as the two men walked together toward the sidewalk.

Manu shook his head. "I have a visit to make," he said. "It will be better to take the subway."

"A visit?" The buru frowned.

"To Don. He and Carlos are preparing to run. That money was for them. I know it. I could feel it in the way he handed it over to us. Carlos is too busy right now to do anything, but Don— I will go find him at work. And say a few words."

The buru nodded. If Manu smelled danger, they had all better look about them.

Veronika slowed down, at last, to consider where she was going and what she wanted. She was outside a bookstore, a bookstore that looked quiet, dark, and softly lit. She needed to think, and this seemed an excellent place for it. Once her eyes had adjusted to the darkness, she passed quickly by the racks of best-sellers lining the entry and stopped at the large sale table in the middle of the store, heaped high with outdated novels, odd cookbooks, and battered children's stories. She touched the spine of each with one delicate finger as she read the titles. Nothing. The next pile contained a selection of dog-eared "how-to" books, most of them involving losing weight or inhibitions or husbands without guilt. Not relevant. Then her finger touched *Become a New You in Eight Days*. That was it. She wanted to become a new her. A different Veronika.

She pulled it out. Chapter 1 counseled her to start with the easy part, to develop a new image from the skin out. In other words, new and different clothes. The idea seemed brilliant and persuasive in its simplicity. If you look like the person you want to be, you will become that person. Why not? She glanced at the price of the book and then took out her wallet. Her stomach growled as she stared at the single five-dollar bill inside it, and she realized that she needed two things before tackling her project: food and cash. She put the book back, grateful for its inspiration, doubtful that in its details it would do her much good, and moved briskly out the door and toward the corner.

The smell of hot dogs grilling at a stand near the corner reminded her how hungry she was. As she pulled out her wallet once more, a softly hesitant voice muttered, "Hey, lady, you got any spare change?" She shook her head, embarrassed, and took out the five.

"One," she said to the vendor, handing him the bill.

"Mustard and relish beside you," he answered in a bored voice, slapping the hot dog in a napkin on her hand and slipping her three dollars in change in beside it.

As she stepped back toward the curb, a man rushing to catch the light smashed into her, hitting her shoulder with his elbow and propelling her directly into the road. She twisted her well-muscled body in an attempt to change direction and fell hard against the panhandler, who was investigating the trash basket closest to the hot-dog stand. She grabbed the edge of the basket, pulled herself upright, and looked over at him in apology. He was thin, dirty, and cold looking, younger than she was and bent over in an effort to keep from being toppled into the traffic. As he straightened up, he reminded her of her cousin Klaus, fallen on hard times. The smell of food under her nose suddenly nauseated her. "Sorry about that," she said. The panhandler looked up, suspicious. "You like mustard? Here, I haven't touched it." She handed him the hot dog, and as an afterthought, the three dollars. Today was a day to start things new.

If the woman in the trust company where her mother had set up an account for her was surprised at a request for $2,500 in cash from a girl in tattered jeans and a sweater that clearly didn't belong to her, she was too inured to surprises to let it show. Veronika took the pile of brightly colored bills and shoved them carelessly in a lump in her pocket, unable to overcome her sense that it was all play money. Not like marks. Marks were real; they bought serious things, like real estate and stocks. Canadian dollars were for splurging on anything you wanted.

"From the skin out," muttered Nikki as she left the trust company and headed into a small lingerie shop where she scooped up panty hose and panties in a variety of colors and patterns. That was the easy part. Her clothing had always been, as it were, anti-clothing. Her mother, for all her wealth and elegance, bought her clothes from conservative shops in Munich and looked exactly like what she was: a well-dressed, middle-class Bavarian. For years, Veronika had refused to wear anything that looked even faintly like something her mother might buy. In consequence, her closet contained almost nothing but jeans. A new Veronika needed something more than that, but it mustn't look like Mamma's clothes, either.

Sanders was sitting in the study face-to-face at last with Clara von Hohenkammer's lawyer. It had been his first piece of luck that day. When he had arrived on the doorstep that morning, he had found Lohr alone in the house, working quietly on something or other in connection with the estate. Now he folded the flimsy white paper he had been reading and handed it back to Sanders. "Yes," he said. "This is from me. It is my most recent letter to her." He smiled affably. "Have you read the rest of our correspondence from this summer?"

Sanders shook his head.

"Then I can understand your confusion, Inspector." Lohr paused expectantly.

"Maybe you could fill me in, then," said Sanders impatiently.

Lohr gave him a puzzled look. "Ah, yes. Fill you in. With information, you mean. Yes, of course." He leaned back in his chair. "I must think a minute. Yes, Clara left Munich on the first of March this year. That was early for her; she did not enjoy Canadian winters. But she intended to stay with friends in Majorca for a month before traveling to Toronto. That would bring her here at her usual time. Normally I would expect to receive one letter from her between the end of March and the middle of October. It would be filled with instructions about her property and investments in Germany and questions of all kinds." Here he paused again, sorting out his ideas. "These letters were dictated to her secretary— that man Whitelaw—and signed by her after they had been typed. She always added a long and affectionate note in pen to both of us when she signed. That is what she had done the previous four summers that she spent in Canada." Again he paused. "This summer was different. I received a letter from Toronto even before she was supposed to have left Majorca, which means that her visit to her friends had been cut short for some unexplained reason. That was odd. Then she requested that I sell a certain large block of shares and transfer the money to a new corporate account that she had established here. I was not happy about that, since I felt that these particular shares should not have been sold at that time, but I was not too alarmed. Then I received two letters in June."

Sanders interrupted him for the first time. "Did you carry out her instructions?"

"Of course. But in my reply I mentioned that I was not sure she was taking the wisest course. But, as I was saying, I received two letters in June, one requesting the sale of a small block of shares and the other asking me to forward an account of her market position at the moment."

"Did that seem reasonable to you?"

"No." He shook his head. "She always has kept very close account of what she owned. I also found the letters odd. There were no handwritten notes, no news of the family. It was as though somehow we had offended her." Lohr frowned. "And then, when I returned from my holiday at the end of August, I discovered a letter that had been written in late July requesting that I sell off several major blocks of shares, representing now the bulk of her liquid holdings in Deutschmarks. I was horrified. Marthe and I decided that perhaps she had fallen into the hands of an unscrupulous lover—although she was a sensible woman, you know, even the most sensible people do bizarre things when they are in love—and he was systematically using up all her funds."

Something else occurred to Sanders as he listened to Lohr speak. "Could another person have written those letters?" he asked.

Lohr cocked his head. "We thought of that. The letters were unlike her, but the signature was hers. Or looked like hers. We didn't have it checked. Instead, I wrote that letter, insisting that I come and discuss all this in person. I was afraid, if she had a lover, that he might open my letters, and so I adopted that rather dramatic trick of sending this one in an envelope addressed in her sister's hand. She liked melodrama; anyway, I believed it would amuse her." For a moment the lawyer looked humanly upset. "She must have received it shortly before she died. I don't know what she thought when she read it."

"I think," said Sanders thoughtfully, "that must have been when she called her accountant."

"Indeed," said Lohr. "Very interesting." The words were spoken in the tone of one who is used to ending interviews and to having his agenda followed. He stood up, and Sanders followed suit.

Just as Sanders was reaching for the handle of the front door, there were rapid footsteps on the gravel outside, and it flew open. He scowled at the vision in front of him. "Oh, hello, Inspector," said Klaus Leitner. "My cousin home yet?"

"Doesn't seem to be," grunted Sanders.

"Oh, that's right," said Klaus, looking at his watch. "She said she was having lunch with Harriet." Sanders, who had been unsuccessful in his efforts to get in touch with the said Miss Jeffries over the past twenty-four hours, glared at Leitner. "But anyway, I was just about to call you, Inspector. I've been at my cousin Theresa's all morning . . . and . . ."

"Yes, Mr. Leitner?"

"Well, it's about her husband. Milanovich. He's gone. And his wife doesn't know where he is."

Sanders headed back to the study and reached for the telephone.

Once returned to the haven of his desk, Sanders checked the time and tried to decide if the agony in his stomach was psychic or physical. Just as he had rather pragmatically concluded that it was probably hunger, the telephone rang. He listened intently to the voice at the other end of the line, scribbling notes as he went, until with a final "Thanks" he slammed down the receiver.

"That's it," he said. There was triumph in his voice.

"What's it," said Dubinsky, sounding even less impressed than usual. "Your horse come in or something?"

"Better than that. That was Tom Gardiner with a message from Volchek. It seems the owner of Rawlinson's Gold Exchange called in. He's just been offered a valuable gold ring containing a large emerald and two diamonds in what they call a fantasy setting. Very distinctive."

"Mrs. Wilkinson's?" said Dubinsky cautiously.

Sanders nodded. "Sounds like it. They have a security camera by the cash, and they taped the person who brought it in. But after a couple of minutes he got twitchy and ran. Volchek's on his way over there now."

"I wonder which one it is?" said Dubinsky.

"Volchek said it sounded like Walker, the one at Mid-City. Get a team to check his alibis. Carefully this time." Dubinsky scowled and picked up the phone. "And then I'm going for lunch. You coming?"

Carlos was beginning to wish that he hadn't changed his clothes when the phone call had come. His shoes were pinching his feet, and his tie had taken on a malevolent life of its own, growing tighter and itchier as he darted back and forth, following the goddamned girl from one narrow little shop to another. Without a chance to close in on her, either, not after that impulsive and abortive try at the corner. So far, she had been into almost every women's clothing store on Bloor Street, and whatever she was looking for didn't seem to exist. At last, she had wandered into a place that sold mostly Irish tweeds; she had been there for over thirty minutes, and now he was getting nervous.

Veronika looked at herself in the plum-colored suit and slightly darker silk shirt and smiled. She liked it. The sales-clerk held her breath. It was the eighth complete outfit she had put together for this girl. "I'll take it," she said.

"The suit?"

"Everything—suit, shirt, belt, scarf." She stepped into the changing room and began to strip. "And I'll wear it now," she added. "Just take the tags off."

"You wouldn't have shoes, would you?" asked Veronika a few minutes later as she stepped out of the dressing room in her stocking feet, carrying her brightly colored cloth purse and Klaus's sweater.

"I'm afraid not," said the clerk. "And that came to thirteen hundred and eighty-nine dollars," she added, handing her the bill.

"Ah," she said, pulling out her cash and peeling off fourteen hundreds. "And could you put this sweater in a bag for me? The rest of the clothes in there you can throw out. Oh, except my running shoes. I'll need them to get to a shoe store."

New shoes and a matching purse took the better part of Veronika's remaining cash, but not of her time. She had an hour and twenty minutes before she was to meet Harriet, and she was, at the most, ten slow, ambling minutes from the museum. She stood on the sidewalk and looked around her for inspiration.

After a brief and unsatisfactory lunch, Sanders sat at his desk, brooding. Volchek had clearly staked out the matter of Mrs. Wilkinson's ring. Dubinsky had dispatched a team to deal with the disappearance of one of the key witnesses in the von Hohenkammer case, although Sanders was willing to bet that Milanovich was flying over some ocean or other by now. His current problems must have made foreign travel seem irresistible. In short, Sanders had delegated himself out of legwork. Everything else to be done was going to require perception, enthusiasm, and thought. He looked at his watch. It was getting on to three o'clock. He reached for the phone and checked the motion. He couldn't face hearing that smug little message one more time. "I'll be back later," he said to anyone in the room who cared to listen, and headed out the door.

The third hairdresser whose establishment Veronika von Hohenkammer visited in this little corner of town admitted that he could arrange for her to have her hair washed and dried, and her makeup done, before ten minutes to four. Since it was, after all, a Tuesday, and Tuesdays weren't that busy. She lay back in the chair, quiet, like an obedient child, and let people do whatever they wanted with her for the next fifty minutes.

*   *   *

Manu stepped off the bus across the street from Mid-City Security Systems and stopped to check the time. Almost three o'clock. He considered what kind of approach was likely to gain him access to Don. Humble friend desperate to see him? He shook his head. Arrogant would-be customer unhappy about an estimate? That was infinitely more promising. But while he was mulling over his approach, circumstance pulled a fast one on him.

Three white-and-blue patrol cars drew up onto the sidewalk in front of the building; six uniformed officers climbed out of the cars. Manu began to stroll along the street away from the bus stop, staring with casual interest at what was happening.

Ten minutes later, as Don Walker was being hustled into one of the patrol cars, Manu left his observation post at the front table of a grubby little café, paid his modest bill, and headed across the street to catch a bus back to the vicinity of his flat.

Once inside the flat, he made a phone call, walked into the kitchen, poured himself a small glass of red wine, and sat down at the table with a pad of paper in front of him. He considered the causes for the alarm he was feeling at the moment and decided that they were sound and real: Carlos was a dangerous fool; Don, a weak, greedy, frightened fool; the fence was on the point of betraying them. He had tried on the bus to reckon up the number of hours that Don would withstand police interrogation and concluded haste was essential. He set down his observations and conclusions in brief, reasoned language, reread them, made a few revisions, reached for a battered copy of the works of Miguel de Unamuno that sat on the shelf, and swiftly cast the letter into a simple code. That done, he showered, shaved, put on a sober business suit, packed one small suitcase, and threw the copy of Unamuno into the briefcase containing the money. From a drawer he took a new passport, slipped it into his inside jacket pocket, picked up the letter, and ran lightly downstairs. Once outside, he turned toward the backyard, where a wiry boy of eleven was practicing indefatigably with a battered soccer ball. He handed him a twenty-dollar bill and the letter, made him repeat the address twice, and watched him head off to deliver his message to the buru. That taken care of, he set off at a brisk pace for the subway and the airport bus.

Completely processed, Veronika glanced at herself in the broad mirror behind the cash desk. She was indeed a new her; so new as to be barely recognizable. She regarded the phenomenon with interest but without emotion or opinion. Tomorrow would be time enough to judge whether she liked the new her or not. The receptionist counted out her change with an automatic smile. "You look marvelous," she said. "Simply marvelous. I hope you have a good time tonight." She leaned back and studied the young woman critically. "Actually, Toni didn't do a bad job on you. Your husband should like it."

"My husband?" said Veronika, and turned to stare, hard, for the first time at her image in the mirror. It was a shock. Considering the violence of the change in her appearance, she would not have been surprised to discover that both outer and inner self had suffered drastic upgrading. Perhaps she had magically acquired a husband, and even an occupation of some sort. She shook her head, bemused.

"He came by earlier to find out how long you'd be," she said. "Made me promise I wouldn't tell you he'd been here. I think he wants to surprise you. I'll bet you didn't even know he was downtown, did you?"

Veronika shook her head slowly. "No . . . no, I didn't."

"Good-looking, too," she said. There was disapproval in her voice. Maybe girls who walked around with shaggy hair and shiny faces didn't deserve to marry handsome men. "You're lucky."

Suddenly, Veronika's brow cleared. Klaus, the seducer of many, in pursuit of his sweater. She smiled. "I suppose he is, if you like the type," she said. "Sort of—"

"All dark and brooding," interrupted the receptionist. She grinned. "Men like that give me shivers down my back."

"Dark and brooding?" Nikki pushed some bills into the little jars on the counter marked with the names of lesser personnel in the establishment and, puzzled, went out the door. You *might* call his soft brown hair dark, she supposed, though it would be a strange description of it, but anything less brooding than Klaus Leitner she couldn't imagine. Besides, how did Klaus know where she was? She stepped onto the sidewalk and looked up and down, searching for her cousin. Not a sign of him. If he had been into that establishment, he hadn't bothered waiting. She shrugged and headed for the museum.

CHAPTER 11

Sanders leaned on Harriet's doorbell. No response. He rang again. Nothing. He raised his fist, hit the door, and stumbled forward as it swung open under the force of his blow. Now he stopped, feeling for the reassuring bulk of his pistol. He listened, motionless, his eyes fixed on the staircase for any sign of movement. Nothing. He stepped across the patch of light flooding in behind him and quietly pulled the door shut after him. He padded silently through the ground floor. Bedroom, darkroom. All empty, all neat and undisturbed, except for a few pieces of clothing draped over a chair and on the bed. Up half a flight, the bathroom was empty. He moved up the staircase without a sound, pausing when his head reached floor level to check the second floor. No one. Even the dust curls were undisturbed. Bloody Harriet, in addition to driving him mad for two days, had walked out for her lunch date with that murdering brat Nikki and left her front door open. He headed for the refrigerator, helped himself to a beer, sat down in her most comfortable chair, and stared out onto the deck, letting his mind roam where it would.

Harriet frowned as she parked behind an anonymous-looking blue car. It had to belong to John. With his usual arrogance, he had abandoned it a foot from the curb right in front of her door, blocking access to her driveway. Unsure whether she was more annoyed or amused, she looked up and down the street to see where he was lurking, ready to pounce, but he must have found waiting too boring and gone off for coffee. Bastard. Now thoroughly irritated, she flicked her hair out of her eyes and began to pile equipment onto the sidewalk. It had already been a frustrating day. She had awakened at nine o'clock that morning in her motel room, looked at her watch, and panicked, positive that she would never get that damn shoot finished today. Everything she had left to do needed morning sun; the project would be a washout after eleven-thirty. She had exhausted herself working well into the night, doing the south and west faces before sunset and then tackling the interior shots of the model suite. She had spent hours shifting enormous pieces of hideous furniture out of her way. But when she had twitched aside the heavy curtains that had allowed her to sleep so late, she saw that the weather had changed. It was raining. She had packed up her gear, eaten breakfast, and headed back to Toronto.

The door opened before she put her key in the lock, and she jumped back, startled. "You sure take a helluva lot of gear with you when you go to lunch, don't you?" said Sanders.

"I haven't been to lunch," she said coldly. "I've been to Orillia."

"Orillia! What in hell were you doing there?" he asked. "And you could have told me you were going. I've been killing myself trying to find you."

"Do you mind if we hold this conversation inside?" she asked, making a futile attempt to push by him.

"Sorry," he mumbled, and reached down to pick up her overnight bag and camera case. She followed with knapsack, tripod, lens case, and cooler.

"Get me a beer," she said, relenting slightly, and headed into the bathroom, "and then I'll tell you all about it. It's very mean and petty. Not the kind of thing you'd want to tell someone whose opinion of you means anything."

"Well, there you have it," said Harriet, settling herself a few minutes later into a corner of the couch with a glass of beer and some crackers. "I took off because I couldn't stand giving any more help and comfort to someone who really needs it. I told you it was mean and petty."

"But why you?" asked Sanders. "That's what I can't understand. I would have thought you'd be the last person in the world she'd go to for help *or* advice."

"What in hell do you mean by that?" asked Harriet, affronted. "Oh, I see. You mean, because of you. Us. Well, I don't think she actually realizes that I . . . that we . . . are whatever we are," she finished lamely. "I don't believe I ever mentioned it. After all, she's only really interested in her own problems at the moment. She never asked me about mine. And if you think about it, the only time she's seen us together we didn't exactly fly into each other's arms, you know."

"Typical," muttered Sanders, ignoring the last comment. "Selfish, spoiled brat. So you decided to take off."

Harriet nodded. "It was very last minute. I just bolted without telling anyone."

"And without closing your door," said Sanders. He had walked around behind the couch and was staring out at the deck as he spoke. "I hate to keep preaching at you, but for chrissake, Harriet," he said, and turned back to the room, "you do take awful chances."

Harriet stopped herself in the middle of a slow stretch. "What do you mean? I checked that door as I was leaving. I always do. It was locked." She dug her back into a pillow propped against the armrest of the couch and drew her knees up to her chest, resting her chin on them and looking sideways over at Sanders. "And you can't resist preaching. It's part of the very fabric of your soul." She tossed that off with a fleeting grin. "Anyway, did you really find it open?"

He nodded.

"Damn. I wondered how you managed to get in, but it didn't seem tactful to ask." She frowned, rescued her drink from the floor, and took a sip. "Must have been the land-lord," she said at last. "He comes in every once in a while, and he's careless as hell. If you look around, you'll probably find a greasy tap he tried to fix, or something like that. And he'll turn up tonight to tell me all about it. He's not a great plumber, but he's a great explainer. He's the reason I have a chain for the door." She pulled her legs up closer to her. "And would you stop looming around all over the place? Come and sit down."

Sanders looked down at his long legs as if he'd never noticed them before. "Looming?" he said, and walked over to the couch. He threw himself down on it, head back, legs straight out in front, and yawned. "Has he done this before?"

"Mmm," said Harriet. "But he's stopped trying it while I'm home. In my bleakest moments I have an awful feeling he creeps around looking for love letters or pawing through my underwear or something like that. But he's probably just checking that my housekeeping is up to standard. I must speak to him about the door, though. That really is too much." She bent forward and stretched an arm along the back of the couch. "Anyway, what's wrong with you? Feeling sick?"

Her hair swung forward and brushed against his hand in thousands of searing fiery sparks. He held himself very still. "No," he said at last.

She pulled her head back. "I see. Then I suppose that look on your face means you're angry," she snapped. "Furious because I went off to work without asking permission, is that it? And I'm not supposed to do that. Would you call and ask me if you could go off and poke around looking for an ax murderer?" The words crackled with anger.

"It's not that . . ." he started.

"Well, then, what in hell is it?"

"It was the—" He stopped, unable to say it, acutely conscious that Harriet's body had stiffened with resentment beside him. "It was the—" Suddenly he started to laugh, deep wrenching gasps of laughter.

"What in the name of God—" Harriet started to speak and stopped again, looking at him in amazement.

He took a deep breath and tried again. "It was the answering machine," he said finally.

"The answering machine," said Harriet, completely mystified.

"That goddamn message on your answering machine," he said, still laughing. "You have to change it. It's too damn cute, and there's nothing worse than cute when you're in a rage. And I was in a rage." She stared at him, and he began to laugh again. "Oh, Harriet," he said, reaching for her and pulling her forward onto her knees beside him. "I am so goddamn glad to see you again." He put a hand through her hair, drew her close, kissed her, and then cradled her face in his shoulder. "How in hell do we get into these ridiculous arguments?"

"They're always your fault, you know," she murmured, and twisted herself gently sideways until she was in his lap.

His hands slipped under her shirt and ran over the soft skin of her breasts, her shoulders, and down her back; she pressed herself up against him with an urgency that twisted his gut and dizzied him. He pulled back and looked at her, touching a finger to her lips as they parted in the beginnings of a question. "Shh," he said. "Is the chain on the door?"

"I'll check on the way to the bedroom," she answered, her voice growing hoarse and faint.

Veronika stood on the broad pavement where the Royal Ontario Museum rose like a vaguely Romanesque fortress and looked around for Harriet. All around her there was a sense of things closing down. The last orange school bus was pulling away from the curb, and the sellers of hot chestnuts and popcorn and small toys on sticks were rearranging their wares, preparing to pack up for the day. She hesitated. Harriet was probably waiting for her inside; there was little point in standing out here. She moved cautiously in her slippery new shoes up the wide stone steps and into the vast lobby.

She looked around. A couple of security guards were

chatting near the admissions booth; two women with a scholarly air strolled past her up the main staircase. No Harriet. She paid her admission fee and wandered into the museum shop to pass the time. Stationing herself in the midst of a collection of terra-cotta reproductions—horses, amphorae, odd-looking beasts and birds—she began to examine each one, methodically checking the descriptions, reading the prices, from time to time looking up through the glass walls in the direction of the admissions booth.

Harriet lay sprawled on her stomach, her head perched comfortably on Sanders's shoulder, one leg tossed over his. "If you're not careful," she said, "I could go to sleep like this."

He lifted her hair out of her eyes and tossed it back, then patted her affectionately on the hip. "I should be at work," he said. "I have no reason at all for being here. It's not even my lunch hour."

"Do they know you're here?"

"Not even that," he said, running his index finger down her backbone for the pleasure of feeling her writhe sleepily against his naked side. "And they can bloody well get on without me."

The telephone rang. "So that isn't for you?" asked Harriet.

He reached over for it. "Leave it," she said, touching his arm. "The machine is still on. We don't have to answer it."

"The hell it is," he said. "Your machine answers on the third ring. I should know. I've listened to it often enough for the past two days."

"Hell," said Harriet, struggling up to a sitting position. "You're right." She reached over and snatched up the receiver, trailing the cold cord over Sanders's chest. She listened for the space of five seconds and snarled, "No." She handed him the receiver and curled up beside him.

"Who was that? Or is it confidential?" he asked, and winced at the hurt vibrating ever so slightly in his words.

"Very confidential," said Harriet, allowing her voice to

drop five tones. "I have this lover," she said. "A girl named Sheila. When she calls, she asks me if I need a new furnace, and if I say no, then— Hey!"

Sanders had grabbed his pillow and was waving it menacingly over her head. "You can be the most irritating, supercilious— "

"My, my, Officer. Such big words." She threw herself up against him and wrapped her arms and legs around him. "I'm cold," she complained. "You have allowed the temperature of the room to drop."

"And at least Sheila—"

"—would have brought a new furnace over. Anyway, there must be hot water. I'd better take a shower," added Harriet. "Or you'll never get back to work. Come and soap my back."

Don Walker slouched in his chair in the interrogation room and maintained a stubborn silence. He had looked up briefly when his lawyer entered the room; but Charlie Mitchell's arrival did nothing to loosen his tongue. It just made him look desperately in Mitchell's direction before refusing to answer. Charlie, meanwhile, ignored his client; he yawned and listened to the questions posed first by Volchek and then, fifteen or twenty minutes later, by Dubinsky, who had also wandered into the room.

Finally, Mitchell raised a hand to stop the questioning, yawned again, and spoke in bored tones: "Could I have a few minutes with my client? I don't think he's quite grasped the situation."

"Sure," said Dubinsky. "Be our guest. Maybe you can talk some sense into him."

It was more a lecture than a conference. Charlie Mitchell's sibilant hiss poured into his client's ear without interruption for ten minutes. From time to time, Walker would nod in miserable agreement and then hunch farther down in his chair. By the time Charlie was finished, Walker seemed to have lost at least half his substance and to be in danger of collapsing into himself, melting into a gray puddle on the chair.

"My client," said Charlie at last, "has one or two things to say that could be of interest to you. But he would like to know first if the Crown is willing to take his helpfulness into consideration when it comes to the laying of charges or the drafting of a sentencing report."

"Just a minute," said Volchek, and disappeared. The men left in the room sat or stood and stared everywhere but at each other until he finally returned. "Crown wants to know are we talking a straight 'guilty' plea on all counts?"

"Could be," said Mitchell, calmly ignoring his client's whisper of protest.

"You've got it. Degree of mitigation depends on degree of helpfulness."

"What does that mean?" asked Walker suspiciously.

"The more you talk, the less you get," said his lawyer. "So let's get going. With luck you can talk it down to two years less a day. Otherwise . . ."

"Uh, yeah," said Walker. "So, what do you guys want to know?"

"Let's start with the robberies," prompted Volchek. "And we can go on from there."

Don rearranged his rodentlike features into an expression of injured innocence and produced his formal disavowal of responsibility. "Yeah, well, I just followed along, like. It wasn't my idea."

"But they couldn't have done them without you, could they, Don?" said Volchek in a silky tone. "You were the one who knew how to get through the security systems."

"Uh, yeah, maybe. See, when you're installing a system, it really costs to make it break-in proof. Like in a house, I mean. With all kinds of windows in stupid places and crap like that. So when someone says to me that no one's gonna try to get in through that little window over the garage, say, it's too small, and it's going to cost a lot more to take the wiring over there, I say okay, and we don't do it, and then we use that window to get in. We're all pretty skinny guys. Then maybe we turn off the system and break a window somewhere else so it looks like *they* forgot to turn the alarm on. You'd be surprised how many people forget to turn on their alarms, anyway." Don was beginning to expand as he worked his way into his narrative. "Rich, stupid assholes."

"What about the house on Rosefall Road?"

"Oh, them," he said dismissively. "They had the whole house done. A fucking cat couldn't have got in there. They had a lot of valuable stuff, I guess. I told those guys not to try that house," he added with an air of righteousness. "And I didn't want to have anything to do with it. I wasn't in on all the jobs, you know. I might've told them how to get in and stuff like that, but I wasn't there." Little beads of sweat were beginning to form on his temples and across his hairline.

"So who ran things if it wasn't you?" asked Volchek.

"It sure as hell wasn't me," said Walker with too much emphasis. "It was the buru."

"The what?" said Dubinsky, who was taking rapid notes as Walker spoke.

"The buru. It means the boss. In their language. They all called him that."

"How do you spell that?" asked Dubinsky. "Buru." Walker shrugged his shoulders. Spelling wasn't part of his bargain with the Crown. "And what language are we talking about anyway?"

"Oh . . . Basque," said Walker. "They all spoke Basque."

"What's that?" asked Dubinsky, looking around.

The various police officers in the room looked at each other. "'It's kind of like Spanish, I think," said Volchek, finally, with more goodwill than accuracy.

"Yeah, kind of," said Walker. "That's where they're from. Spain. Anyway, the buru—he's this kid, really smart kid. Reads all the time. Philosophy and stuff like that. He figured out what to do. And when. And he knew the guy who fenced it all for us."

"And who's that, Walker?" asked Volchek softly. "Where

did you get rid of it all? We were wondering about that. And we were wondering just where we could find it, too. It's gonna make things a lot easier on you when we find all the goods."

A line of sweat trickled down the side of Walker's face. "I don't know what happened to it." Real anguish shook his voice. "We took it to the buru, and he stored it at this house he had until he could get to the fence. And I never knew where the house was, so there's no use asking me," he added vehemently. "I was only inside it once, when we had to pick up a vanload of stuff, and Carlos and me, we were riding in the back of the van and never saw where we were going. And it was dark out. But it was a really big, new-looking house, like in Thornhill or Aurora. Places like that. You could hear all these animals around and stuff. It was in the country, sort of. That's all I know about it." More sweat gathered on his forehead. "Then he got rid of it in New York, or at least in the States somewhere. I think New York. But listen, I never even saw the guy."

"And does the buru, the boss, have a name?"

"Not that I know," said Walker. "No one ever said his name."

"How about an address?"

Walker shrugged.

"So," said Dubinsky, "who shot Constable Underhill? You, Walker?"

"Listen, I never killed no one." His hand jerked spasmodically, and he grasped it tightly with the other one. "Especially not a cop. You gotta be crazy to do that. I wasn't even there that night. I was working. I told you, I never liked that house. I wouldn't have gone if I could. You guys already asked me about that weeks ago. And you checked it out. You go look at your records." His voice began to rise in pitch, and he paused to pull himself back in control. "I was working. Carlos would've done that. He's crazy. Real crazy. I dunno, I think he saw too many Rambo movies or something. He can't keep his hands off of a gun. But I dunno who did it, because when they were talking about it, it was in goddamn Basque, and I never knew what they were saying. But it must have been Carlos. It can't have been Manu. Jesus, he's so scared, if he saw a gun, he'd piss himself." Walker paused uneasily for a moment as he remembered Manu's knife, but he shoved the humiliating picture back into the deepest recesses of his brain. "It must have been Carlos."

"And Mrs. Wilkinson?"

"I wasn't there neither. You guys checked me out on that one, too. I was clean. I was in on a game that went on all night."

"So where did you get her ring, Walker? Someone mail it to you?"

There was a panic-stricken pause. "Manu took it," he blurted finally. "And asked me to raise money on it. He thought he'd make people too suspicious. With him having an accent, you know."

"So tell us about this, uh, Manny. Is that his name?" said Dubinsky.

"Yeah. Something like that. He's a Basque. Real patriotic," he added, remembering the knife once more. "He's kinda tall, skinny, not real dark, but he's got this long black hair. And a mustache. One of those little ones. And he's twitchy as hell."

"And Carlos? What does he look like?"

"I dunno. Nothing special. He's shorter than Manu. And he's got black hair. And a tan. I guess he's about thirty, maybe." Walker was beginning to sweat profusely.

"And where do we find these guys?" asked Dubinsky softly. "Because unless we can find them, your story isn't worth a pinch of shit. Or two days off a sentence. Think about it, Walker. Armed robbery. Murder. Very big words. Long words. Fifteen, twenty, twenty-five years long."

"Christ," muttered Walker. He seemed to be counting. "I don't know where the fence lived. I think he was an American or something. And the other guys . . ." His eyes shifted sideways in panic, and Dubinsky jotted an extra note on his page. "We used to meet in an apartment on Lippincott Street, a third-floor apartment. It was 1872 Lippincott Street. I think Manu and Carlos lived there. And look, you gotta give me protection. These guys aren't just stealing stuff. They're terrorists. They don't give a damn what happens to anyone; they'll have me killed. Tortured to death." By now the sweat was pouring off Walker's face and collecting in unpleasant pools around his flannelette shirt.

Veronika put down the last piece of pottery in the museum shop and walked over to the door. The lobby was even quieter than it had been when she entered, almost deserted except for two security guards chatting to a third man, dark haired and handsome, with an ominously familiar air. And that meant it was time she left for Munich. When security guards and their friends in a foreign city start to look familiar, it is time to go.

She wandered back inside the shop and drifted over to the jewelry counter. Her eye was caught by a medallion, enamel on copper, in brilliant greens and the amethyst of her new tweed suit, which depicted a ferocious bird with red garnet eyes. "How much is this?" she called to the shop assistant, who was wandering about in a desultory fashion, tidying up piles of sweatshirts and stacking boxes that had been knocked over.

"The copper medallion?" she answered, pausing to put down the boxes in her hand. "Two hundred. No, sorry. Two hundred and ten. That's because the garnets—"

"I'll take it," said Veronika. "Don't wrap it up. I'll wear it. Here," she said, dropping a pile of bills on the counter. "I just want to see if my friend has arrived. I'll be back for the medallion and my change in a second."

But the lobby remained deserted except for the bored-looking staff and two little girls clutching sketch pads who came giggling down the broad staircase, followed more slowly by a weary-looking mother. For the first time, it occurred to

Veronika that Harriet might not have found her message on the machine yet, might not have remembered that she had promised to visit the museum with her today. She had promised, hadn't she? Nikki tried to remember exactly what had been said, but the words were blocked out by the haze of exhaustion and sorrow that lingered just below her excitement. Tears sprang to her eyes.

"Miss? Oh, miss?" said a tired voice behind her. "Your medallion. And your change. Are you sure you don't want a box?"

"No," she said abruptly, and winced at her discourtesy. "This is fine. Thank you very much."

She fastened the heavy piece of jewelry around her neck and looked at her watch. It was past four-thirty. Now that she was here, it would be silly to leave without looking at the exhibits. Biting her lip to hold back the tears, she returned to the admissions booth. "Where are the Greek and Roman collections?" she asked.

The attendant looked up from her novel, yawning. "Third floor at the back."

"If my friend comes in and asks for me, could you say I'm up there?"

"Sure," she replied. "What name—"

But Veronika was already gone, running up the staircase.

Carlos moved from the coat-check counter where he had been half-leaning, half-sitting, and raised a farewell hand at the woman seated there. "See you later, Bettina," he said. "I'd better go see if I can round up the boss. Don't work too hard."

"Never fear," she said, and plucked her novel out from a carton on the rack beside her.

Carlos strolled over to the telephone and dropped a quarter in the slot. After a brief murmured conversation he hung up and started up the staircase in long, easy strides.

Veronika stopped at the head of the stairs to catch her breath. She was offered a choice at this point between Truth and Beauty on her right, and the Classical World on the left. "Truth and Beauty later," she said firmly, and plunged into the other corridor.

Roman pottery and statuary took up the first gallery, all fascinating, no doubt, but she found that she could not force herself to stop long enough to look at anything. She walked rapidly along, unsettled at being in the center of a huge space where all the sight lines were broken up by pillars and false walls. She shivered. She shouldn't have come here alone. Not now. This was worse than being alone in her mother's house, with her mother's ghost murmuring sorrowfully no matter where she went. Here there were thousands of ghosts sighing and shuffling along the marble floors. And invisible footsteps, always near her, belonging to no one.

The ambient lighting became darker as she penetrated farther into the classical exhibits, until she turned a corner and stopped, almost blinded by the sudden brilliance. To her left, a stone bridge crossed a vast, light-filled space in the center of the building. She walked across it, giddy from a sense of floating precariously three stories above the ground, but the door at the other end of the bridge was locked, and she turned back to the dark enclosure of the exhibit area.

Right in front of her was the Etruscan collection, housed in its own set of walls, leaned on by the Greeks from one side and the Romans from the other. And a strange device, the gentle powdery green of old copper, hung on the wall directly before her eyes, in the center of the collection. Some long-dead Etruscan artisan with a malevolent sense of humor had decorated its handle prettily in graceful spirals; and then he had finished it in a circle out of which protruded half a dozen or more curving spikes, each one viciously long and sharp. Veronika stared at it, unable to turn her eyes away. She moved forward toward the monstrous thing, drawn by curiosity and grim fascination, until she could read the neat card beneath it. "Etruscan meat hook," it said primly, "or *kreaga*." Her stomach turned; she gagged and turned rapidly to study a large amphora, decorated with the more disciplined swirling designs that she associated with the Etruscans, breathing deeply until her stomach calmed.

She turned to the case opposite the amphora and conscientiously studied each vase, each utensil, each painted pot, as if her life depended on it, finally letting her gaze drift over the passageway, out onto the stone bridge, where there was light and an absence of nightmarish visions. But in a cloistered passageway on the other side of the atrium, leaning on another stone parapet, watching her, was the man, the dark-haired man with large dark eyes, whom she had seen in the lobby. And suddenly the description of her "husband," the person who had asked after her at the hairdresser's, leapt into her mind.

"For God's sake, Veronika," she said aloud in the empty room. "Don't be stupid. The man probably works here. And there are thousands of men in this city with dark hair and eyes. As many as there are in Munich." Resolutely, she turned to her right and headed for classical Greece. The exhibit was much more brightly lit than the Etruscan gallery had been, and the pale statuary gleamed reassuringly in the artificial day. She stopped in front of a collection of copper pans from Grecian south Italy, transfixed between amusement and admiration. The handle of each one consisted of a delectable nude male, lying faceup, toes pointed, arms stretching panward. Now, if reproductions of those were available in the museum shop, she thought with a grin, they would be worth paying for. Somewhat cheered, she wandered without noticing where she was going through the darkened galleries behind the Etruscans.

"Would you like a beer?" asked Harriet. She was walking around the living room, energetically drying her hair with a large purple towel.

Sanders yawned. "Coffee is more like it. I have to do something useful before I fall asleep."

"You seemed useful enough to me," she hissed, and bumped

him out of her way with a swing of her hip as she headed for the stove to make the coffee. "But if you want to be genuinely handy, you might check the answering machine and see why it isn't working." She turned on the tap to fill the coffeepot and pointed over to her desk with one foot to indicate where the thing lived.

"First of all, it isn't on," said Sanders in a slightly muffled tone as he bent over the desk. "And secondly, you seem to have wrenched the top off in one of your fits of temper. In addition, there aren't any tapes in it. And," he said, turning around and holding up a long gray wire, "it isn't plugged in."

"What?" said Harriet as she flicked the heat on under the coffee and turned to look. "What in hell have you done with it?"

"Me? I haven't done anything. Come and look at it. Do you think your landlord might have been messing around with it?"

Harriet looked down at the gaping wound in the top of the machine. "Look, he's not the world's handiest guy, but he wouldn't have done that." She frowned and turned toward Sanders. "I don't like this. I left that machine in perfect order, on. I even went back and checked as I was leaving. Just the way I double-checked that front door. Why would someone break in and rip apart my answering machine? I mean, look around you. Absolutely everything else in here is exactly the way I left it." She sat down and looked around the room with an intensity of gaze that totally excluded him.

He watched her eyes move purposefully from deck, to kitchen, to desk, and finally, to the answering machine. Then she looked down the stairs, paused and nodded. She dropped her head onto the chair back and stared up at the ceiling; after a moment she closed her eyes. He sat down on the couch and waited impatiently for her to return her attention to him.

Just as he was deciding that she must have fallen asleep, she spoke with an irritating lack of relevance. "What did you mean by that crack about taking a lot of stuff to lunch?"

"What in hell has that to do with anything?" asked Sanders, and shook his head. "Leitner told me you were having lunch with Nikki. So I came over to wait for you to get back."

"Why did he say that?"

"Presumably because she told him she was having lunch with you," said Sanders.

"Omigod," said Harriet. "Did I tell Nikki I'd have lunch with her today?" The towel dropped off her head, and a strand of wet hair fell onto her lip. She picked it up and began to twirl it around nervously. "Just let me call her. Get yourself some coffee, and some for me too, please."

Sanders found himself slamming cupboard doors and running water to prevent himself from listening to Harriet's murmured words. He was just heading for the sliding door onto the deck when she hung up and walked over. "She isn't home, John. She hasn't been home since this morning, apparently. And she did tell Klaus that she was having lunch with me."

"Did you say you were going to have lunch with her?"

"Of course not! At least I don't think so." Harriet shook her head impatiently. "Maybe I did, just to calm her down and get rid of her. I was hellishly unpleasant to her yesterday. Damn that girl! No matter what happens, she always leaves me feeling guilty."

Veronika suddenly realized that for the last ten minutes she had been staring at the same collection of pottery without even seeing it. Another wave of exhaustion and sudden nausea swept over her; she stretched and took a deep breath. Then, suddenly, reflected off a sheet of glass, she saw the dark-haired man again. And now not in reflection but distorted through two sets of glass cases. His head moved as he searched the room, slowly, methodically. She stepped back farther into the darkness, and when she raised her eyes again, he had disappeared. She looked frantically around, her view blocked by pillars and displays and heartlessly beautiful statues. He was nowhere.

Suddenly, there he was, in front of the pans she had laughed at minutes before, looking not at them but through the cases, searching.

She turned, began to run, and then stopped in a panic. Her footsteps resounded on the stone floor, each one giving away her location. She kicked off her little shoes and skidded around the next exhibit, aware of a blur of statues on her right and blank temporary walls everywhere else. Now she could hear footsteps behind her, easy, rapid, confident footsteps. She ducked behind a wall and found herself surrounded by three more walls. She whirled around. She was facing a mural in beige and burnt umber depicting a maze of hideous complexity. It towered over her, mocking her confusion. Horrified, she turned and ran toward what she hoped would be the front of the building, slipping on the floors in her stocking feet, once careening off a display case, once hurtling off the fragile-looking false wall of the Egyptian exhibit area and discovering it to be solid enough to hurt. Suddenly, in front of her, there was bright light coming from another open area. One more accessible to the public, she prayed. She ran toward it and with a sob of relief saw an escalator. The metal grillwork of the steps snatched painfully at her stockinged feet, but she kept running until she reached the second-floor landing. As she skidded across it to get on the escalator again, she stopped dead. At the bottom, looking up at her with a terrifying, gentle smile, was the handsome face of a man she knew, waiting for her as surely as the man behind her was chasing her. She reversed and bolted into the exhibit area on the second floor.

Veronika was aware of cases and cases of animals and birds; she brushed by one small girl, but otherwise, no living being who could be of any help. Ahead of her, past glassed-in forests and snarling stuffed predators, an exit sign glowed. Light-years away. As she ran toward it, on her left she saw an opening to an area of blackness and plunged in, panting. Velvety darkness enveloped her, and she leaned against the wall to catch her breath.

She was in a simulation of a cave, dark, with grottoes carved into the walls, some tiny, some vast enough to hold a party in. Pale illumination filtered down into them, allowing the visitor to see coiled figures of snakes and small mammals and various crustaceans sheltering in the rocky configuration. Above her head bats hung peacefully from the ceiling, and she felt safe. He would think she had left by the emergency exit and would follow. When he had gone, she would creep out and go down the main stairs again. In the distance she could hear the ringing of a bell. Closing time. Security guards would come around soon to clear out loiterers; they would protect her. She pressed herself against the wall and started to edge a little deeper into the cave.

She heard a voice in the distance. "Just a *minute*, Mummy. I'm going in the bat cave one more time. I'll meet you at the top of the stairs." Veronika began to move forward toward the voice. Then, suddenly, out of the darkness, a powerful hand seized her arm; her head jerked to one side with the force of a blow to the temple.

Carlos looked down at the crumpled girl. He was mildly surprised to discover that she was still breathing. Tough skull. He dropped the cosh into his pocket, reached into his jacket, and took out a thin knife. A sharp little voice from close by said, "*Wait*! I said I was coming right out." He grabbed the limp Veronika by the hair, pulled back her head far enough to get his hand under her face, and made a rapid slashing movement. With satisfaction that lasted only a split second, he felt the familiar sensation of silent yielding flesh under his knife. Suddenly, the weapon caught noisily in something metal and wrenched itself out of his grip. Before he realized what had happened, his fingers were sliding through a pool of warm, sticky blood.

"Shit," he muttered, and picked her up. He tumbled her headfirst into a darkened corner of the grotto beside them. She landed with a satisfactory thud. By the time anyone discovered her, he figured, between the knife wound and the head injury, she'd be long dead, anyway.

*　　*　　*

When the little girl was finally chased out of the cave by the security guard doing his check and restored to her mother in the front lobby, she was filled with excitement. "You know, Mummy, I never saw it before, but they have this really realistic body in the cave, too, all crumpled up on the floor of one of the things in the wall. It's creepy. It's even creepier than the snakes. Can we come back tomorrow?"

"That's nice, dear," said her mother vaguely. "Now hold on to my hand before we get into the subway. It's crowded. I don't know what your daddy's going to think when he finds out we're not home yet," she added. "Did you say come back tomorrow? Certainly not. I have to work late tomorrow. Maybe next week. But you must promise not to hide like that again. Mummy was worried."

CHAPTER 12

Constables McNeill and Collins walked back into the room and threw down their coats. Dubinsky looked up at them and scowled. "You could've called in," he said. "Or did you forget how? We were kind of interested in knowing what was going on out there."

McNeill yawned and sat down in the chair beside Dubinsky's desk. "What was the point of calling in? To tell you we found zip all?" He stretched his legs out in front of him. "There was no one home but Grandma and a kid. Grandma doesn't speak any English, Collins here forgot to take a course in whatever the hell language she does speak, and Ma was at work until eleven. At the hospital. Which hospital? Who knows? Anyway, the kid never saw anyone who looked remotely like those two guys, never heard their names, never saw Walker around the house. Nothing."

"Maybe he's lying," said Dubinsky.

"Maybe he is," said McNeill. "You want me to go back and beat it out of him? He looks about ten, skinny, underfed. Just the kind the papers love to get hold of. I could break his arm, maybe. They'd love that. Anyway, we left a guy out there to keep an eye on the house." He sat up and looked around. "I'm going out for something to eat. The inspector back yet?" There was silence. "Where is he, anyway?"

"How in hell should I know?" asked Dubinsky sourly. "Dead. Disappeared. On ten years' leave. You think he ever tells me anything?"

"Well, give him my love when he gets in," said McNeill. "If he does. And tell him I'll be back in fifteen minutes or so." And he heaved himself back up to his feet and stalked out of the room.

"Where does McNeill think he's going?" said a familiar, testy voice. Dubinsky turned his head slowly in the direction of the door and stared impassively at Inspector Sanders. "We need everybody."

"He's just come in from the west end; he's past due for a supper break," said Dubinsky. "And where have you been?"

"All over," he said vaguely. "Actually, I was tracking down some ideas I had in the von Hohenkammer case," he added in a mumble. "Didn't realize how late it was." He sat down and began leafing through reports on his desk. "Anything come in on Milanovich?"

Dubinsky shook his head.

"The girl's disappeared, too," said Sanders. "No one seems to have seen her since this morning. We'd better start looking for her."

"Maybe she's wherever her brother-in-law is," said Dubinsky. "Could be they were planning on running off together on Mummy's money or something. Or then again," he added, "maybe she's at the movies. Or shopping. It's a bit early to panic."

Sanders gave him the look of a man whose best lines have just been stolen and picked up the telephone. He dialed twice, spoke briefly each time, and hung up. He looked at his watch. "Long movie," he said. "Check the airport."

"While you're waiting for that," said Dubinsky with barely concealed sarcasm, "you might be interested in what we got from Walker. He can see a very long stretch in his future, and he's been spilling his guts out to Volchek in there." He pushed some papers over in Sanders's direction; the inspector sighed, picked up his chair, and moved over to Dubinsky's desk.

"What's been done about Walker's accomplices?" asked Sanders with a twinge of guilt in his voice.

"McNeill and Collins went out to the address on Lippincott—nothing. They've left someone there. Volchek is circulating a description. He's sent teams out to the airport, bus depots, and so on. He figures they might be trying to make it back to Spain. If they heard we picked up Walker."

"What do those two guys do?" asked Sanders. "I mean, when they're not breaking into houses. They must have some job or other or they never would have got into the country."

Dubinsky shook his head. "Dunno. No one ever asked him."

"Then send someone to ask him, for God's sake. We might be able to find them that way." But Dubinsky wasn't listening. He had already picked up the phone.

Twenty minutes later, the telephone rang on Dubinsky's desk. He listened, jotted down some notes, muttered briefly, and hung up. "Interesting," he said, looking over at Sanders. "Carlos is a security guard; he used to work for Mid-City, but quit last January or February."

"Too early for Volchek to include him in those people he was running a check on."

"That's right. And the other guy, Manny ... Walker thinks he worked in a restaurant as a waiter, or maybe even a chef. He's not sure."

"Wonderful," said Sanders. "How many thousand restaurants are there in the city?"

"Enough," said Dubinsky. "Enough so that by the time we'd checked them all he could have changed jobs three or four times. Anyway, I'll send Collins out to Mid-City to find out what they have on Carlos."

Harriet opened her refrigerator door and decided that nothing in it was worth the trouble of eating, much less cooking. She grabbed a piece of celery, ran it under the tap, and nibbled at it as she wandered around the apartment. A sick sense of guilt was hovering somewhere around her stomach, and she was trying very hard to isolate it, somehow wrap it up and tuck it away somewhere. It can't have been just that she felt that she had been unpardonably rude to Nikki, could it? Most of the unforgivable things that she had thought had remained silent screams in her head. She had had the tact, surely, to suppress the most obvious signs of her impatience. May she *had* told Veronika she would meet her for lunch, but where? She went out onto the deck and shivered in the cold September wind while she ran through a mental list of all the restaurants she could have possibly suggested. None of them rang a bell.

She walked back in, rubbing her arms briskly against the chill, and decided that perhaps she was suffering from hunger, not guilt. She opened the refrigerator again, looked seriously this time, and finally pulled out a piece of aging cheddar wrapped in plastic. It felt unpromisingly hard, as though it had been drying out in her refrigerator for weeks, but it might just be grillable. She set it down, and it hit the counter with a thud. "Really, Harriet," she muttered, "that cheese isn't just old, it's mummified." She stopped dead. "Good God. The museum. I was supposed to meet her at the museum. This afternoon." She looked at her watch and then walked quickly over to the telephone.

Carlos tucked the yellow parking tag into his pocket and got into his car. In spite of all that had happened this afternoon, he drove with his usual judgment; he couldn't understand the stupidity of people who drew attention to themselves by parading their aggressions on the road. As he wheeled the car neatly into an opening in the traffic on St. Clair, the faint stickiness on the fingers of his right hand caught the steering wheel unpleasantly, and he frowned. He should have been wearing gloves. That was stupid. He wondered where his knife had fallen. Not onto the floor. He'd looked. So he must have kicked it into one of the grottoes, and that meant it might be found today or lie there until the next major renovation of the area. But the whole goddamn scam was coming apart, anyway. It was time to drift on. Before he was connected with it. It should be safe enough back in Arizona. He could work in the antiques store for a few months; that would make his mother happy. Besides, another winter in this place and he was going to crack. Just clean out the papers and things he'd left at Manu's, pick up as much cash as he could get from the fence, pack up his suitcase, and he'd be gone. They'd still owe him plenty, but under the circumstances . . .

He saw the police cruiser almost before he had made the right turn onto the street. He took a deep breath, completed his turn, accelerated very gently, slowed, and turned into a narrow alleyway that provided access to the shabby garages behind each house. Still at the same measured pace, he took another turn between two houses that led him out onto the next block and began a tortuous path back to his own little flat.

Meanwhile, the bored constable in the cruiser jotted down the license number of the car that had driven into the alleyway. On this quiet street of hardworking families, once the sun had set and day shifts were over, there wasn't much activity. He recorded it all.

The clerk at Iberia Airways was doing her best. Yes, a flight had left for Spain over an hour ago. The constable read out the description on the page in front of him, looked up, and smiled hopefully.

She stared at him with an expression that mixed exasperation and amazement. "I'm sorry, sir," she said, "but half the men on the flight could be described like that. Slender, dark haired, brown eyes, and moderately tall. Not young, not old. With a small mustache. You haven't anything else?"

"Well," said the constable unhappily, "his name seems to be Manny or Mano or something like that."

"Manuel?" prompted the clerk hopefully.

"Yeah, that sounds right," said constable. "You got anyone like that on your passenger list?"

"I'm sure we do," muttered the clerk. "Several, in fact. Manuel isn't an unusual name, you know. Here," she said, running her finger down the page. "One, two, uh, no, I remember him, he was just a little kid, and that one was quite elderly, in a wheelchair. Could your person be elderly?" The constable shook his head. "Then"—she flipped over a page—"three. Three men who might fit your description, all named Manuel."

"Then how about someone who looks sort of like him, but shorter. Named Carlos."

She muttered something that, perhaps fortunately for his morale, the constable did not catch. "Not a very helpful description," she snapped. "It covers about every other male on the plane. Including the crew. Dark hair and eyes are fairly common in Spain, you know, sir. And Carlos is about as common a name as Manuel." The constable shrugged his shoulders unhappily. "We'll see what we can do," she added, remembering her obligation to be helpful. "I'll put you in touch with security."

While the harassed team at the airport were plodding through their unenviable task of tracking down two Spaniards with dark hair named Manuel and Carlos, Collins was contemplating throwing the man on evening shift at Mid-City Security Systems in jail for the night. It had taken ten minutes for the man to be convinced that he had to call someone in authority; it had taken twenty minutes for him to locate the relevant telephone lists and, finally, to reach a vice-president, who promised the imminent arrival of someone else with keys to the personnel files. Fifteen minutes after that, a very irritated personnel manager, smelling slightly of scotch, turned up and tried his best to look cooperative.

Harriet was about to slam the telephone down, drive over to the shiny new police building on College Street, and run up and down the halls screaming Sanders's name when she finally got him on the other end of the line. "My God, but you're a hard man to reach, John," she said. "I was beginning to think your story about being a cop was just an elaborate excuse for never being available."

"Sorry," he muttered. "I really do work here. Sometimes, anyway. All hell broke loose while I was over at your place." His voice had dropped so low she was having trouble making out the words.

"So people noticed you were gone, eh? Well, don't fret. This call is legit. I just remembered something about Nikki. I promised to meet her at the museum today, I think. I can't remember if we actually set a time or not, but she may have gone there looking for me."

"The museum? Well, she wouldn't be there now, would she?" He looked at his watch. "It's eight o'clock. When does it close?"

"I'm not sure," said Harriet. "Some nights it stays open late, I suppose. Do you want me to call?"

"No. Official business. I'll call you when I know something. But I wouldn't count on anything. She won't still be there, even if she did go to meet you." Sanders cut the connection and looked up.

"Now what?" said Dubinsky.

"It seems the von Hohenkammer girl might have gone to the museum this afternoon. We'd better put someone on it."

"Listen, she's been gone less than twelve hours. She's not a five-year-old kid," protested Dubinsky.

"Maybe not. But she's still a possible suspect in a murder case. And an essential witness," he snapped. "I'd like to keep tabs on her. Get someone to call the museum." He scribbled down the relevant information.

"Here," he said. "You, what's your name?" A blond young man who was lounging uneasily against a desk in the middle of the noise and confusion jumped and reddened slightly.

"Lucas, sir. Rob Lucas. I was sent over in case—"

"Right. You might as well beat your head against this one and find out what it feels like. Call the museum and ask if Veronika von Hohenkammer, five foot three—"

"I know what she looks like, sir," he interrupted.

"Oh, keen, eh? Then find out if she was there this afternoon and when she left." He handed him the piece of paper with his indecipherable scrawl on it. The telephone rang again, and this time Dubinsky reached over and picked it up. "It's Collins," he said, looking over at Sanders. "He's got something." Dubinsky took neat and rapid notes for a minute or two. "Great," he said. "Bring me back a corned beef on rye." He glanced up, caught Sanders's signal, and added: "Two corned beef on rye."

"What's he got? Besides food," said Sanders.

"Ah, he has a name, address, and previous employer for Carlos. Very interesting, too."

"Well, for chrissake, don't just sit there grinning. What in hell did he find out?"

"His name is Carlos Ramírez. He gave as a reference his previous employer. He used to work at the Royal Ontario Museum as a security guard. Coincidental, eh? And his address was 142 Palmerston Avenue. That sounded familiar to me. Didn't a witness in this case live on Palmerston?" Dubinsky reached for the file.

"Call Volchek and find out," said Sanders. "It's faster."

"Mrs. Maria Figuerao," said McNeill from his position a couple of desks away. "I interviewed her; 142 Palmerston Avenue. Same number as my sister's house in Oshawa, different street name. I noticed it at the time. She was the owner of the house where Walker spent the whole night playing cards when Mrs. Wilkinson was getting killed. And what do you want to bet that Volchek's other two witnesses are our disappearing Spaniards?"

"Basques," said Dubinsky. "That's what Walker called them."

"Basques?" said Sanders. "You didn't say they were Basques."

"Volchek said it was all the same thing," said Dubinsky. "It seemed easier to call them Spaniards. I mean, they are Spaniards, aren't they?"

"Sort of," said Sanders, reaching for the phone.

*   *   *

Ten minutes later, the tired and irritated clerk behind the desk at Iberia Airways swore in exasperation as the same young police constable, looking considerably less lively this time, walked over to her. "Now what?" she said. The obligatory smile refused to emerge.

"We have some more information on those two men I was asking you about before." She reached for a piece of paper, just in case. "The name of the second man is Carlos Ramírez."

She ran her pencil down the passenger list rapidly. "No. No Carlos Ramírez."

"And apparently these two men are Basque." He said the word with a certain hesitation. "Does that make a difference?"

There was a long pause as she continued to stare at the list. Then she looked up at him and smiled very sweetly. "Constable, if you were looking for a Canadian named . . . oh, let's say John or Bill . . . and all you knew was that he was six feet tall, wouldn't it be helpful to find out he had purple hair and spoke only Swedish?"

It took a few seconds for the sarcasm to penetrate. The constable reddened.

"Yes, Constable, it makes a difference. A hell of a difference. I will inform security. They will be *very* interested." As she reached for the phone, she smiled again. "And you can be damned sure his name isn't Carlos Ramírez, either."

"Are you certain of this?" Sanders asked. He was staring down at the piece of paper that Rob Lucas had just put in front of him.

"Yes, sir. I talked to three of the six people who were on duty in the public areas of the museum this afternoon. The guards didn't notice her, but the woman at the admissions desk certainly did. And so did the woman in the gift shop. She bought an expensive bronze medallion and paid for it in cash. Quite late in the afternoon. She was apparently waiting for a friend and kept looking out the windows of the shop for her. And according to the woman selling tickets, she wanted to know where the Greek and Roman collections were and asked her to direct her friend there when she came. But she didn't give a name. The description fits."

"And no one saw her leave."

"That's right. No one. It didn't strike them at the time, but they noticed it when I asked. The guards had done a check, chased one little girl out of the bat cave—kids always hang around the bat cave—but saw no one who fit the description of Miss von Hohenkammer loitering about."

"Could she have gone out a back door?"

"Only with a key. Otherwise, she would have set off the alarms. When I asked if she could have slipped out when one of the staff were leaving, they admitted that it was possible. But not likely."

Sanders stared down at the neatly written notes. "What do you know about the Basques, Constable?" he asked.

"The Basques?" said Lucas, momentarily startled. "Spanish or French Basques, sir?"

"Spanish. No, both."

"A bit. They speak a non-Indo-European language which is very difficult for non-Basques to learn. And let's see, they've been fighting for their independence from France and Spain for centuries. And the Spaniards feel about the ETA—that's the Basque separatist organization—about the same way that Margaret Thatcher feels about the IRA. There are some excellent Basque restaurants in town if you're interested—Basque cooking is very good—and quite a few Basques emigrated from Spain to the American Southwest. What else did you want to know?"

"That'll do. Where in hell did you get all that from?"

"A history course I did. I wrote an essay on independence movements in the Iberian Peninsula. Want to know something about Catalonia?"

Sanders glared. "No thanks. Telephone the people at the

museum and tell them we'll be there in ten minutes. Get a car, Constable. I'll meet you out in front."

"Do you know exactly where she would have been in the museum? What sections?" asked Sanders into the telephone.

"Greek, I suppose," said Harriet. "That was what she was interested in. Did she go to the museum?"

"Oh, she went, all right. And no one saw her leave. Which means there's an outside chance that she still might be there. I'm going to see if I can find her now."

"I'll come with you," said Harriet firmly. "I can help you search for her. And if she's there and hiding for some reason—my God, but that sounds bizarre, doesn't it?—she might come out if I'm there." Harriet paused in wonder. "I never realized she was that squirrelly."

"Squirrelly?"

"If she's hiding in the museum, she's squirrelly, let me tell you. Normal women don't do things like that. I'll meet you in front of the building."

The crowd that met in the lobby of the Royal Ontario Museum looked small and insignificant, dwarfed by the shadowy heights of the totem pole that rose almost to the ceiling three floors above and by the curling staircases that surrounded it. Their feet echoed on the marble floor, and Harriet shivered. Power, primitive and menacing, seemed to emanate from the darkness around that great stolen symbol, and in spite of the imposing bulk of five police officers standing near her, she felt uneasy.

Sanders was in low-voiced conversation with the security guards and two additional administration people, while Harriet tried to avoid looking at the fierce totemic figures carved in wood beside her. She gasped, startled, at the sound of his voice in her ear. "We'll do the public areas with Mr. Arkwright here," he said, nodding at one of the university students who work as guards during the night. "The rest of the guards and Collins and McNeill will do the areas that are closed to the public." Two of the police officers walked over to the knot of museum security officials. "We'll start on the third floor. Lucas, you come with us, and you," he said to the last two officers, "stay down here and make sure our pigeon doesn't fly out the front door unnoticed."

Mr. Arkwright made an admirable guide. He took them carefully through every section of the third floor that a member of the public could possibly penetrate, accompanying the search with scandalous and funny tales of oddities he, or somebody, had encountered. Until Sanders told him rather coldly to keep quiet. "If she's here, which I doubt, there's no point in warning her that we're coming, is there?"

Harriet glared at him, and the party proceeded in silence. She would have infinitely preferred any kind of chat to this silent procession through the pale, glimmering figures of the past.

"Well," said Mr. Arkwright as he peered around the last pedestal holding up the farthest statue, "if there's something alive up here bigger than a mouse, I'll turn in my badge. Let's try the second floor. More places to hide down there." And the party stalked, ran, or clattered its way down the stairs.

The statues on the third floor were unsettling enough, but they were nothing compared to the cases of stuffed predators glaring dimly out at her in the natural history sections. She felt eyes boring into her back and hot breath brushing her neck as she followed along behind John, resisting the impulse to run over and hang on to him. But her pride was more powerful than her nerves, and she stayed a deliberate eight or ten paces back, in the aisle to the left of him. Rob Lucas was over on the right, and Mr. Arkwright was moving quietly along up ahead.

At the end of the display, they stopped and looked at Mr. Arkwright; he raised his hand to point to his right. Then the unnatural silence of the room was broken by a rasping moan and a sharp, retching cough.

"Omigod," said Harriet, "what was that?"

"Shhh," said Mr. Arkwright. There was another cough. "The bat cave," he said. "The goddamn bat cave." He ran over to the wall with his keys in his hand, searched out one, and inserted it into a metal plate. The dark mass ahead and to their left revealed itself as an archway ablaze with light. He ran toward it, followed by the others. At the entrance, he turned to Lucas. "Go to the other end. Check all the grottoes." Lucas disappeared.

Before they were past the first bend, they heard Lucas shout, "Up here."

Veronika was facedown, one knee close to her chest, the other leg straight. Her hands were just above her head, and she lay like a small child asleep. As they stared down, she made a slight effort to raise her head, and her rasping breathing echoed in the enclosed space.

"What's that?" said Harriet quietly, pointing down at her.

"Blood," said Sanders. "She's hurt, but she's still alive. We'd better get—"

"The guard's gone for an ambulance," said Lucas. "And to get the keys to open up the exhibit to get her out."

"No, I realize that's blood," said Harriet. "I'm not completely stupefied. I mean that thing sitting at ten o'clock to her head."

Sanders looked down for a moment, then vaulted over the railing and landed, much harder than he had expected, in the sharp and nasty surface of the exhibit. He felt Veronika's neck with a delicate touch, then took off his jacket and slid it gently under her face. Lucas reached over the rail and handed him a plastic bag. "Thank you, Constable," he said, and leaned over to pick up Carlos Ramírez's knife from the floor of the exhibit. "You have good eyes, Miss Jeffries," he said with a glance in her direction. "But then you always did, didn't you?"

An hour later and Sanders had done everything, for the moment, that he had to do. "Come on," he said to Harriet. "I'll take you home."

"Don't be silly," she said. "I've got my car. If I leave it out there, I'll get a fifty-dollar ticket. If I haven't got one already."

"Give me your keys," he said. Harriet was too tired to resist. She pulled them out of her pocket and handed them over. Sanders removed his own keys from his rumpled and dirty jacket, restored to him once the delicate operation of removing the injured girl had been completed, and tossed them over to Lucas. "Take the car back, will you, Constable?" he said. "I'll see you in the morning."

"I'd be glad to follow behind and pick you up once you've dropped off Miss Jeffries," said Lucas. "It's no trouble."

"No, thank you, Constable. That won't be necessary." If the words hadn't told him, the glare would have; Lucas, suddenly enlightened, waved the keys cheerfully in the direction of the two of them and left.

"Tired?" asked Sanders. They were sitting in a small restaurant with bowls of goulash and a large basket of bread in front of them.

Harriet shook her head. "Starved. I had no idea how hungry I was," she said as Sanders refilled her wineglass. "I wonder how Nikki is," she added. "I still feel—"

"Just a minute." Sanders got up and left the room. In less than two minutes he was back. "She's okay. Not great, but she'll do. There was a botched attempt to cut her throat; hence, the blood. Probably caught the knife in that pendant she was wearing. She has two head injuries, the one at the point of impact, where she landed in that grotto, and another on the side of the head. Which means he coshed her, probably aiming at the temple, tried to cut her throat, and then dumped her into the grotto. She has a concussion, but she didn't lose that much blood, apparently."

"When did it happen?"

"Before closing time. Otherwise, the guy is still in there; he couldn't get out without setting off alarms. Anyway, she probably would have been seen if she'd been walking around after closing."

Harriet shook her head. "I can't understand why no one saw her. I mean, she was just lying there! Large as life."

"Well, even with full lighting the cave has strange shadows. And the guard said that when he checked the area he was so busy chasing a little girl out that maybe he didn't look as carefully as he should have. But basically they really don't expect to find bodies in the exhibits." He looked over at her pale and unhappy face and covered her hand with his. "Listen, it isn't your fault. Did you make a definite appointment with her to go to the museum? Do you remember?"

Harriet shook her head again. "I don't think so. She was supposed to call me, and we were going to set a time. But then my answering machine was all screwed up and—"

"And so, if she did call and tell you to meet her there at four or five or whenever, you couldn't possibly have gotten the message."

"Do you think that whoever tried to kill her knew she had telephoned me? And knew who I was and knew where I lived? And took the tape out of my answering machine so I wouldn't go to meet her? That's a lot of ands," she added with a shaky smile. "You know, John, I don't care for this very much. It sounds like someone living in Clara's house," she said, thinking of the handsome and plausible young man whom she had so generously offered to help and to whom she had given her business card.

"Eat your goulash like a good girl and drink your wine. I'm not leaving you alone tonight. You'll be safe."

This time she didn't protest.

At one-thirty A.M., Eastern Daylight Time, Manu Iturralde stepped out of the Iberia Airways 747 and blinked in the pleasantly cool continental dawn of the airport at Málaga, far to the south, the other side of the country from his native San Sebastián. He walked briskly over to passport control, where the usual customs and immigration officials

had been bolstered by an unusual number of members of
the Guardia Civil. Three unfortunates ahead of him, whose
names happened to include the given name Manuel, and one
gentleman with a slightly Basque-sounding last name, not
terribly long hair, but a definite mustache, had all been
called over to one side, for what was probably going to be a
lengthy investigation of their luggage and discussion of their
papers.

But Manu, whose passport identified him as Pedro Albornoz
y Miró, received only a perfunctory glance. The officer in
the Guardia Civil took in his erect carriage, his sober gray
suit, his elegantly cut hair, and his clean-shaven face, and
nodded politely. Señor Albornoz gave him an almost im-
perceptible, chilly smile and walked away, unmolested, to
catch the bus that would take him into the center of town.

CHAPTER 13

John Sanders stood in the middle of the hospital room, feeling awkward and out of place. Ed Dubinsky was leaning on the windowsill, managing to look unobtrusive; Veronika von Hohenkammer lay in corpselike silence, her face gray except for deep black smears under her eyes. With white bandages around her head and throat, she looked to Sanders as if someone had started to mummify her and then left for his coffee break. "I thought you said she was conscious and fit to be interviewed," he hissed at the white-coated woman standing beside him.

"She is, in a manner of speaking," the resident answered in normal tones. "She's just asleep. You said it was urgent, so the best thing is to wait around a bit and catch her while she's awake. She drifts in and out, but basically she's all right."

"Can she remember anything?" asked Sanders with some apprehension.

"You have to expect a certain amount of amnesia with head injuries. Hers doesn't seem to be too severe. She knows who she is, and she was surprised to find herself here instead of at the museum. By the way, was she at the museum?"

Sanders nodded. "That was where we found her."

"Then it sounds pretty good to me. I wasn't sure where she'd been when she injured herself; if the visit to the museum had been six months ago, then you'd be in real trouble." The resident laughed cheerfully. "Why don't you sit down instead of looming over her like that? She'll wake up in a minute. And don't shake her. Her head hurts." She moved over close to the door and leaned against the wall, determined, it seemed, to monitor the interview.

Sanders picked up a chair and set it beside the bed. This was the second woman in the last twenty-four hours who had accused him of looming. "Were there facial injuries?" he asked, looking over at the doctor.

She shook her head. "Back and side," she said, sounding like a barber and touching her own head to indicate the site of the blows.

"Then why the black eyes?"

The resident snorted with laughter. "Mascara and God knows what other kinds of goop. Don't look at me like that. She was wearing a lot of eye makeup, and it got smeared. The nurses will clean her up today, don't worry. We took the worst of it off just to get a look at her skin color, but we didn't bother with the eyes."

Before Sanders could comment, those same eyes flew open. Veronika stared up at Sanders's face, puzzled for a moment, and then smiled. "Hello, Inspector," she said, her voice rather hoarse and weak.

"How's your head?" asked the doctor.

"Bad," said Veronika. Her eyes swam with tears.

"Keep this short," said the resident, turning toward the door. "I'll be back in ten minutes."

"Who attacked you, Miss von Hohenkammer?" asked Sanders. If he was going to be hurried out of here in ten minutes, he had no time for idle preliminaries.

"I didn't see him."

"Him? It was a man, then."

"I think so. A man had been following me."

"In the museum?"

"And before. A man asked for me at the hairdresser's."

"And where was that? Which hairdresser's?"

"It had an Italian name, near Bloor and Avenue Road. I can't remember . . . it reminded me of the wine . . ."

"Chianti?" said Dubinsky, his pen poised but idle for the moment.

That brought a small smile. "Wrong wine. Orvieto—it was Arvieto's or Orveto's or something like that. I had my hair cut before I went to the museum."

"Can you describe the man who followed you?"

She started to nod her head and stopped again. "Yes. I saw him several times." She shut her eyes and went on speaking. "He's almost as tall as Klaus. He has dark hair, almost black, curly, but not very. Cut stylishly, but short. Big eyes, dark brown, thin eyebrows, and the one on my right is arched, the other is straight. His nose is thin and long. He has those cheeks that sink in, almost with a line down them, you know? And his chin comes down in a point that is squared at the bottom." Dubinsky was scribbling rapidly as she talked. "He is thin, but his shoulders are not— They are wide, uh, broad. He walks like a dancer. If you know what I mean."

"Perhaps you could explain," said Sanders, who didn't.

"No, I'm too tired." She opened her eyes again; they were moist with tears.

"Rest for a minute." Sanders turned to his partner. "Get the artist over here right away." When Dubinsky had left, he turned back to the injured young woman. "I'll just tell you what we're doing. Don't bother to answer. I'm sending for our sketch artist. We will give him that description; he'll do a drawing and then ask you how it should be altered to make it accurate." Her eyes drifted shut again, and Sanders realized he was pouring his words into a vacuum. He moved his chair over by the window, stared out over the rooftops of the downtown core of the city, and considered what she had been saying. Chances were that this fantastically de- tailed description was pure hogwash. Witnesses could rarely recall anything with such clarity and detail. Yet she just might be that one in a hundred with a strong visual mem- ory. He wondered if the medicos would let her sit up and look at mug shots. She ought to be able to pick him out, if he existed. Who in hell was he, anyway? And why did he want to get rid of her? Maybe her sister, after all, had hired him, making one last attempt to get the whole pie.

Dubinsky walked quietly into the room. "He'll be here in an hour or so," he said. "He's doing someone for Volchek. She say anything else?"

"Not a word. She's asleep again."

"No, I'm not asleep." Her voice was clearer now, and stronger.

"Can you tell me what else happened yesterday?" Sanders spoke as gently as he could. "We're trying to figure out why someone would want to attack you."

"Nothing," she said. "Nothing happened yesterday. I went shopping and had my hair done and went to the museum."

"Who knew you were going?"

"No one knew, except I left a message on Harriet's answering machine. We were going to meet at the museum but hadn't set a time. I told her I'd be there at four. She never came." Again her eyes filled with tears.

"She didn't get the message," said Sanders. "Her answering machine was broken."

Dubinsky raised his pen and then his eyebrow as he looked over at his partner.

"Who was in the house when you left? And could have known that you were going out? Maybe heard you leaving that message?"

"No one. Bettl was out, and Klaus had gone over to my sister's."

"Ah, yes, so he said. When did you leave the house? Right after he did?"

"No, I was very cold, and I got changed first." A patch of hectic color flared up in her gray cheeks and then started to fade again.

Sanders paused. What had happened while she was changing to cause such a reaction? "Then tell me precisely everything you did." As she talked, her voice growing hoarser and more hesitant, he wondered why he was putting her through this. Except that he was void of ideas. "Who else did you see in the museum? Besides the man with the thin cheeks. Was he with anyone, did you notice?" Stupid question. Why in hell would you take a friend to help you hit a small female over the head?

Veronika von Hohenkammer reddened again. Once more she forgot and shook her head. The color drained rapidly from her cheeks, leaving them even grayer than before. She closed her eyes in pain and then opened them once more. This time their gaze was wide and candid. "No, of course not. I saw no one else. Just the people I mentioned."

The door flew open. "Out," said the resident briskly. "Before I put you out."

"Why is she lying?" asked Sanders as they waited for the elevator.

Dubinsky looked over at him. "Who knows? Any number of reasons. How about, she knows who he is, she saw him talking to her sister or whoever, and she doesn't want to blow the whistle on them."

"Then why the detailed description?"

"Yeah, well, wouldn't you? I mean, family feeling only goes so far. The guy tried to murder her. There's a difference between fingering your own sister, or cousin, and having us catch them in the course of our investigations. Right? If we do get this bastard and if he points the finger at Theresa baby, then that's not her fault, is it? So she's done what she wanted to do. Saved her own skin without doing anything mean or nasty, like squealing on a sister."

"Jesus, but you have a cynical view of mankind, Ed. It's a wonder you can get up in the morning."

"I can't. Sally throws me out of bed. Let's go get some breakfast."

When Milan Milanovich walked out of the room in the Royal Bank, where he kept his safety deposit box—his other safety deposit box, not the one for which his wife also had a key—he was greeted not by a friendly teller wishing him good-bye and a good day but by a pair of police officers. Not especially friendly. Wishing to speak to him. Not here, but down at the police station. With his briefcase.

As he climbed sulkily into the cruiser, he had only one question. "How in hell did you guys find me? No one at this bank even knows me."

"We noticed that, sir. But you parked your car outside the bank. On the street. In a no-parking zone."

"Jesus," he muttered. "I was in there only five minutes."

"Long enough, sir," said the driver cheerfully, and Milanovich subsided into silence.

The three remaining members of Veronika von Hohenkammer's family were now sitting in separate rooms, guests of the Metropolitan Toronto Police, a study in variations on anger. Milanovich remained sulky; Theresa, imperious; Klaus, combative. "What did you get from them?" Sanders asked Collins, to whom had fallen the brunt of the questioning.

"Short version?" Sanders nodded. "Milanovich has a girlfriend. He's been in the city all the time, with his car in her garage. But her husband's coming home tonight, and he had to make his move. The briefcase contains $60,000 in U.S. dollars. His own money, he says. Like a savings account. Just in case."

"I'd be interested in finding out exactly where that money came from. Considering that he's damned near bankrupt. And his wife?"

"She spent the day at home, she said at first, looking after the kids and talking to her cousin, Klaus. But the nanny doesn't lie, and when we poked around a bit, it seemed Madam had gone out several times. And so did Leitner. If the girl did leave the house between eleven and eleven-thirty, any one of them could have been over there and known that she was going to the museum. Klaus went out before eleven to see their lawyer. Theresa remembered the safety deposit box at their bank and popped out to have a go at it. We've witnesses for all that. Either one of them could have gone to the house, heard her on the phone, known where she was going and when, and set up whoever he was. Of course, Milanovich's girlfriend was at work during the day as well. His alibi is nonexistent."

Collins's recital was interrupted by the telephone. Dubinsky reached over lazily and picked up the receiver. "Yeah, it's Ed." He listened for a minute in silence. "You're sure? Well, okay, bring the picture in. We'll show it to Walker. You never hear of coincidence?" He set down the phone and looked over at his colleagues. "MacVey says that the sketch he did of the suspect the von Hohenkammer girl described is identical to the sketch he did of Walker's pal, Carlos Ramírez. According to him, it sounds like the same guy."

"He's sure?" asked Sanders.

"That's what he says."

"I wonder . . ." And Sanders picked up a pencil and began to draw little boxes and surround them with bigger boxes on the piece of paper in front of him. Dubinsky shrugged and went back to the work on his desk; Collins muttered something about checking up on those statements.

For almost an hour the business of the department whirled past John Sanders, having as much effect on him as the water in a trout stream does on a boulder sitting in the middle of it. Over the long run, no doubt, considerable; in the short run, none at all. Finally, he pulled the telephone over and punched in a number without bothering to look it up. Dubinsky put down his pen to watch.

"Harriet?" That Dubinsky heard quite clearly. "Do you have . . ." and here his voice trailed off; several people walked in and out of the room, slamming doors and talking. "Could you bring them over? Now? Yes, it's important or I wouldn't have asked, would I?" There was a slight pause. "If I were just feeling sentimental, I would have asked for pictures of you, not of some building, for chrissake. See you in half an hour."

But Harriet was there in twenty minutes, holding a manila envelope in her hand and looking slightly out of breath. "You found your way up, then," said Sanders, taking the envelope from her.

"Not without a lot of help," she complained. Sanders didn't hear; he was laying the contents of the envelope out on his desk. Dubinsky got up, curious, to have a look. "Hi," she said, holding out her hand. "Remember me? Harriet Jeffries. That long night at Clara von Hohenkammer's."

Dubinsky took her hand and tactfully refrained from mentioning that he had already memorized her features and her name, and now that he had pieced together exactly where Sanders had disappeared to yesterday afternoon, he was tucking away her address and telephone number.

"These ones," said Sanders. "Send them over with the sketch and see what Walker has to say about them. Have them call me." As an afterthought, he turned to Harriet. "Thanks. You had any lunch?"

She shook her head.

"Find someone, Ed. Two corned beef on rye."

The call did not come until the corned beef had been commissioned, fetched, delivered, and consumed. Dubinsky answered the phone and then graciously handed it over to Sanders. He listened and nodded several times. "Look, ask him one more thing, will you? Is the buru a woman?" He stared up at the ceiling, ignoring the curiosity emanating from everyone around him. "That's it," he said at last, and put down the phone.

"What's what?" said Harriet. "And would you stop being so goddamn mysterious?"

"I just had an idea, and it could have been a very stupid idea, but I thought I'd try it out. I mean, suppose the house where Walker said they kept all the stolen goods wasn't in the suburbs at all but in the city? You know any big houses in the city that are surrounded by enough land that they sound and smell as if they're in the suburbs?"

"Clara's?" said Harriet. "That's a hell of a long shot."

"So? It would give a connection between Carlos and Nikki. Anyway, Walker says the guy that Nikki described is Carlos, all right. And he identified your interior shots of Clara's house with the house in the suburbs where they kept all the stolen property."

"I don't believe it," said Harriet firmly. "Clara would never have anything to do with something like that."

"The person who ran the operation wasn't a woman. Walker met *him* several times. When they asked him about it a minute ago, he said, more or less, 'Don't be stupid. He was a guy, just a kid.' She wasn't even there most of the time, Harriet. She probably knew nothing about it. But I'll tell you who did."

"The gardener," said Dubinsky. "He's the only one who was there all the time. And you could call him a kid."

"Come on. Let's go have a word with Paul the gardener. We'll drop you off on the way."

"Oh, no, you don't. I have to go over to Clara's house, anyway, to pick up some things for Nikki. She called me just before you did. Said she couldn't reach anyone there, or at her sister's."

"That's because they're all here," said Sanders. "Stewing."

The house was emptier than any house Harriet had ever been in, devoid of any trace of life. Much emptier than when she had taken possession of it to photograph it. "I'm going up to Nikki's room to get her things," she said firmly. She didn't like feeling spooked by atmospheres.

Dubinsky had taken Lucas with him to look for the gardener in his flat above the garage, since Lucas appeared to be less intimidated by the prospect of having to cope with dogs than Collins was. Sanders looked around the front hall, told Collins to keep an eye on things on the ground floor, and headed toward Harriet and the stairs. "I'll come with you," he said. "We need to find the housekeeper."

Harriet emerged from Veronika's room with a suitcase filled with nightwear and other necessaries just as Sanders was descending from Bettl's room. "You find her?"

"She's gone," he said. "Didn't leave so much as a hairpin or a blond hairnet behind. Probably in Germany by now." He shrugged. "Get what you were looking for?"

Harriet nodded, but her reply was cut short by the sound of Lucas running up the stairs.

"The sergeant would like you to come over to the gardener's flat, sir. If you don't mind."

"Right behind you, Lucas," he said. As he headed out the kitchen door, something suddenly occurred to him. "And what did you do with the dogs, Lucas? Hypnotize them?"

"Not a dog on the property, sir, as far as I can see."

Dubinsky was standing in the middle of a pleasantly shabby, immaculately clean room. One corner held a spotless kitchen; another, a bed, stripped down to its mattress. There was a table pushed against the wall next to a window; on it sat a typewriter and some books. Sanders picked up the top one: *Obras* de Miguel de Unamuno was stamped on the cover. He flipped through it idly, not understanding a word. "This was sitting on top of that book," said Dubinsky, holding out a standard business envelope with "Inspector Sanders" typed on the outside.

The envelope was not sealed; when he lifted the flap, two sheets of paper slid out. "A lot to say for himself," said Sanders, and began to read:

Tuesday, September 17

My dear Inspector,

It is clear to me that you have been moving closer and closer to us. If you are reading this, you have discovered my apartment. Therefore, as a courtesy, I write this to you before leaving the country, because I fear that I have left you no physical evidence of what has happened; for that you will have to go to the address listed below, where, if you are quick enough, you will find enough to satisfy even you. For I perceive that you are a careful—indeed, a fastidious—man in these matters. Not like some of the policemen in my country, who do not worry about small matters like evidence if your name is Basque.

I sincerely grieve for the death of Doña Clara. She was a great lady, and a very gracious one when in good temper. She reminded me very much of my own mother. I would never have harmed her, nor permitted my associates to harm her. If she was not murdered by the housekeeper, Bettl, then she was poisoned by her daughters or her nephew. Any one of them would have killed for a few pesetas, not to speak of Doña Clara's fortune. All I know is that her death came at a very awkward time for us.

We had a beautiful scheme, Manu and I. I do not expect you, as a policeman, to appreciate it, but I do expect you, as a human being, to understand that in theory we intended as little harm as possible. We would steal from the rich and well insured, store the fruits of our labors safely in the house of Doña Clara, sell them at our leisure, and take the money back home. Without touching anyone. That is always the problem, is it not? In theory. In practice, we needed to consort with criminals in order to steal efficiently and to dispose of our goods at a sufficient profit. I am not sure if I chose badly or if bad choice is inherent in the activity. Through Doña Clara's thieving household, I found someone to dispose of expensive works of art. But through that person, I was encumbered with Carlos, who is a madman, and Don, who is a coward.

I knew they were not honorable men, but I had not expected them to be unprofessional, so unprofessional that in a crisis they would kill. Carlos for amusement, Don to save himself. It was Don who killed Mrs. Wilkinson with a blow on the head, using a statue of a Viking warrior. When Carlos shot her, she was already near death. Or so Manu tells me, and he is observant and truthful. Carlos shot one policeman; Don killed the

other with a blow on the head. Don told me it was an
accident. That is difficult to believe. The tragedy is that
had I been there, I would have been able to control
him, I think, but having drugged the entire household
so that we could get the last shipment out, I found it
necessary to drink some of that coffee myself. Otherwise, you would have been very suspicious. And with
those actions they have destroyed our hope of raising
enough money to help fund a significant political resis-
tance in our own country. A futile hope, in all events,
you will say. But I am young enough to believe that
such things may be. If not now, later.

This morning we rescued what remained of the last
consignment of goods. Doña Clara's daughter had discovered our simple hiding place, although I do not
think she knows who we are. I sent Carlos to keep her
away from home—women seem to find him enchant-
ing, strangely enough—while we moved it. Now I have
misgivings about what has happened to her. Carlos
asked for help to deal with her, and it occurred to me
that he intended to keep her from the house by removing her permanently. I went myself to the museum,
hoping to avert another death. She took fright when she
saw me and ran before I could get to her.

Now there is no time to do anything but leave. You
have Don already, Manu tells me. You are welcome to
him. If you do not find Carlos at his apartment, look
for him in Arizona. I do not know what his mother
called him, but he has passports in the name of Ramírez
and Ugalde, and also Garcia, first name Carlos always.
As for me, I am tired of gardening. I shall locate Manu
and return to university. You will forgive me if I do not
tell you where. *Euzkadi ta Askatasuna*, Inspector.

> Yours faithfully,
> Ixtebe Etxebarrieta (Paul Esteban)
> (or as Don knows me, the buru, the boss)

P.S. Manu has never killed anyone in his life; he is a brave but essentially peaceful man. Although he is not fond of the Guardia Civil. I sincerely trust that by the time you receive this letter, he will be far from Canada. And the dogs are at the kennel; you will find the receipt on Doña Clara's desk.

The letter was neatly typed, including the signature. "Son of a bitch," said Sanders. "There's nerve for you. What does that mean?" he said, turning to Lucas and pointing to the words at the end.

"Hey, I don't speak Basque," said Lucas, taking the letter and reading it. "Oh, it's the name of the political party—ETA," he said, grinning as he came to the end. "It means something like 'Country and Freedom.' He's an *etarra*. Member of the party." He handed the letter over to Dubinsky and looked in the envelope. "Sir, there's another slip of paper in here." He pulled it out and whistled.

"What's on it?" asked Sanders.

"A couple of addresses: on Palmerston and on Acacia Crescent."

Sanders snatched the paper from him and glanced rapidly at it. "Come on. Back to headquarters. You can finish that in the car," he said to Dubinsky. "Let Lucas drive."

Sanders blew into the room like a hurricane. "I need warrants—now. Get someone onto it."

"For what?" asked Collins innocently, reaching out his hand for the slip with the addresses on it. "This one is Carlos Ramírez's flat, you know. We've already sent someone over there."

"Someone isn't enough," snapped Sanders. "Anyway, the bulk of the stuff is probably at the other address."

Lucas slowed to a moderate pace as they approached the building on Acacia Crescent; he pulled up some distance away and stopped. "You want to wait here until Sergeant Dubinsky arrives, sir?" he asked.

"No. He won't be long," said Sanders with more assurance than he felt. "And it may already be too late." He opened the car door and looked carefully around him before striding up to the high-rise on the south side of the street. Not a bad sort of place to live, he reflected. Not as homely as some, better kept than most, and close enough to Bathurst and Eglinton that you could walk to restaurants. Art theft was prospering these days. As they stood by the entrance waiting for the superintendent, Sanders peered through the glass into the lobby and revised his estimate of profits by a few hundred thousands. All those green trees, heavy pieces of furniture, and fountains lurking in there didn't come cheap.

Sanders paused in front of the door of the apartment on the seventeenth floor and listened. Inside he could hear music playing—tasteful, delicate music—and soft, muffled footsteps. It would seem that luck was with them. Their bird had not flown. Sanders raised his hand and knocked, firmly, definitively. An official knock. A knock that any pimp or pickpocket in the world would recognize.

The music was turned down. The footsteps moved closer, and the door opened on a chain. "Well, well, well. Inspector. You tracked me down to my little hideaway. How very clever of you." The door closed, there was a rattle of a chain being taken off, and the door opened once again.

"I had some help," said Sanders as Frank Whitelaw stood to one side to let the two men pass.

This was an even different Whitelaw, affable and charming, wearing an embroidered silk smoking jacket over a cream-colored silk shirt. Behind him the apartment glowed richly in the September sun. The Oriental rugs made Sanders want to give his shoes a wipe; the furniture looked like the antiques they don't turn out in factories and then pepper with fake wormholes, and on the flat white walls was a collection of paintings that might just be real. Lucas stood quietly by the door; Sanders walked in and across the room and then stationed himself in front of a richly swirling landscape with horses whose sweat he could almost smell and whose labored breathing seemed to ring in his ears.

"Impressive," he said flatly.

"Isn't it?" said Whitelaw, smiling. "A Géricault. But not a great one. It's a rather tentative study he did for something else during one of his better periods. I'm fond of it, though, in spite of its lack of finish. Quite extraordinary power and motion, wouldn't you say?"

Sanders grunted something that could be taken for appreciation. On the opposite wall, he noticed two rectangular white spaces, surrounded by the dust marks, the marks left by paintings after they been taken down. "And what was here?" he asked. "A couple of Rembrandts?"

Whitelaw smiled faintly. "Not at all. Just some of those Victorian landscapes that are two a penny at any gallery. I thought they might do for here, but they didn't work. I'm still looking for replacements."

"What did you do with them?" asked Sanders, genuinely curious. What did one do with a two-a-penny Victorian landscape that wasn't up to snuff? Put it out on Thursday with the trash?

"Oh, I shipped them to New York. They should be able to get me a thousand or two each for them. I mean, they weren't Constables, but they were decently done." This time his smile was dismissive and end-of-conversation-like. "Now what can I do for you gentlemen?"

"Just a few questions," said Sanders amicably, glancing at his watch. "Nice apartment you have here." He looked down the hall as he spoke; there was room for at least two huge bedrooms down there.

"Not a bad little place," Whitelaw said. "Adequate for a bachelor existence." With a restrained wave of the hand, he indicated the modest proportions of his dwelling.

The time had come to alter the mood. "Why the secrecy?" asked Sanders, his voice suddenly probing, suspicious. Any moment now the sweat should be breaking out on Whitelaw's forehead.

But Whitelaw's brow remained smooth and unsullied. He shrugged his shoulders and continued, with a gentle smile, "Clara expected me to live in the house, you know. She liked to have people right there under her nose. The little flat on Wood-lawn was a compromise. Within walking distance, but off the property. Still, one has to have a place of one's own, you know. Not just a room. A real place. One has, uh, possessions. Investments."

"How much did Mrs. von Hohenkammer pay you?" said Sanders abruptly.

"I beg your pardon?"

"Come now, Mr. Whitelaw," he answered with quick savagery in his voice. "Paintings by artists *I've* heard of? Antiques? Oriental rugs? An apartment you must be paying three thousand a month for? You don't get all this on the minimum wage."

"You don't get all this on what my employer was paying me, either," said Frank Whitelaw with a touch of bitterness. He looked steadily at the two policemen for a few moments and then walked over to the window. He stared out over the rooftops of the city, turned and half-sat on the windowsill. "Sit down," he said. "Let me explain. The problem is that you are confusing capital and income. When I first met Clara von Hohenkammer, I was a partner in a very profit-able business in art and antiques; hence, the rugs—there are more in the bedroom and study if you care to check—the paintings, the furniture. Unfortunately, my partner attempted a particularly senseless bit of fraud—it's a hazard in the antiques world, as I'm sure you know—and was caught. He couldn't face the consequences and killed himself. The busi-ness was ruined. By the time it was all over, I had to sell off everything, inventory, the building, the lot." He leaned his head back and stared up at the ceiling for a tragic moment before looking back at them and continuing. "But I still owned my flat in London and all this furniture. I had a choice between selling everything and living on the proceeds until I had nothing or finding some sort of work and keeping at least some of my most beautiful pieces. I had been the financial person in the antiques business—my partner was the art expert—and finding a position as business manager for an arts group wasn't very difficult." His voice became louder and brisk. "And from there to my job here. I sold my flat in London and bought this one. Therefore, rent is not an issue. And Mrs. von Hohenkammer paid me forty thousand a year plus travel expenses when necessary."

Sanders's confidence in Paul Esteban's letter was beginning to crumble. Whitelaw was purring like a cat, inviting him to search the place, warrant or no warrant. "So you're an expert on art, are you?" he said, trying to fill up the silence. "Now I find that very interesting."

"It is, Inspector. Very interesting. A precarious livelihood at times, but never dull. One meets a great many people."

Sanders studied the man carefully. He was still sitting comfortably on the edge of the broad windowsill, looking peaceful and calm. Too calm. "Didn't you find working as a secretary a comedown?" he asked with deliberate harshness. "Only forty thousand a year? Taking orders from Mrs. von Hohenkammer night and day? Like Bettl, the housekeeper?" A hint of extra color crept up into Whitelaw's cheeks. "Or did you reckon on marrying the widow and getting the lot? And when that fell through, you had to find other ways to build up your self-esteem, didn't you? And your bank account." For a brief second, Sanders thought he saw fury written across the man's face and smiled. He had hit a nerve. "May I use your telephone for a moment?" he asked, with a slight nod in Lucas's direction. The constable walked unhurriedly across the room and joined Whitelaw at his post by the window.

Ten minutes later, Sanders was still on the phone, trying to extract some conclusions from the team at work on Clara von Hohenkammer's books and files. "Look, I know you haven't got enough to go into court with," he said in exasperation. "What I want to know is, have you uncovered enough so *you* know what's going on?" There was a pause, and another smile spread over Sanders's face. "I thought so. You're sure of that? Excellent." He set the telephone down and turned back to Frank Whitelaw, who was still lounging by the window. "There are interesting discrepancies in Clara von Hohenkammer's financial records, it seems. But that doesn't surprise you, does it, Mr. Whitelaw?"

"Well, you know, it does," said Whitelaw. "Clara was careful about her records. Very careful about her money. Of course, her children could have been messing about. That's always possible. They had entirely too much access to her private affairs. Greedy brutes, those children are."

"Greedy enough to write fake letters to her lawyer asking him to sell stock and deposit the proceeds in a special account?" said Sanders, apparently studying the notes from his telephone conversation. "Greedy enough to forge her name to those letters? And then to drop three hundred milligrams of cyanide from a folded piece of paper into the pot with the herbal tea in it because the accountant was coming and they were about to be found out? Leaving the paper under the table wasn't a bad trick. It made us concentrate for a while on people who had access to the cup. But Bettl likes to do things well ahead of time, doesn't she? It's one of her flaws as a cook. That pot had been sitting in the kitchen for over an hour, ready, waiting for her to pour boiling water into it. And for that last hour, several people stayed right next to Mrs. von Hohenkammer, nowhere near the table with the cup, long before the tea came out of the kitchen. Milanovich. His wife. And you, Mr. Whitelaw."

"Is this fanciful tale supposed to be an accusation, Inspector? Because if it is—"

"Oh, no. Just an explanation. It was that first letter, you see, Mr. Whitelaw." Sanders continued, his voice developing an almost hypnotic rhythm. "Whoever wrote it should have waited until Mrs. von Hohenkammer had arrived in Toronto. Because that's where the letter was postmarked, and her friends in Majorca insist that she was still with them when she was supposed to be in Toronto writing it. I call that careless, don't you, Mr. Whitelaw?" Sanders looked at his watch again.

The sun disappeared behind a cloud, and Whitelaw's face seemed to take on the pallor of the sky, matching the whiteness of his knuckles as he clutched the edge of the windowsill. He cleared his throat. "Worried about the time, Inspector? Don't let me keep you if you have another appointment."

"Not at all," said Sanders. "I think I hear him now. Let Sergeant Dubinsky in, Constable." And Lucas walked over to the door.

With Dubinsky's arrival the atmosphere changed again. A certain briskness swept through the apartment as soon as he drew the document from his pocket. "I have a warrant here to search these premises, Mr. Whitelaw," he said cheerfully. "Would you like to examine it?"

"That wasn't necessary, Inspector. All you had to do was ask," said Whitelaw, ignoring Dubinsky. "I have nothing to hide."

"Volchek's coming over, too," said Dubinsky. "He's afraid you'll miss something."

"Won't bother me," said Sanders. "Mr. Whitelaw and I are going to carry on this interesting discussion downtown, aren't we, Mr. Whitelaw?"

Whitelaw shrugged his shoulders. "If you like, Inspector. I'm not particularly busy today. Though I would appreciate the opportunity to change into something more appropriate," he said, lifting the edge of his silken jacket between his thumb and forefinger.

"Lucas," said Sanders. "Keep Mr. Whitelaw company, will you?"

Rob Lucas marched stolidly after the business manager into his bedroom. The constable walked over to the window to occupy himself discreetly while Whitelaw got ready. Out of the corner of his eye, he saw him slip off the jacket and drape it on the bed, adjust his cravat carefully in the mirror affixed to a large wardrobe sitting in the corner, and then push aside its sliding door. "It's in here," he said, his voice muffled as he stepped inside. There was a rattle of hangers, a certain amount of stamping about, and then silence. Total silence.

"Oh, shit," said Lucas, his imagination busy with a vision of Whitelaw's corpse, filled with cyanide, lying among his well-made shoes. He shoved the door open as wide as it would go, pushed the clothing on hangers roughly aside, stared down at the floor, and gasped. There was nothing there. Whitelaw had disappeared into thin air.

Sanders looked up as the constable pounded into the room. "I've lost him, sir," he said miserably. "In the wardrobe."

"What? How in hell can you lose someone in a wardrobe?" By the time he had finished the sentence, he was inside the offending piece of furniture, tossing clothes out onto the floor. "This particular wardrobe doesn't have a back, Constable," said Sanders in an ominous voice. "A fact that had escaped you, perhaps, when you let Whitelaw wander into it. And as a bonus, there's a door, a locked door, in the wall behind it."

"Do you want me to try to break down the door, sir?"

"For chrissake, no," spluttered the inspector. "What do you think we are? Shove aside that piece of furniture and let's have a better look. Dubinsky!" he yelled. "Give us a hand."

"It's not a very fancy lock," said his partner, breathless from the effort of helping push the wardrobe across the room. "Look in the kitchen and see what you can find, Constable. A hammer and a chisel will do."

They were interrupted in their search by a knock on the door. "Answer it, Lucas," growled Sanders. "On your way to the kitchen." Fury still dripped from his tongue.

"I wasn't sure if you had finished questioning Mr. Whitelaw or not," said a voice from the hall. "I thought I'd better check."

"Well, look who's here," said Sanders. "Thank you, Sergeant Volchek. And I think, once we relieve this man of his keys, we might have something for you. Constable, cuff him, will you, and this time, keep an eye on him?" Sanders reached into Frank Whitelaw's pocket and extracted two sets of keys.

The bachelor apartment that connected with Frank Whitelaw's more spacious premises by the door in his bedroom was clearly not designed to hold everything that had been put there. There were paintings stacked against the wall, crates filling the space under the window. Volchek was crouched on the floor, unpacking the first crate, removing each piece, and checking it against the list he had drawn from his pocket. "No question," he said after a few minutes. "There's more than enough here already," he said, nodding to the table covered with sterling silver, "to charge him. At the very least with receiving. That will do to go on." He rose to his feet and started in the direction of the business manager, who was slumped in an elegant chair, glassy eyed, staring at the door to the outer hall through which he had escaped once already today. Into the arms of Adam Volchek. "Just what is your relationship with Carlos Ramírez, Mr. Whitelaw?" said Volchek, perching on the edge of the table covered with silver.

"Carlos Ramírez?" said Whitelaw, as if puzzled, and then thought better of it. "I didn't really have a relationship with him. Paul Esteban mentioned to me last year that he was looking for a possible partner, someone who understood antiques, and I put him in touch with Ramírez. I had run into him a year or so ago at an auction. It just so happened that they were both Basques. A lucky coincidence, that was."

"And what is all this? Another lucky coincidence?" Volchek's wave took in all the extraneous wealth in the room.

"No, just a favor for a friend, that's all. Carlos and Paul planned on opening an antiques shop in Toronto, and I was keeping some of their stock for them until they could get their premises ready. I don't use this apartment much. Basically, I keep it as a guest room."

"And if I were to tell you that everything in this room, with the possible exception of your rug and furnishings, was stolen sometime this summer, you'd still say you were just doing a favor for a friend."

"Of course." He straightened up and crossed one leg jauntily over his knee as his shattered confidence began to rebuild itself. He smiled ruefully at Sanders. "It may have been stupid of me not to have investigated what they were up to, but it's true. Ask Paul and Carlos."

"I don't have to ask them," said Volchek softly. "I already have Esteban's version of events."

Whitelaw's hand tightened around his ankle. "Surely you don't believe that man," he said with a desperate attempt at another smile. "You must realize by now that he's part of a Basque terrorist group; he's even been in prison. Those Basques, they're taught to lie and steal as children." His voice wavered slightly. "They'll say anything to protect themselves and their confederates."

"Really?" said Sanders. "Interesting. Then you're not one of his confederates, I take it. Because he says he saw you, Whitelaw. He was standing in the kitchen door when you thought you were alone. He saw you dump the cyanide into the teapot."

"The hell he did!" screamed Whitelaw. Now the sweat was pouring from his forehead. "I was alone when— Anyway, that wasn't cyanide. It was just an herbal sleeping powder Clara took sometimes. I used to lace her tea with it whenever she got excitable and overtired."

"Let's find out, shall we?" Sanders turned and walked into the other apartment. In a few seconds he returned with a rumpled dinner jacket in his hand. "I predict that when we're finished with this jacket, we'll have found traces of cyanide in the pocket, won't we? I was wondering why I couldn't lay my hands on what you were wearing the night of the party when we looked through your apartment. In fact, I'm so sure we'll find it that as soon as Sergeant Volchek finishes charging you, I'm asking for you back. In the matter of the murder of Mrs. Clara von Hohenkammer of . . ."

And the machinery of the law slid into motion yet one more time. But Rob Lucas was still standing in the hallway of the apartment when Sanders finished his final conversation with Adam Volchek and headed for the door. "Paul Esteban can't have seen Whitelaw put cyanide in the teapot, sir, could he? I mean, he said he didn't know who—"

"He could have, Lucas," said Sanders. "Everyone said he was around all evening, here and there. He could have seen a lot. And Whitelaw thinks he did. Which in itself is revealing, isn't it?"

"Mmm," said Lucas. "I hadn't realized you were looking for Whitelaw's dinner jacket, either. I would have brought it out right away if I'd known. Did you check everyone's clothes for traces of cyanide?"

"That's what a careful investigator does," said Sanders sententiously. If he's awake enough to remember what he's doing, he added silently.

CHAPTER 14

"Did you get her onto the plane?" asked Sanders. "Actually onto it?"

"Yes. Actually on the plane," said Harriet, sitting down. "And her cousin, too, you'll be happy to know. Klaus decided at the last minute that family was more important than career and so—swoosh. Off to Munich on a first-class ticket. Just like that." She smiled automatically at the waitress and accepted a menu. "Which gets him out of my hair, thank God. I was afraid I'd end up spending the winter teaching him how to make a living. Anyway, I know why I'm glad to see them leave, but I still don't understand why you dislike Veronika so much."

"Why do I dislike her?" He pushed his chair back and straightened out his legs in front of him. "Because she used you. And because she kept screwing up my investigation. And because I can't stand that little waif look that says, I'm lovable and incompetent. Please protect me." He shook his head. "I don't know. I also have the feeling that if she'd told us everything she knew, we could have put things together days earlier."

"Did she really believe her mother was mixed up in it all? She should have known better." Harriet shook her head and turned her full attention to the typewritten list in front of her. "What are you having?" she asked.

"The special," said Sanders. "It looks better than it sounds. And yes, that's what she said. What can you do? She still doesn't believe it was Whitelaw, because her mother trusted him, she said."

"Well, you have to admit that it is hard to believe," said Harriet. "I'll have the special," she called to the waitress, who had by now given up all hopes of getting an order from her. "And whatever he's drinking."

"Why?" asked Sanders.

"You mean Whitelaw? Or what I just ordered?" She raised her hands in mock terror to ward off an imaginary blow. "How could anyone take him seriously? You know, typical twit, all pomposity and bad culture. A character in a really good British farce. I can see him as a fence, if you're right about his expertise in art, but I cannot see him as a murderer."

"The right outside pocket of his dinner jacket had enough cyanide in it to do in a lumberjack," said Sanders. "Or at least more than enough to keep the lab people happy. I don't know why it would be there if he hadn't been carrying a little paper package of the stuff around for the evening, waiting for a chance to dump it in the teapot."

Harriet shook her head. "But why would he want to kill Clara?"

"He was embezzling from her," said Sanders. "Or at least that's what the accountants are finding. One of those quick-in, quick-out schemes that's supposed to net a huge amount of money before the auditors come in."

"But Clara twigged?" said Harriet. Sanders nodded. "She was awfully shrewd, you know. Not one of your sweet, confused little widows; not by a long shot."

"And called in her accountant. That wasn't the only scam Whitelaw was running, either. There was artwork moving in and out of that apartment faster than apples in a fruit store. They haven't figured out yet whether it's fake or stolen. Mostly fake, they think. He'd been doing that for two or three years, apparently. He simply fit the stuff that Esteban gave him right into his network for disposing of paintings. Just increased his volume a bit."

"Have they caught Esteban?" asked Harriet.

Sanders shook his head. "The Spanish are positive that neither Esteban nor his sidekick went back to Spain. They've suggested that they're probably hiding out in Brazil or Argentina with a lot of other fugitive members of ETA. I don't suppose we'll ever see them again." He shrugged. "But thanks to Paul the gardener, Carlos Ramírez aka Garcia, aka Ugalde, was picked up in Arizona this morning. Behind the counter of a store his mother owns that sells antiques and Indian artifacts and stuff like that. Esteban must really have hated him. And Walker."

"Well, why wouldn't he? They ruined his chances to raise money for his cause, after all. I sort of liked Esteban, or whatever his name is."

"You would," said Sanders. "But I wouldn't count on Esteban not having that money, you know. We've traced a lot of the stolen merchandise. Some very valuable stuff was sold over the summer and the money transferred up here. Someone has the cash, and as far as we can tell, it isn't Whitelaw. Maybe Esteban just stuffed it in an old pair of gardening gloves."

"And took it back to Spain," said Harriet triumphantly. "Where the Spanish authorities aren't looking for him because they don't want to believe he could get into the country without anyone knowing about it."

"Harriet," said Sanders, picking up her hand from the table where it was lying. She looked up. "Let's get the hell out of here."

"Here?" she said, looking around the small restaurant where they were having their late lunch. "I haven't eaten yet. I'm hungry."

"No, you irritating woman, out of the city. Let's go down to the coast. It's September. It'll be beautiful. You can even take pictures if you like, and I'll carry the equipment."

"Cape Cod would be nice," she said. "But I'll need two days to finish off that assignment in Orillia." She turned her face away from him and stared out the window. "Actually, John . . ." She looked back.

"Yes?" He tried to keep his voice light and unconcerned while he braced himself for the inevitable excuses.

"Do you like islands? And ferries? I have a passion for them, you know. Why don't we go to Martha's Vineyard? There are gorgeous old houses there, and all the summer people will have left. It sounds—"

"Two days?" The sunshine seemed to gather itself into a giddy golden bath inside the drab little room. "That should give me time to pack," he said casually. "What would you like for dessert? The pie looks good."